BEN O' BILL'S,
THE LUDDITE

BEN O' BILL'S, THE LUDDITE

DANIEL FREDERICK EDWARD SYKES, GEORGE HENRY WALKER

ISBN: 978-93-93693-65-5

Published: -

LECTOR HOUSE LLP

LECTOR HOUSE LLP
E-MAIL: lectorpublishing@gmail.com

BEN O' BILL'S, THE LUDDITE

A YORKSHIRE TALE.

BY

D. F. E. SYKES, LL.B.
AND
GEO. HENRY WALKER

ABOUT THE AUTHOR.

D F E Sykes was a gifted scholar, solicitor, local politician, and newspaper proprietor. He listed his own patrimony as 'Fred o' Ned's o' Ben o' Billy's o' the Knowle' a reference to Holme village above Slaithwaite in the Colne Valley where many of the events in the novel take place. As the grandson of a clothier, his association with the woollen trade would be a valuable source of material for his novels, but also the cause of his downfall when, in 1883, he became involved in a bitter dispute between the weavers and the mill owners.

When he was declared bankrupt in 1885 and no longer able to practise as a solicitor he left the area and travelled abroad to Ireland and Canada. On his return to England he struggled with alcoholism and was prosecuted by the NSPCC for child neglect. Eventually he was drawn back to Huddersfield and became an active member of the Temperance Movement. He took to researching local history and writing, at first in a local newspaper, then books such as 'The History of Huddersfield and its Vicinity'. He also wrote four novels. It was not until the 1911 Census, after some 20 years as a writer, that he finally states his profession as 'author'.

In later life he lived with his wife, the daughter of a Lincolnshire vicar, at Ainsley House, Marsden. He died of a heart attack following an operation at Huddersfield Royal Infirmary on 5th June 1920 and was buried in the graveyard of St Bartholomew's in Marsden.

INTRODUCTION.

Although the book was initially credited to D. F. E. Sykes and G. H. Walker, G. H. Walker's name is missing from the third edition, and it is essentially Sykes' work.

First published in 1898, it is a novel which deserves wider recognition as it deals with surprisingly contemporary issues, but it is as a social history of the period that it stands out. Sykes' use of the local dialect, the entertaining asides that he includes and his skill at sketching characters and their lives, at a period of such turmoil in the Colne Valley, add to its value.

It is interesting that, as a historian, Sykes chose to embellish the facts, that were available to him at the time, with fiction, and his purpose must have been literary. Historians rightly take issue in this matter, but he is clear on his sympathy for their cause and the background and reasoning behind these events, though he draws back on the murder of Horsfall. The Luddites were not mindless machine breakers but desperate men, in poverty and despair, fighting for a voice to be heard against uncaring mill owners and a corrupt government.

This is undoubtedly Sykes' best novel, a sound history of the Luddites and a good read.

PREFACE.

AT the York Special Commission in 1812, sixty–six persons were tried for various offences in connection with the Luddite rising against the introduction of machinery. Of these sixty six seventeen were executed, one reprieved, six transported for seven years, seven were acquitted, seventeen were discharged on bail, fifteen by proclamation, and one stood over but was not called on.

The story, Ben o' Bill's, is mostly true, and the authors have not felt called upon to vary in any material respects the story as it was gleaned in part from the lips and in part from the papers of the narrator.

It is proper to say that the Ben Walker of the narrative was of kin to neither of the writers.

The thanks of the authors are tendered to Dr. Edwin Dean, of Slaithwaite, and to the Justices of the West Riding for permission to reproduce the portraits of Dr. Dean and of Sir Joseph Radcliffe.

DEDICATED
(Without Permission)
TO
MARY LOUISA SYKES,
THE FRIEND OF BOTH,
AND
WIFE OF ONE OF
THE AUTHORS

CONTENTS

CHAPTER I.

IT HURTS me sore that folk in these days should so little understand the do-ings of us Luddites. To hear young people talk, the Luddites were miscreants that well, deserved the hanging they got—a set of idle, dissolute knaves and cut–throats the country was well rid of. Nay, worse, many young lads with a college learning seem to know next to nothing about them, and talk as though all great deeds were done in far–of parts, and as though of heroes and martyrs England has none to show. I am little apt at writing, and my hand is stiff and cramped with years. But my memory is good still, and I can remember better the things of fifty years ago than those of yesterday. So, before hand and mind fail me altogether, I will set on record all I call mind of those memorable days that closed so black after that bloody York Assize. And if to any reader I should seem garrulous or egotistical, be it remembered in excuse that I can only tell the tale as I now recall it, and that I write of things I saw and things I knew, and of doings I took part in. I risked my own neck, and had the good fortune to escape with my life, and with honour, too, which not all who escaped whole and safe could say. When I was a boy, in the last days of the past century, our folk lived at Lower Holme, above Slaithwaite, in the old homestead in which my father's father and his father before him had lived. We were tenants of my Lord Dartmouth. The house is still there, and when I close my eyes of an evening, before the fire and my pipe goes out as I sit thinking, I can see the old place yet, as I knew it in my boyhood's days. My father, William Bamforth—Bill o' Ben's—was a manufacturer, a small manufac-turer we should say now; but no one thought of calling him a small manufacturer in those days. He was as big as most men thereabouts. He bought his wool of the stapler at Huddersfield—old Abe Hirst;—it was scoured and dyed in the vats in the farmyard; my mother and my cousin Mary, and Martha, the servant lass, that cleaned the house and milked the cows, and kept my mother's mind on the rack and her tongue on the clack from morning till night, helped with the spinning. The warping and the weaving we did at home in the long upper chamber. We had four looms at home, and, moreover, we put our work out to the neighbours. It was a busy house you may be sure, what with the milking and the churning, and the calves, and the pigs, and the poultry, and the people coming for milk, and the men coming for their warps, and the constant work at the old hand–looms in the long, low chamber above, with its windows stretched right across the front to catch the precious light. What stir, too, there used to be when father and I set off for the fairs at Nottingham and Macclesfield and Newcastle, for all those markets did Bill o' Ben's attend regular as the almanac itself. There was the loading, overnight, of the great covered waggon with the pieces of good linsey, and here and there a piece of broadcloth for the clergy and the better classes, and the grooming and shoeing of "Old Bess," the stout grey mare. Then the start at early dawn, with the first lark in summer, in the starlight of the winter mornings. Oh! it was grand in the summer across the moors, when the roads were plain to see, and only the crusted ruts to jolt our bones; but in the dark mornings of November, when the wind howled about the waggon's arch, and the rain beat like pellets about the tarpaulin, and the waggon wheels sunk deep in slush, and in the set winter–time, when the roads were lost in snow, it was cruel work for man and beast. It was gamesome, too, at the slimmer statutes at Nottingham and Macclesfield, when I had nothing to do but stand at the stall in the market–place and cut the suit–lengths for the customers, or carry their parcels to their inns. And grand it was to see the men servants and the buxom country lasses at the hiring, making their half–yearly holiday, and spending their money right cheerfully. My father had an old connection, and scarce ever had to return with pieces unsold. Then, when the fair was over, and he sat in the parlour of the Angel at Nottingham, or the Swan at Macclesfield, smoking his long, "churchwarden" and drinking gin and water, I would off into the town to see the booths, and the actors, and the giants, and the fat women, and the dwarfs and two–headed monsters, and many other curiosities that may not now be seen. I used to sit for hours in the winter nights at home telling Mary of the bearded woman, and the hen with five legs, and the learned pig, but of the country lasses, whose cheeks were so rosy and lips so ripe, she cared not to hear.

The times were bad for most people, but at home we did not feel the pinch very much. We had the cows and the poultry and the pigs, and though oatmeal was terribly dear, twenty shillings the hoop, I never knew what it was to miss the oatmeal porridge and the abundant milk for breakfast and bacon and potatoes for dinner. On Sundays we nearly always had beef or mutton and Yorkshire pudding, and my mother's home–brewed was famous throughout all the country side. Mr. Wilson, the parson of the church, always called when he came to Holme, though my father had grieved him sore by taking a pew at Powle Moor Chapel, and sitting under that godly man, Abraham Webster; and Mr. Wilson always declared to my mother's own face that her home–brewed was better drinking than any to be got even at the Black Bull Inn, at Kitchen Fold, which boasted the best "tap" outside Huddersfield itself. Sometimes on Sundays, too, my mother had a guests' tea–drinking, and then we had buttered tea–cakes and eggs, and salad, and tea, and out were brought the silver cream jug and silver sugar tongs and spoons and the little fluted china cups and saucers, with little, pink primroses on them, that belonged to my great aunt, Betty Garside. The women–folk drank tea, but not so much, I think, that they liked it, for they had not the chance of getting used to it, but because the quality drank it, and it served to establish their rank and dignity. My father would never touch it, and I can't say I was ever partial to it myself. So you see we were not so badly–off at home. My father's custom lay mainly in the country market towns, and the high price of corn caused by the ceaseless wars kept squire and farmer in rich content, and they paid for their cloth like men. It was the manufacturers who had made and relied on a foreign market for their goods, who cursed Napoleon, and cursed, too, our own Government, that was ever at daggers drawn with him. Why could we not let the French rule their country their own way they said. What was it to us whether king or Directory or Emperor ruled in France? My father was a Whig, and swore by Mr. Fox; yet I think at first he was not sorry to see our corn so high, prices so good, and money so plentiful among the farmers. But in time the war told on all of us, our ships could not sail the seas, the mills and warehouses groaned with piled–up merchandise, and the pieces fetched so little, it was scarce worth while to cart our goods from town to town. Then every manufacturer in the West Riding called for peace, and, in time, peace at any price.

I think it was at Nottingham, in the back–end of 1811, I first saw any signs of a stir because of the new machinery. A man was shot at Bullwell, near that town, when trying to get at some new stocking–frames, I saw his body brought into the town on a stretcher by two constables I can see his eyes and open mouth, with the yellow teeth, and the tongue thrust out between them, and blood trickling down the sides of his chin and his hands, the fingers of one wide outspread, the other gripping tight some grass and sand he had clutched, and his right knee drawn up so rigid they could not stretch the body, and he was buried in a chest. They laid him on a table in the tap–room of the first inn they came to, and I saw him through the window. When we rode home to Slaithwaite, I remember my father was very silent, and would not talk about the new machinery, but I was soon to hear enough of it.

I remember, as tho' it were yesterday, one winter's night about that time, my father was sat by the fire–side, smoking his pipe and taking a thoughtful pull at times at the yellow pewter pot from which he drank his ale; my mother in her rocking–chair knitting a pair of long, grey stockings for myself. I was reading by the candle–light a copy of Mr. Thomas Paine's "Rights of Man," which I had bought at Nottingham, and which, despite the groanings of Mr. Webster, our pastor at Powle Moor, I found a very sound and proper book, as, indeed, I still maintain it to be; and Mary was looking at the prints in Mr. Miller's Scripture History, with lives of the most celebrated Apostles, and wondering for the hundredth time how it came about that the frontispiece exhibits Father Adam with a full beard, whilst the very next print depicts him, after the fall, with a chin as smooth as an egg: for there is no mention of razors in the Garden of Eden. Martha was down in the village at a prayer–meeting; and Siah, the teamer, had had his porridge and his pint and had gone to bed. We could hear him, through the rafters, snoring in the room above. It must have been a Tuesday, for father had been to Huddersfield to market, and had come home, as he always did on market–days, more talkative than his wont.

"Aw rode as far as th' Warrener, wi' Horsfall, o' Ottiwell," I heard my father say. "He could talk o' nowt but th' new machines 'at he's bahn to put i' Ottiwells. He's bahn, to ha' all his wark done under his own roof, he says. He's sick o' croppers an' their ways. An', he says, too, 'at it 'll noan be long afore there 'll be a new kind o' loom 'at 'll run ommost by itsen, an' pieces 'll come dahn to next to nowt. He says time's noan so far off when th' old hand–loom weavers 'll go dahn their own slot."

"How long did you stop at th' Warrener?" asked my mother, who had her own way of putting a point.

"Tha' means it wor th' ale were talking; but tha's mista'en. He meant it every word. An' he said, 'at them 'at lagged behind mun go to th' wall, an' he, for one, meant movin' wi' th' times. Him an' Enoch Taylor's mighty thick, an' Taylor's putting th' new machinery into Bradley Mills, and Vickerman's. All th' market's talkin' on it. Aw called at th' Pack Horse—".

"I warrant yo' did," observed my mother.

"At th' Pack Horse," proceeded my father, superior to innuendo, "an' Horsfall wor there, an' he said 'at th' era o' manual labour wor over, an' th' triumph o' mechanic art had come. These were his very words. Aw thowt aw'd remember them to tell, yo'."

"An' little aw thank yo' for yo'r trouble, William Bamforth," observed my mother, "for that nor any other o' your fine tales from th' Pack Horse. Little it seems yo', or Horsfall either, dandering about th' Pack Horse after th' market's done, an' me toiling my blood to water to make both ends tie. Th' triumph o' mechanic art, indeed! Triumph o' fiddlesticks. Th' hand–loom's done well enough for thee, an' for thi father afore thee, an' where would you put yo' new machines if yo' got 'em, I'd like to know."

"Ther's that bit o' money lying idle at Ingham's, an' we could build on th' Intack, an' ther's a fine run o' water, as Horsfall says it's a sin an' a shame to see running to waste, an' ther's that fortune of your Aunt Betty's, at's out at mortgage wi' Lawyer Blackburn."

"Aye, an' there it 'll stop for me," cried my mother, "let well alone, says I. Wasn't tha tellin' me only th' other neet' o' that poor man at Nottingham, 'at our Ben couldn't sleep o' neets for seein' him starin' 'at him? Dost tha want bringing home on a shutter, an' me lonely enough as it is, what wi' thee an' Ben settin' off nearly every week, an' when yo'r back stopping at th' Pack Horse every Tuesday till it's a wonder a decent man an' a deacon isn't ashamed to be seen coming up th' broo. I'll ha' na building wi' my brass. There's enough to follow as it is, an' that girl, Martha, that soft as she thinks every man as says 'It's a fine day,' means puttin' t' spurrins in, and na, nowt 'll do but havin' th' masons and th' joiners all ovver th' place, an' them so fond o' drink too. Aw'm moithered to death as it is, an' 'll ha' none on't, so tha' may put that maggot aat o' thi yed, William Bamforth."

"But Mr. Chew says" .....

Now Mr. Chew was our new vicar, Mr. Wilson being not long dead.

"Oh, Mr. Chew. It 'ad seem him better if he washed th' powder out o' his own yed i'stead o' puttin' stuff an' nonsense into other folks!"

"If yo mun talk your own business ovver wi' all th' countryside why can't you go to Mr. Webster, as is well known to ha' more o' th' root o' th' matter in him than all th' clergy, an him a weaver hissen, too."

"Why, and so I will," exclaimed my father, rising to wind up the clock, a solemn act that, in our house, served, except on Sundays, instead of family prayers, and sent us all to bed.

The very next Lord's Day my father and mother, Mary, and myself, with Martha and 'Siah, must go to Powle Moor in the afternoon to hear a discourse by Mr. Webster, my father and I walking side by side, a thing which I liked not so much as to walk with Mary. But it chanced that on this very Sabbath my father explained to me what I had often pondered upon, why we should trudge a good two miles across the moor by a rude footpath to the Baptist Meeting House, when the Church lay on a broad and good road almost at our feet, and we had there a large pew, our own freehold, which had been used aforetime by my grandfather and my great–grandfather. Whatever the reason was it had not been apprehended by our old collie, for such is the sway of long habit, that every Sunday when the cracked bell chimed for morning service at the church, it would rise from the hearth, yawn, and stretch itself, look about it as though enquiringly and reproachfully, and then sedately descending the hill, would enter the church, walk decorously to the old pew, now generally empty, and stretch itself by the door, in the aisle. Nor, I confess, was I much wiser than the old dog, for my father's explanation of our desertion of the church of our fathers. "You see, Ben," he said to me, when pressed on the point, speaking slowly, for he breathed with some difficulty in our way up the hill, — "you see, blood is thicker than water."

Now this is a truth there is no gainsaying.

"And I shall allus hold," continued my father, "I shall allus hold 'at Parson Wilson had no reight to stir th' magistrates up to refuse th' license to th' 'Silent Woman' because some o' th' Baptists 'at belonged to th' Nook Chapel used to go theer o' wet neets to sing an' pray an' expound for mutual edification, an' if one or two on 'em did happen tak' too mich ale at times, it's well known talkin's dry wark. Then about them hens o' your mother's half–cousin, Sammy Sutcliffe, Sam–o'–Sall's. Tha' knows it were agin all natur' for Parson Wilson to gi' it in as he did, an' it were but nateral we should side wi' our own kin."

Now it was about these hens I wished to learn, for it was because of them that it has ever been said that schism was hatched in Slaithwaite—that th' dissenters layed away like Hannah Garside's hens, and had laid away ever since.

"Yo' see it wor this way," explained my father, "Hannah were allus a very fractious woman, more particular as, do what she would, could never get wed, an' such drop o' th' milk o' human kindness as God had ge'en her to start wi' seemed to ha' soured on her. Her an' Sam–o'–Sall's lived neighbour, an' it were like enough 'at her hens strayed into Sammy's fowd, and into th' shippon too. Hens is like other folk, they'll go' wheer they're best off, an' if Hannah threw th' fowls nowt but bacon swards yo' needn't blame 'em if they went wheer they could get out o' th' reach o' her tongue an' a grain of meal an' corn as weel. Onyway she pulled Sammy up afore Parson Wilson for th' eggs, an' Parson Wilson gave it agen yor' mother's cousin. An' what I say is," said my father, pausing to' get his breath, and striking his stick into the ground by way of emphasis, "What I say is, there's no swearin' to eggs. Moreovver Hannah gloried ovver th' decision to that extent it wer' more nor flesh an' blood could bear, an' when she cam' an' set i' church, reight i' th' front o' yor' aunt, wi' a Easter egg fastened i' her bonnet, Sammy saw no way for peace but to join th' Baptists. An', as I said afore, blood's thicker nor water, an' yor' mother an' me havin' prayed on it, and yor' aunt sayin' beside 'at no money o' hers, an' it's well known she's tidy well off, should ever go to th' Erastian idolators, our duty seemed clear both to yo'r mother an' misen. Not but what aw liked th' owd Parson well enough, tho' he wer' a Tory, an me a Whig."

We were by this time in the road that strikes across the top of the hill towards Salendine Nook, and by the side of which the Powle Moor Chapel was built, with the house and outbuildings for the minister. We could see the men quitting the burial ground and the little public—house hard by, and, all in their Sunday clothes, folk were coming from every part for the afternoon service, not hurrying, and with no air of business, but solemnly and seriously, talking little, and with thoughts, like their faces, set Zion—wards. When we exchanged greetings, as we did with most, it was in grave tones, for it was not counted decent in my young days to be over cheerful on the Sabbath Day. And tho' as I have said, we at home had not felt the pinch of the hard times more than we could bear, there were few there so well off. Most that went to th' Powle were hand—loom weavers, with here an' there a little shop—keeper, and tho' meal was neither so bad nor so dear as it had been in Barley time, nor work so scarce as it became later, yet most knew the pressure of want, and the shadow of worse things still to come seemed to brood over us all.

It was a sight to see Powle Chapel at an afternoon service. Every pew was filled, and every eye was fixed on Parson Webster as he gave out the hymns line by line, verse by verse, for few of us could read, tho' most made a point of having a hymn book. Up in the loft was the music, the double bass, the viol, and the clarionet. Between Jim Wood—Jim o' Slack—who played the double bass, and his colleagues of the viol and clarionet contention had raged from the very foundation of the church at Powle. Jim o' Slack maintained that in every true view of harmony wedded to divinity, the notes of the double bass stood for the wrath of Jehovah, and were designed to inspire awe and inward quaking. The feeble and futile utterances of the viol and the clarionet, he conceded, might represent the tender qualities of mercy and compassion, and, as such, might be worthy of some consideration among the Methodies, whose spiritual food was as milk for babies, but in High Calvinism, Jim maintained, nought but the bulky instrument his soul loved could convey adequate conception of the majesty of God and the terrors of hell. It was grand to hear the singing. We all sang for our lives, and we all had a notion of singing in tune. Then the praying! oh! it was fine to hear little Parson Webster. How he rejoiced over the elect! How he lamented over the unregenerate! It was very comforting to hear, for we were the elect, the Erastians of the Church and the Arminians of the chapel in the valley we well understood to be those in outer darkness. With what a solid satisfaction, too, did the elders settle down to the discourse of an hour and forty minutes by the hour glass, which was the least we expected from Mr. Webster. I remember still his text of that very day, "Behold I was shapen in iniquity, and in sin did my mother conceive me." Who could deny, he asked, the utter and natural depravity of man? Why only he who by the very denial stood confessed of the sins of arrogancy and self—sufficiency. Was not the natural man, since the Fall, prone to murder, lust, evil imaginings, covetousness, hardness of heart, vain glory, malice, and all unworthiness, all being, by nature, the children of wrath, and only that small handful of the dust of Zion, of all that great valley, called forth and justified before the foundation of the world that we should be holy and without blame before Him in love. How awful, too, was the lot of those that went down quick into hell, whose steps took hold on the eternal fire whose flames were never quenched. But we were not of these, tho' on this we must not plume ourselves, for salvation was not of him that willeth nor of him that runneth, but of God that sheweth mercy, for the potter had power over the clay, of the same lump to make one vessel unto honour, and another unto dishonour. I was very glad for my part to have been made a vessel unto honour, and of this there could be no reasonable doubt, for when my father, moved thereto by my mother, after the split about Hannah Garside's eggs, finally asked for admission to the community of the Powle and was dipped, cousin Mary and I were required to state on which side we elected to stand. Mr. Webster, in a long and earnest discourse in the parlour at home, and with much praying, set before us, as he said, life and good, death and evil, blessing and cursing. I waited to hear what Mary had to say, being for my part little troubled in my mind at that time about religion and not rightly understanding on what points of doctrine Mr. Chew differed from Mr. Webster, and liking the chapel the better because the singing was heartier, and the Church the rather because the sermons were shorter, and it seemed to me your soul might be saved there with less pother. Now Mary, I know not why, said she should go with her aunt, and was commended for a good girl by Mr. Webster, and I, not wishful on the Sunday to turn down the broo' to Church whilst Mary toiled up the hill to the Powle, announced my resolve to walk in my father's steps. So Mr. Webster, much pleased, praised my filial obedience, and he being well content to take this as a sign of grace and effectual calling, I e'en took his word for it and joined the Baptists.

I say I remember well the text of that afternoon, and by this reason. My father and mother and Mary were set in the one pew whilst 'Siah and Martha and myself were set behind them. Now as I looked upon Mary that afternoon it came into my mind very strongly that it was strange so fair and dainty a specimen of the potter's craft should be shapen in iniquity, and I was marvelling greatly to myself that out of the same lump of clay two vessels so unlike as Cousin Mary, and Martha, our serving wench, should be fashioned by the potter's hands. For Martha was broad shouldered and squat, and had coarse towzelled hair, very red, and her mouth was large and her lips thick, and her arms were rough of skin and red, and she waddled in her walk, and her breathing was heavy, and her eye dull, and her voice was not tuneful, tho' she would sing in the hymns, albeit my mother frowned at her and would have had her hold her peace, for my mother did not think it quite proper for the serving man and maid to sing with their betters: but as my father said "If you go to chapel, you must do as chapel does."

But Mary, oh! my children, you will never know what my cousin Mary was like in those days, with her brown eyes, so warm and soft, and her brown hair all wavy, and with little love ringlets about the neck and her little hands not white but creamy brown, and her rosebud mouth, and her voice so musical, and her smile so sweet. And so, I say, thinking, perhaps, too much of these things, and wondering, too, at the marvellous skill of the potter, and opining, belike, that there must be a difference in the clay, but quite certain that Mary was not fashioned in iniquity, and the day being hot and the air very heavy, and two suet dumplings I had eaten for dinner sitting heavy on me, I fell into a sort of doze as Mr. Webster reached his twelfthly. Now, Mary, seeing this, and being ever full of mischief, having looked to see that my father was intent on the discourse, and that my mother's eyes were closed—in thought—did lean over the pew and put into my mouth a lump of good–stuff and, I chancing at the moment to throw back my head, the sweet rolled into my gullet and had gone nigh to choke me. I had much ado to stifle my cough-ing, and all the congregation did look hard at me, save only Mary herself, who listened with sweet gravity as Mr. Webster proceeded with his twelfthly.

I walked home that evening with 'Siah, for Mary dallied behind with Martha, and father and mother had gone on before with Mr. Webster, who was to take his supper at our house, as was now his almost weekly custom of a Sunday. 'Siah was a silent man, and was a good servant, loving his beasts and careful for them, but over fond of ale, and much to be feared when overtaken with drink, and noted that he had fought a great fight at the Feast with one arm tied behind his back.

"Aw believe awn getten it, Ben," said 'Siah, as we went across the fields in the wintry gloom, homewards.

"What's ta getten, 'Si?" I asked.

"Th' conviction," said 'Siah.

"Conviction, what conviction?"

"Why, th' conviction o' sin to be sure. How many convictions does ta' think there are?" said 'Siah, in a pet.

"Why, 'Siah, th' last conviction tha' had were afore Justice Ratcliffe at th' Brigg, and more by token if my father hadn't sent me wi' th' fine, in th' stocks tha'd ha sat for six mortal hours by Huddersfield Church clock."

"That were a different sort o' conviction all together, Ben, that were for feigh-tin', and this aw mean naa is th' conviction o' sin."

"Well, fighting's a sin," I said.

"Aw dooan't know as it is—not if it be for feightin' such a thing as th' ostler at th' Pack Horse for sayin' Martha's bow–legged, when aw know better, but aw do believe at aw gat my conviction o' sin much i' t' same way."

"How does ta' mean, 'Siah," I asked, for I saw our teamer was in deadly ear-nest.

"Why, bi wrastlin', to be sure. So th' missis munnot tell me agean there's no gooid i' wrastlin'. It were after aw came back fra th' village last neet. Aw leets o' Martha an 'oo gav' me a bit o' her tongue for makkin' a swill tub o' mysen an' for lettin' a little chap like th' ostler at th' Pack Horse ha' th' law on me, an' so aw went into th' shippon an' set by mi' sen for happen two hours i' th' hay at aw'd pulled for th' beasts. An' aw said to mi' sen 'at it were no use tryin' to be good for aw were clear born to be damned. Aw could ha' ta'en that hop o' mi thumb at th'

Pack Horse awmost atween mi finger an' thumb an' pinched him i' two if it hadn't been at aw were mazed i' drink. An' so th' text com' into mi head at aw wer reight served for mi fuddlin' an' 'auv made up mi mind to just pay him aat next time aw goa to market, an' then awst turn religious an' happen gi' up drinking, except at th' Feast an' Christmas time, an' mebbe when aw get treated an' at a chersenin' or a weddin' or a wake, an' mebbe occasional o' a Saterday, not to lose th' taste an' feel on it, an' i' th' way o' dooty as yo' may say."

This was the longest speech I ever heard 'Siah deliver. I thought his resolution a good one, only advising him when he brought the matter off with the man at the Pack Horse to be sure to make his opponent touch a button so as to have law on his side, and if possible to have witnesses that could be relied on to speak the truth, I mean, so as to make it a case of what lawyer Blackburn called provocation.

It was after supper that the momentous consultation about the machines began. Full justice had been done to that evening meal. There had been cold beef and a chine, oatcakes that had been dried on the creel over the big fireplace before which a bullock might have been roasted whole, cheese and apple pie, and, to drink, a quart or more of my mother's famous home brewed. Mr. Webster, by grace of his office, was privileged to drink his ale out of the large two–handled silver flagon, a hundred years old at the least, that no common lips had ever touched. I do not think the supper was the worse for that we took it in the house instead of the parlour. There was the sanded floor to our feet and the smoked rafters above, and in the sill of the long diamond paned windows were red earth pots of geranium and musk and fuschia, that made the room smell sweet as a nosegay. The spinning wheels were away in the corner, a list hearthrug made by my mother's own hands stretched before the grate, a cushion whose covering worked by the same tireless fingers imaged the meeting of Jacob and Rebecca at the well, adorned the long oak settle under the window. The walls, washed yellow, were relieved by the framed funeral cards of departed relatives; the calf bound family Bible containing entries of births, marriages and deaths for many generations back, my own birth being at that time last entry of all, tho' there have been added a goodly list since then, reposed on the chest; a celery glass, highly cut, on the one side and a decanter on the other. A beautiful enamelled tray, with hand–painted roses, was reared behind, and best pictures of all, my father always vowed, and richest ornaments of any room, a prime flitch of bacon and two sturdy hams hung on the hooks near the door, so as to catch the air to keep them sweet. I have been in many a fine room since then, notably when I went to Woodsome Hall to see my Lord Dartmouth and give the tenants' greeting to his bonnie bride; but for real home feeling and snug comfort never have I seen ought to compare with the old house at Holme when it was tidied up for Sunday.

Supper was over. Mr. Webster was sat in my father's arm chair, his little legs, with their worsted stockings, hardly reaching the ground, and I make no doubt he would have been more comfortable on the settle, which was lower; but it was a point of civility with my father to surrender the master's chair to an honoured guest. A long churchwarden sent its reek up the broad chimney, and a little glass of weak gin and water stood by the parson's right hand convenient on the table.

Not that Mr. Webster took much of either ale or strong waters; but this was Sunday, and it is well known that when a minister has preached two sermons, with many a long prayer thrown in, to say nothing of hymns, sing he never so badly, his throat must needs be dry. My father sat opposite Mr. Webster on the other side of the hearth, my mother, in her low rocking chair with the iron rockers, swaying gently to and fro, and fingering her handkerchief for lack of her knitting needles, which must not be used on Sundays. The case reserved, as a lawyer might say, had been put by my father with much aiding and commentary from the mother, who justified her interruption, under a look of remonstrance from both pastor and lord, by saying that a woman could jump over a wall while a man was going round and round seeking for the gate.

"It is no small matter, friend Bamforth," at length said Mr. Webster, "and one that I doubt not you have taken to the Lord in prayer. Well pleased too am I that you have seen fit to take counsel with me in this weighty business. For it is laid upon me to feed the sheep of our Master's fold, and tho' you would not look to me for the bread that perisheth, but rather I to you, for it is written that the labourer is worthy of his hire, and ye may not muzzle the ox that treadeth out the corn, yet perchance in doubtful and perplexing times a pastor's counsel may be the more needful nourishment. Now I would have you take heed against the besetting sin of this latter–day and corrupt generation, which I take to be that very making haste to be rich against which the Book doth expressly warn us. You speak of building a mill for these new methods. Hast thou not thought within thyself, like the man in the parable, saying 'What shall I do, because I have no room where to bestow my fruits? This will I do: I will pull down my barns, and build greater; and there will I bestow all my fruits and my goods.' And mark what to that man God said: 'Thou fool, this night thy soul shall be required of thee: then whose shall those things be, which thou hast provided? So is he that layeth up treasure for himself, and is not rich toward God.' And now I ask you, brother Bamforth, can you be rich toward God, if you build up your fortune on the ruin of your fellow men. You say one o' these new finishing frames will do the work of four, may be of six men. Aye, also is there talk of looms that shall need neither skill nor care. It may be true, I know not. But oh! it will be a sore day for this hillside, and all the country round when that day shall be. What is to become of those who now keep a decent roof over their heads, and tho' times be bad can still give bit and sup to wife and bairns. You may make new machines but you cannot make new men to order. And see to it that it be not now with thee as in the days of Pharaoh of old, when Aaron's rod swallowed up the rods of the wise men and the sorcerers, and thy rod too be swallowed up. If that came to pass of which I have read and heard, there will be no room in this valley for men of but moderate means. Yo' may build a mill, but bigger men will build bigger mills, and the bigger mills will swallow up the less, and thou and thy son, and even Mary yonder may be fain, thou in thy old age and they in their prime, to take wage at another's hand, and to do a hireling's task in another's mill."

"If I do may I be—"

"William," said my mother, before my father could conclude, and we could only guess what awful doom my father was about to invoke upon himself. But enough had been said. Whether the mind of our household's head were the more moved by the picture of his friends and neighbours reduced to want, or by the picture of himself and his working for others, who had always puts out work ourselves, I know not; but from that day forth there was no more thought for many a long day of any change in the ways we had used of old, and, for the new machines, my mother died in the belief that the curse of Scripture was upon them.

CHAPTER II.

IT WAS not often my father missed the Audit Dinner at the Dartmouth Arms, but for some reason I do not remember, he could not go to the November Audit of 1811. So I went in his place, as was but my due, seeing that in the course of time and nature the homestead would be mine, and I tenant to my lord in my father's stead. So to the dinner I went in great state and no little fluster, having donned my Sunday clothes, and showing as fine a leg (though I say it that should not) as ever passed Slaithwaite Church. I went by the churchyard corner where old Mr. Meeke rested in his grave, and I did not fail to doff my beaver, for was I not taught all I ever knew at the Free School, founded by Mr. Meeke, and I was, too, ever a lover of the Church, though we had joined the Hard–bedders. There had been a wedding that day, and I should have been there, but none were invited save only family friends, owing to times being so bad. Jack o' Jamie's had wed Sue Lumb, and I knew Jack o' Jamie's and Sue both, as indeed I knew every mother's son and lass in Slaithwaite; and my mother could tell their pedigree for generations back. Opposite the door of the Dartmouth Arms I came across a crowd different from ordinary, for in the midst was Jack donned in his Sunday best, and a great white rosette at his breast, and there was Sue with a white veil over her head and clinging to Jack's arm and crying and coaxing, and Jack fuming and swearing and waving his arms and shaking his fist at his own father. Sure a rare sight for a wedding day, and I stayed to hear what might be the meaning of it all. I knew Jack for a decent, hard working lad that kept his father, a drunken neer–do–weel, from the rates. Old Jamie had a hang–dog look to be sure, as he kept away from his son's reach and cowered behind his new daughter–in–law.

"It's too bad," Jack was crying, "It's too bad; yo' all know 'at awn kept mi father awmost even sin' aw could addle a meg, an' him doing nowt but tidy th' house up an' go a rattin' with th' dog an' happen bring a rabbit home betimes—an' aw never grudged him owt, for he's mi own father, an' mi mother 'at's dead an' gone left him to me. But, its too bad aw say—gise 'ang, it ud make a worm turn—here its mi wedding day, an' aw thowt we'd have a bite an' sup by ordinar. So aw off to Ned o' Bill's an' bowt three p'und o' good wheat flour, tho' it's well known, what price it's at, an' ill aw could spare th' brass. But a felly doesn't get wed every day. We calc'lated it ud mak ten cakes, an' that ud be one round apiece an' two to put bye for Sunday. Mi father baked 'em hissen three days sin', for we thowt we munnot eit 'em till they were stale, new uns crumble so—an' aw bowt a piece of th' skirt o' beef at lay me in five good shillin'—so when aw set off to take Sue here to th' chuch aw left mi father to watch th' beef afore t' fire, an' we borrowed some plates an' knives an' forks an' three chairs, for aw thowt we'd all have a feast at 'ud make th' weddin' party remember mi weddin' day as long as they lived. An' after th' knot wer' teed an' we were walkin' th' village so all could see what a lass awd gotten, we just looked in at th' house door to see if th' meat were nearly done—an would yo' believe it, th' owd glutton 'ud supped welly a gallon o' th' weddin' ale an' were wipin' his chops wi t' back o' his coat sleeve, 'at weren't his own, but borrowed o' mi uncle Ben; an' ther' were nobbut four cakes left an' a good p'und cut off th' joint an' th' pan as bare o' gravy as if it had been new scoured. Oh! tha' brussen guts; if tha' weren't mi own father!" And here Jack shook his fist over Jamie's head, and Sue tried to turn aside his wrath and to play the peace–maker, as a good woman ever will.

"For shame o' thissen," said one; "It 'ud sarve thi reight to put thee i' th' stocks," said another; "Let's stang him," a woman cried. "Many a decent body's been cucked for less," said Moll o' Stuarts, who knew what the cucking stool meant full well. And all felt that Jamie Thewlis had done as scurvy a trick as ever he had done in a scurvy life. Even those that drank with him, the loafers and vagabonds of the village, got to the outskirts of the crowd, and left him alone to his defence.

"Yo' see it were this way," said Thewlis, when he could get a hearing. "Th' table' wor set all ready for th' weddin' party. Aw'd laid a clean cloth on th' table. There were a plate an' a knife an' fork for every one that were comin'. Th' house were tidied up an' as clean yo' could had etten yor dinner off th' floor. Then Jack started off to fetch Susan. Th' cakes were on th' table, one bi each plate. Aw put th' joint on th' jack afore th' fire just as he'd told me bi th' clock. Then aw set me dahn to watch it. It wor a grand joint. Aw could ha' fair hugged it when aw took it up, so plump an' red and firm, wi' streaks o' fat runnin' in an' among th' lean like rivers o' cream in a bank o' strawberries. Th' fire were just reight, banked down an' hot, an' aw ca–ered me dahn first o' one side o' th' hearth an' then on t' other, an' began to watch th' hands o' t' clock an' wish it wor dinner time. Dinner time it were bi reights, but we'd put th' dinner back so's Jim an' his frien's could walk through th' village. Then th' skin o' th' joint began to crack, an' th' fat to fizzle an' ooze 'aat an spit. Aw looked at th' clock. Aw'll swear th' han's hedn't moved for half–an–hour, an' yet it were tickin' reg'lar—aw nivver felt hauf as hungry i' mi life afore. Aw'd had no breakfas', for awd said to mi sen it 'ud nivver do to shame yar Jack's weddin' dinner bi not doin' reight bi it. Then all at once th' jack gay' a click an' summut splurted aat, an' all at once there wer' a smell at fair madi mi belly leap inside me. But aw'd promised yar Jack at aw'd do fair—so aw went to th' cellar–head to see if ther' wer' happen a crust or owt to stay mi innards, but ther' wer' nowt. Then ther' wer' another click, an' another spurt, an' th' room wer' fair full o' th' smell. It awmost turned me dizzy. Aw looked at th' clock agen, an' guise 'ang me, if th' hand had stirred aboon an inch, an' dinner seemed as far off as ivver. Then aw thowt awd fetch th' ale. So aw got th' jug an' a milkin' can an' started off to th' Globe. Aw tried hard to strap a gill, but th' owd skin–flint wouldn't trust me. Aw'd awmost talked her into it when t' thowt cam' into mi head at happen one o' th' naybors 'at hedn't bin axed to th' weddin' might be after th' joint; an' aw span home as fast as aw could for fear o' spillin'. Then when aw oppened th' door ther' war' a fair blast o' th' smell o' gravy right i' mi face. It just took mi breath away, an' aw had to tak' a pull at th' jug to steady misen. That heartened me up a bit, an' aw just took one o' th' cakes, mi own at wer' to be an' set i' my own place at th' table, so it were no robbery,—an aw put it i' th' pan under th' meat; an', by gow, it wer' a sop an' gradely. Aw think aw mun ha' put too much salt on it, for aw felt as dry as a lime–kiln. Then aw had another swig at th' jug, an' looked aat for th' weddin', but aw could see no' signs on 'em. Then aw bethowt me at th' fiddler were' nobbut a little un, an' could mak' hauf a cake do, so aw made hauf a sop. Then th' gravy began to run red an' brown into th' pan, an' ow knew th' meat wer' near enuff—an' still ther' wer' no signs o' anybody. Howsomever, aw thought my share shouldn't be spoiled for any tomfoolery such as walkin' th' village wi' a lass o' my arm, as if yo' couldn't do that ony time. So aw just cut a slice aat an' put it on a shive an et it o' mi knee, an' had a swallow out o' th' piggin' to make it equal wi' th' jug. Then aw thowt aw meight as well be hanged for a sheep as a lamb, an' aw ate mi fill. Tha' ma' poise me, Jack, if tha' likes, but tha'll noan poise th' meat out o' me, that's one comfort. It's th' first time for six months 'at mi back an' mi belly ha' not shakken hands, an' aw'll ta' thi poisin', an' thank yo' for it."

But long before Jamie had done his story he was out of danger of a hiding. There was not one there that did not feel hungry with the very story, and the party trudged homewards with a laugh and a cheer to make out as best they could on what was left—Jamie, forgiven and impenitent, not last in the joking throng.

The partition of the upper story of the Dartmouth Arms had been removed, and thereby room was made for the poorer tenantry who came this year in great numbers, many there being who came to plead the hard times and escape their remit, but joined in the rude scramble for the thick slices of meat and bread and the brimming pewters that were their yearly gift from the lord. But in the long room, on the top floor, was more decent seeming and good manners; for the tenants of the larger holdings at that time paid to the host of the inn each man eighteenpence that there might be a well–spread board. Mr. Joseph Scott, who lived at Woodsome (none of my lord's family being then in residence), did sit at the head of the table, and gave us the health of the king, which we drank with a good will, for there was none that did not grieve for the old man so sore stricken in his latter days. Then did Mr. Scott call upon us to toast His Royal Highness, the Prince Regent, and many did drink the health with a hip, hip, hurrah but for my part, though I hate to waste good liquor, I poured my ale into the spitoon, for stories not a few had come to our ears of the wild doings of the Prince and of his cruel treatment of his consort. Mr. Fox, to be sure, and other leaders of the Whigs in Parliament, did excuse the wildness of the Prince, and some did even bear a railing tongue against the hapless princess; but for me, who am perhaps too little learned to judge of princes and courts, I deemed such naughtiness should not be in high places more than in men of less degree, and my loyalty went into the sawdust. But I took a double draughty to the health of my lord and his lady.

There was no lack of subjects for our tongues to wag upon when the ale had loosed them, and a well–lined waist set the oil of gladness on our faces. There was, for one, the never failing theme of Lord Wellington's doings among the Dons. But a few days previous, General Marmont had raised the siege of Ciudad Rodrigo, and our spirits had been greatly stirred by the discovery of one of his dispatches, in which he boasted that he would have pursued the British forces to the lines of Lisbon "if the moment designed for the catastrophe of England had arrived." That put our English up, and was as good as a score of recruiting sergeants to our army. Catastrophe, we knew well, might come to us as it has done to other nations; but never, we vowed, should or could it come through a frog–eating Frenchman. We gladly turned from that topic to news nearer home. There was the great fight at Thissleton Gap, for instance, which showed what British grit and muscle and pluck could do; and we were all ready to wager all we had that if you searched France from north to south you could find no champion like Crib, who had near been the death of Molineux in a fight near Grantham, breaking his jaw, and leaving him senseless on the field. There had not been a bed to be had for love or money for twenty miles round Thissleton Gap the night before the fight, said the "Leeds Mercury," and all the nobility and gentry of the county had been there; and after his great victory Crib, carrying away a purse of £400, had driven to London in a carriage and four, the postillions decked with blue ribands and streamers, and the whole populace in every town and hamlet by the way turning out to cheer the wearer of the belt. Then, too, there was much talk of the progress making with the cutting of the new canal that was to tie the eastern and the western seas; and we had not yet done marvelling at the boring of the waterway under Stanedge. Then, again, we must gossip to one another anent that strange portent of the skies, the wondrous comet, that still made our early morns so beautiful and yet so fraught with dread. The wise men said its tail was over twenty million miles long, as it streamed away from Charles's Wain across the distant sky, and Mr. Mellor, the schoolmaster, did try to show me how the calculation had been made; whilst Mr. Varley, of the corn mill, who had a merry wit, did say that coals would soon be cheaper, for the Welsh were counting on the comet coming so near, they might toast their cheese by it. Mr. Mellor was somewhat ruffled that his serious discourse should be turned to levity, and said that as perchance Mr. Varley could not be expected to understand the deep subtleties of astronomy, he would try him on a subject nearer his heart.

"I will, to–morrow," said Mr. Mellor, "bring to your house twenty golden guineas, and in return you shall give me your written bond to give me therefor, one grain of good wheat, two grains and no more on the day following, four on the next, and so on each day thereafter for six months by the calendar, every day doubling the number of the day before."

"Done, and done to it," cried Mr. Varley, and all the company exclaimed that so rare a bargain the miller never made in his life before and for an hour after that I saw Mr. Varley was doing sums in his head, and chuckling feebly to himself but in time he ceased to laugh, and his brow wrinkled and his eye was anxious, and he was seen to add figures secretly in his bulky pocket–book, and ever as he worked he grew sadder; till at length he cried that not all the corn that grew that year in Yorkshire could pay his wager, and he was fain to fill our measures round with best ale to be quit of his bargain. And all that went away sober that night told their wives how the schoolmaster had bested the miller, and were the more resolved their lads should mind their books and be good at figuring. And I was very glad that my old master had come off with so great credit, for Mr. Varley, by reason of being the lord's agent, was something prone to give himself an air.

But Mr. Webster was not too pleased that Mr. Varley should have jested of the comet. It had exercised him sore in the searching of the Scriptures, and oftentimes had he pointed to its presence in the heavens, and many a restless night had he given to my mother.

Mr. Webster would have it that the comet did foretell the coming of the Son of Man in a cloud with power and great glory, and the good man rejoiced thereat, seeing nought to cause us grief, but rather joy, that there were "great earthquakes in divers places, and famines and pestilences, and fearful sights and great signs from heaven." And he would exultingly call us to witness the fulfilment of prophesy for that there were signs in the sun, and in the moon, and in the stars, and upon the earth distress of nations, with perplexity; the sea and the waves roaring; men's hearts failing them for fear and for looking after those things which were coming on earth. But my mother lived to laugh at her fears, and even to wear a dress that became the fashion, of which the body was of pale red silk, a star of gold thread standing for the comet's head, and a fan shaped tail of silver spangles spreading out in likeness of the comet's tail.

It was my great honour after the dinner, and whilst the company sat over their cups, to be invited to the head of the table by Mr. Joseph Scott, of Woodsome, who was then lately become a magistrate, a handsome man of some forty years. He asked most kindly after the health of my father and mother, and bade the tapster who waited on the upper end of the table charge me a bumper of the wine of Oporto, which did fill my heart with a great warmth. Then when I would have returned to my seat by the schoolmaster he bade me remain, and I listened with all my ears to the talk of my betters. I noticed that Mr. Scott spoke mostly with Mr. William Horsfall, of Marsden. I knew Mr. Horsfall well by sight, having seen him often on the road as he went to or returned from market, a man in his prime, with a keen, resolute look; not easily turned from his purpose, I warrant you. Impatient of opposition, I judged him even then, brusque, and a little petulant, but not unkindly of heart as I had heard, for those that worked for him had ever a good name for him—but a masterful man.

The talk between these two was much of the coolness there then was between America and England. Mr. Horsfall was very bitter about this. "It is all the fault of those accursed Orders in Council," he said. "Before our benighted Government issued the Orders in Council, America took twelve million pounds worth of our manufactures—now not one penny–worth. Withdraw the Orders and you conciliate America; you bind her to us by the closest tie of all, the tie of self–interest. So long as these Orders remain in force it is futile to talk of negotiations. It is beating the air. We are alienating our own flesh and blood, we are running grave risk of having another enemy on our hands, and that of our own household, our cousins if not our brothers. Here are we pulling our own nose to spite Napoleon's face. It is suicidal, it is criminal!"—and I know not how many other hard names Mr. Horsfall hurled at the poor Government whilst Mr. Scott, with the ink scarce dry on his commission, fidgetted in his seat and was, I thought, hard put to it to defend the Government. At last when Mr. Horsfall grew more vehement in his denunciation of ministers, Mr. Scott bade him remember that it was the Whigs who in January, 1807, issued the first counterblast to Napoleon's Berlin Decree; and then did these two Englishmen, the one a Whig and the other a Tory, get so warm about Whiggery and Toryism that I had much to do to get to the truth of the matter. In a lull of the storm I did so far presume upon the great condescension that Mr. Scott had shewn to me, for my father's sake, as to ask him what these same Orders in Council might be, and how they bore upon us humble folk in Slaithwaite, for save that every one did speak of them as the cause of much of our bad trade and sore distress, I knew little for certain about them. "You must know then," explained Mr. Scott, "that in 1806 Napoleon issued from Berlin a proclamation, addressed to all the world, declaring the island of Great Britain in a state of blockade, all British subjects, wherever found, prisoners of war, and all British goods, wherever taken, lawful prize, and excluding from all the ports of France every vessel which had touched at any British port, no matter to what nation such vessel might belong." — —

"But surely, sir," I said timidly, for I knew little of such great matters, "surely, that was to declare war on all the countries of the world."

"'Rem acu tetigisti' — thou hast touched the point with a pin," cried Mr. Mellor, who had drawn near, whereat I blushed mightily, for I knew a little of the Latin, thank to much persistence of my good dominie, and by this time all the company had ceased their jesting and coffing and idle gossip, and all ears were cocked to hear what Mr. Scott and our neighbour Horsfall were so hot about.

"Then did the Whig Government," continued Mr. Scott, triumphantly, "issue an Order in Council, declaring that England was authorized by the Berlin Decree to blockade the whole seaboard of France; to prohibit all vessels which had touched at a French port from entering our harbours, and making their cargoes fair prize. It was that Order which estranged America, and has made it so that all our foreign trade has been cut off as with a knife."

"Nay but," said Mr. Horsfall, "you should not forget to say that Mr. Percival, your Tory minister, has not only continued the Order but extended it; that the Whigs have admitted the error of their policy, that petition after petition has gone from the manufacturers of Yorkshire, praying for a Repeal of the Order's, and that Mr. Brougham is never weary striving for that good end. But we know how it is—the war may ruin us manufacturers, but it pays the landowner. It keeps up the price of corn and stock, it finds pay and promotion for the young bloods of the aristocracy, it distracts the minds of the people at home from domestic reforms, it keeps up the hideous system of privilege, by which peer and prelate batten on the spoils of a people oppressed to the limits of endurance, and it is mighty convenient to keep Napoleon as a bogy man to frighten the people withal when they cry for reform." And then did these two good men at it again hammer and tongs, and others joined in, and the ale and the wine talked louder than sense and knowledge, and you could make neither head nor tail of all the talk. But presently they simmered down, and Mr. Horsfall was drinking to the health of Mrs. Scott, whom he vowed he knew when she was the beauty of Storthes Hall, as if nothing had come between them to raise a dust, and all the more that, as good chance would have it, they hit on a subject on which they had little variance.

"I hear," said Mr. Scott, "that you are trying these new finishing frames of the Taylor's, at Ottiwell's."

"I am that," said Mr. Horsfall, "and well content I am with them. They finish the cloth better far than the best croppers ever did or could, and one machine can do the work of four men."

"Then you will need less men," said Mr. Scott, "and this is no time to be sacking men—I remember what happened twenty years ago when Grimshaw, of Manchester, arranged with Dr. Cartwright, the new Bishop Blaize as they called him, to set up four hundred looms at Manchester to be run by a steam engine. Grimshaw received hundreds of threatening letters, he was fired at more than once, his wife nearly fell into a decline from constant fear, and just when the mill was built, for four hundred looms, and part of the machines were in, mill and looms and all were swallowed up in a fire, and who made the fire you may well guess. It ruined Grimshaw, and now he goes about saying he wishes Bishop Blaize had been in blazes 'fore ever he had tempted him with his fine stories. But you Whigs will never be content with the wisdom of our forefathers. You must have something new fangled, either in mill or state"—and so they off again into politics; and having promised my mother to be home by milking time, and fearful if I stayed longer the fumes of the tobacco and the wine would be too much for an unseasoned head, I took my leave of Mr. Scott and won my way into the open air.

By the stepping–stones that crossed the river, who should I see but Soldier Jack and a merry party that had been out with the harriers. They had come trooping down Kitchen Fold from over Crosland Moor way, and were in high feather, shouting and singing, while the hounds bayed in chorus. Soldier Jack was no man's lad, a bye–blow. He had been left on the Workhouse steps tied in a bundle, and nought to show who was his father or who his mother. Then when he was a lad of ten years old the Overseer had 'prenticed him out to a shoemaker in Huddersfield, but he had been a sore trial to his master—disappearing and appearing when he liked, and neither fair words nor the strap, of which his master was not sparing if Jack spoke truth, availing to make him follow the old adage and stick to the last. Then one fine day the recruiting sergeant, in all his bravery, had put up at the Rose and Crown, and called on all gallant lads to take the king's shilling and fight for glory and their country. "That's the colour for me to dye," thought Jack, and braving the law, which would have laid him by the heels for breaking his writings, he 'listed in a foot regiment, and was off for the wars with a heart as light as the heels he showed his master. Then many a year passed. Jack was unseen and forgotten in the haunts of his youth, when lo! he appeared, from God knows where, straight as a picking rod, brown as a berry, minus the left arm, and with a limp of his right leg; but otherwise sound as a bell and tight as a drum. He had some money, in the coinage of all the countries of Europe well nigh; and, as I heard tell, right royally did Jack live while his money lasted. He had no fixed quarters in the early days of his return from the wars, but of recent years he had dwelt much among the Burn Platters, an uncanny race of outlaws that some said were Frenchmen and some said were gypsies, that lived at Burn Platts on the moors on the edge of Slaithwaite, and of whose savagery and evil ways many stories were told. But Soldier Jack ever kept himself spruce and trim, and was a welcome visitor at every house on all that country side. How he lived none did know for gospel. At times in his cups he talked mysteriously of golden crosses and rare stones that he had lighted on in the sack of holy houses in Spain; but this, I think, was mere embroidery of his adventures. Lord! what a life had been Soldier Jack's—what sieges he had seen, what pitched battles he had fought in, what prisoners he had taken, what forlorn hopes he had led, what distressed damsels he had rescued, how many haughty hidalgos he had slain with his own hand! Even Lord Wellington himself had been under obligation to him, and he had all but seized with his own hands the awful person of Napoleon himself. How he lived I say I know not. Belike he had some small pension from the king. At haymaking time, too, he turned a good cock and an honest penny, despite his one arm. He never missed a market or a fair, could be trusted above the common to carry a message, and was something of a farrier. But set job he had none, and yet never wanted. To be sure he had free quarters in nigh every hostelry all the country round, and if truth were told could hang up his hat when he would, for good and all, at the Black Bull; for widow Walker, who kept that house, was known to be widowing, and a fair and buxom dame withal.

Now on this night of the Rent Audit Soldier Jack was pleased to leave the hunters and walk homewards with me, though his comrades were clamorous for him to join them in another bout at the ale. Though times were never so bad, it went hard with the weavers if they could not leave their shuttles and follow the hounds; and somehow they had ever wherewith to guzzle at the inn. But Jack was maybe wearied with the trail, and we took our way past the church and up the hill towards Holm. For some short distance Jack walked with never a word, though I wanted news of the hunt, where they had killed, and whose hound showed the truer scent. Then without prelude Jack began.

"Ben, I want a word with thee. You and me has ever been friends, and your mother, God bless her, ever the soft word and the open hand. And yo'r father, a good man, though over hard on the slips o' youth"—now Jack was forty if a week— "But there are things brewing it is right yo' should know on; for them tha's 'kin to yo' are like to be tangled in em."

"Whatever do yo' mean, Jack?" I asked, trying to speer at him in the gloom, for I thought maybe the ale had got into his head.

"There's a deal o' sufferin' about these parts, Ben. More nor yo' think on. Yo' happen think 'at because th' lads about are after th' hounds an' have a bit to spend on drink 'at they're better off nor they are. But yo' see I'm more about nor yo' an' more intimate like. Folk is sellin' their bits o' stuff quiet like. Mony a decent woman 'at wouldn't have it known has sent me wi' 'owd keepsakes an' heirlooms like to th' silversmith i' Huddersfelt an' Owdham. They put a brave face on it an' talk little, but aw know there's scores o' fam'lies i' this valley and on these hill sides, 'at's welly clammin'! It isn't them as goes 'afore the overseers 'at's the worst off.

There's scores an' scores livin' on the town 'at go reg'lar every week for th' town 'lowance. They'n got th' length o' th' ovverseer's foot, an' its not for the like o' me to blame 'em."

"Crows shouldn't pike crows' 'een, eh Jack?" I put in.

"Th' ovverseer's fair game," continued Jack, unmoved. "But he's a fool for all his stuck up ways. Aw tell yo' 'at there's hundreds awmost sucking their finger ends, like bears do their paws, 'at winnot go on to th' parish. An' mark yo', th' poor ha' borne wi' slack work an' mullocked on as best they could, as long as they thought th' wars and bad harvests were to blame. An' they've bided in hope, for harvests winnot all be bad, an' we'st beat the little Corporal yet. But now th' mesters are for makin' bad worse wi' this new machinery. They're crying 'Every man for hissen an' devil take the hindmost.' They're bringing wood and iron to do the work of willing hands and arms, an', by gow, the lads about won't see their craft ruined, an' them an' theirs pined to death, wi'out a blow struck. Aw tell yo', Ben, there's mischief brewin', or my name's not Soldier Jack; an' if yo' want to know more, yo' mun ask yon mettlesome cousin o' yours, Judd Mellor, o' th' Brigg." —

"What! George Mellor?" I cried; "why, what has he to do with it?" For such an ending to the soldier's tale I never thought nor dreamed of.

"I've said my say, Ben, and yo'll get no more out o' me. It's no use pumpin' at a dry well tha' knows. So aw'll say good neet, an' my duty to thi father an' mother." And resisting my entreaty that he would go onwards to our house and take pot luck at supper, Jack wheeled off into the dark, and I heard his stride, firm and martial still, despite the gamey leg, as he made across a footpath to the left, and his voice humming a stave of Lillibulero.

CHAPTER III.

IT WAS the Christmas Eve of 1811, a night beautiful, bright and clear. The moon was high in the heavens, and a myriad stars gemmed the sky. Flakes of snow fell gently, like the lighting of grasshoppers, but not so thick as to cloud the air. It was cold, but not bitterly cold. The snow crunched cheerfully under your feet, the hedges were rather frosted than cumbered; but the wild waste of hill all around and above Slaithwaite was white with a coverlet smoothed as with careful hands. The little homesteads on the hillsides stood out stark and black on the pale setting, their slender lights of lamp or candle declaring that many this night waked, who every other night in the year went to bed with the sun. We sat in the house, kitchen you would call it now—all our household save only 'Siah, who, we made no doubt, was faithful to his yearly custom of honouring Christmas by getting more ale than was good for him. Only a candle burned on the table, but the fire was piled high, and cast a lurid light about the room, the yule log saved from last year's fire blazing bravely. My father was fidgeting and looking at the clock. He would have rather been in bed. We had had our supper, but a great currant loaf and a round of cheese was on the table, and the biggest pitcher of all our ware was ready for Martha to fill from the barrel in the cellar, when the right moment should come. Mother and Mary had speculated, and wondered and then wondered again as to whether the Church singers would this year sing a verse or two by our door. My mother argued they would not, as a mark of reprobation for our joining the Baptists. Mary, who knew that the hearts of the young men of a choir, church or chapel, are not in the keeping of vicar or minister, had her own reasons for maintaining a contrary view. My father stoutly declared he did not care a brass farthing one way or another. Meat and drink and five good shillings were waiting them, he said, and if they were fools enough to turn up their noses at good victuals and good brass, that was their look out, not his. All the same we all knew he would have felt it keenly that our house should be passed over for the first time within the memory of any of us. Then came the further problem—which set would be likely to reach us first, the church, who must sing first at the Vicarage and Dr. Dean's, and at Sammy Sykes's, who was churchwarden; or the waits from Powle Moor, who had further to come and a rougher way. Anyhow we hoped devoutly the two parties would not arrive together. We could hear, in the still night, the sound of music in the air, sad and wistful, floating among the hills. However we should soon be out of doubt, for midnight was hard upon us.

The old clock warned the hour with a staggering click, and its clear metallic voice had rung out but six of the twelve hours, when we heard a footfall on the carpet of snow in the yard. There was no murmur of voices, none of the hawking and tuning and chuntering of a band of lads and lasses, but right out upon the still air, firm, strong and deep baritone, as from a singer well set up and fearless, music of itself, and with instrument neither of string nor reed to back it, came the grand old words and tune, like which no other words and tune do ever stir my heart—

> "Christians awake! Salute the happy morn,
> Whereon the Saviour of Mankind was born.
> Rise to adore the mystery of love
> Which hosts of angels chanted from above;
> With them the joyful tidings first begun
> Of God Incarnate and the Virgin's Son."

And then again.

> "Of God Incarnate and the Virgin's Son."

Who could it be? Some lone wanderer surely that had stolen a march on church and chapel alike.

"It's happen 'Siah," hazarded Martha. No 'Siah had a voice like a frog.

"It's th' sexton," said my father.

Now the sexton was sixty years old, with a piping treble, and the voice of our midnight visitor was rounded, full and mellow.

I looked to Mary for a hazard, for no thought of who it could be came to my mind, and I was not best pleased that anyone should outstrip the choirs. And as I looked the voice without took up another strain.

> "Then to the watchful shepherds it was told
> Who heard the Angelic herald's voice 'Behold.'"

And Mary's face was a sight to see. She had dropped her knitting on her lap, and her hands were crossed over the work, and her face was as though the morning sun shone on it, and a soft smile was on her parted lips, a look half–glad, half sorry, was in her eyes and her bosom seemed to flutter.

"It's George," she said, very softly, "George Mellor, fra' th' Brigg."

And then came a thundering knock at the door, and my father rose to open it right heartily, and in came my cousin, George Mellor, with a great red muffler round his neck, and his coat all flaked with snow, and his short brown beard and moustache wet with half–melted flakes; now stamping his feet and now kicking them against the door–post, and bringing with him a gust of cold air and a sprinkling of tiny feathery sprays that whisked in at his back.

"A merry Christmas to you, Uncle William, and a happy New Year." "And to you, aunt, with my mother's love." This with a hearty smacking kiss. "And to you, Mary, and here's a Christmas Box for you," and I thought George would have kissed Mary too, but she was away to the other side of the table.

And so all round, with a noble smack at Martha's lips, Martha being nothing loth, and giving kiss for kiss with a good will that set us all laughing. "A right proper lad is George Mellor, and knows how to win a lass," I heard Martha tell

'Siah afterwards, when she was rating him by way of curing his aching head.

And a right proper man George Mellor was. Six feet by the stick, and with shoulders well back, and strong, firm, warm hands that gripped you to make you tingle. His eyes were brown and full of fire, and dark auburn hair curled close upon a rounded head. He had a temper, if you like, but he never bore malice, and I never knew him do or say a mean thing, and if he was at times unjust he was quick to make amends. He was a prime favourite of my mother. Her own sister was George Mellor's mother. His father was dead, and my Aunt Mellor, to my mother's surprise and indignation, had married John Wood, of Longroyd Bridge, a cloth finisher, in middle life, somewhat younger than my aunt, and a man it was hard to like. Whatever could have possessed my aunt capped us all. She had a bit of money of her own, and could have pulled along in a middling way without a second marriage. But my father said, "You mun wait till yo're a widow yoursen, if yo want to know what makes a widdow get wed again." Anyhow Aunt Matty had a hard time of it, for John Wood was a hard man, cold–blooded and spiteful. He soon found out that he could hurt his wife through George, and he always seemed to rub George the wrong way. The lad ran away once, and none of us knew what became of him till long afterwards, not even his own mother, who nigh fretted herself into her grave over him. But he turned up again as suddenly as he had vanished, taller, stouter, firmer set, quieter. John Wood thought his spirit was broken, made him so quiet. But he found out his mistake when he began to slur at him.

"See here, John Wood," George had said, for he would never call him father, "I have come back home for my mother's sake, because it was made clear to me my place was by her side. I will work for you, and do my duty by you, and I will pay you fair for my board and ask no favour of you as man or lodger. But you must speak me fair, and treat my mother kindly, or you'll rue the day you ever crossed George Mellor." He had a quiet way with him when he was most roused, a sort of cold heat, had George; though over what you would have thought concerned him least, he would flare up and flush, and his eye would blaze and out his words would come like a pent–up torrent. I never feared George when he was in a temper, but it was dangerous to cross him when his cheek and lips paled and his words came soft and slow.

"Aw walked up th' cut side," he explained. "It seemed an age since aw saw yo' all; an' our house's none too cheerful just now. Trade's fearful bad, an' John Wood's as sore as a boil—an' I bowt this sprig o' mistletoe of a hawker for yo' to hang on th' bowk, an' who' should let you Christmas in if not your own nevvy, Aunt Bamforth."

"Sakes alive, aw nivvir thowt on it," cried my mother all of a sudden. "Ben, whip outside this minnit—doesn't ta see George's hair is awmost red an' it's black for luck—whatever could'st ta be thinking' on, George?" And so nothing must do but I must step outside and enter with due Christmas greetings, to cross the luck, and the waits from Powle Moor arriving at the very nick of time, we all went in together; and Mary and George and myself were soon busy enough handing round the cheese and cake and ale.

George and I slept together that night, and next morning, we all, save my mother and Martha, who must stop at home to cook the dinner, went to church, for we wouldn't for anything have missed hearing the Christmas hymn; and near all Slaithwaite was there, Methodie and Baptists and all; and even folk that went nowhere, Owenwites they called them, made a point of going to church that one morning of the year. They said it was to give them an appetite for the beef and plum pudding; but I think it was more by way of keeping up a sort of nodding acquaintance with what they felt they might have to fall back on after all, for you may ever notice that the parson treads very close on the heels of the doctor.

Now after dinner my father must needs have a glass of hot spirits and water, and presently was fast asleep in his chair, and I would have been glad to have done likewise, for I was not used to sitting up half the night, and had dozed off more than once in church, only to be roused with a start by a nudge from Mary. But George was all for a walk over Stanedge to stretch his legs and get a mouthful of home–fed air after the foul smells of the town. I thought Mary pouted a bit, and asked her to go with us, but she said two were company and three were none, and George maybe was too fine to walk out with a country lass. I expected George to disclaim any such slanderous thoughts, but he only laughed and said something about the wind being too nipping for the roses on Mary's cheeks. So off we two set towards Marsden at a good swinging pace. When we had dropped down into the village, and were thinking of calling at the Red Lion to get a glass of ale and a snack, whom should we come on but Mr. Horsfall, of Marsden.

"What, Ben, lad!" he said to me heartily and shaking my hand most warmly — "A right good Christmas to you, and my compliments to my good friends at Holme." A pleasant man was Mr. Horsfall when he liked, but one you must not lightly sour or cross. He had an iron hand, folk said, but he kept it gloved.

"And who's your friend, Ben?"

I made George known to him, and Mr. Horsfall could tell him of knowing his mother, my aunt, when she was a blithe young girl courting with my uncle Mellor that was dead. But what surprised me was that George, generally so cheery and ready to meet civility more than half–way, seemed to freeze up and would scarce give his hand in greeting to Mr. Horsfall.

"It'll be cold on the top, Ben," said Mr. Horsfall. "Come along to Ottiwells and taste our spiced ale. My wife will be glad to have a crack with yau, and it'll be cozier by th' fireside nor ovver th' top I'll warrant you."

My own good will went with this invitation, for I got enough and to spare of Stanedge in my business rounds; but George hung back strangely, and Mr. Horsfall, not used to have his advances coldly met, ceased to press us, and with awkward apologies on my part, and a curt nod from George, we went our several ways.

"I wonder you can speak civil to a man like yond," said George, when we had our faces straight set to climb the hill.

"Name o' wonder, why, George?" I asked, thinking nothing but that some private quarrel must have sprung up, of which I knew nothing, but ready enough to side with George, for in my young days families stood by each other, right or wrong.

"Don't you know that Horsfall is foremost of all in pressing on the use of the new machines? Don't you know that he has put them into Ottiwells? Don't you know he is sacking the old hands and will have none but young 'uns that will and can learn, for it isn't all that will that can, how to work the new frames? Don't you know that there's many a family in Marsden now, this very merry Christmas that we're wishing each other like prating parrots, that has scarce a fire in the grate or a scrap of meat on the table, or warm clothing to the back, just because of Horsfall and such as he? Don't you know that in Huddersfield Market Horsfall has sworn hanging isn't good enough for the Nottingham lads? If you don't know, you live with your eyes shut, Ben, and your ears waxed, for aw'll never believe 'at your heart's shut, lad. And then you ask me why I couldn't take him hearty by the hand."

"But what does it matter to thee, George?" I asked, wondering at his warmth and hardly keeping pace with him as he strode on in his excitement.

"It matters nowt to me in a sense, Ben, and yet it matters all to me. I suppose th' upshot would be that John Wood might as well shut up shop, and little I'd care for that. John Wood's cake's baked, and if it warn't, there's enough for my mother 'bout his brass. But it's not o' Wood nor myself I'm thinking, Ben, and I don't take it too kindly you should look at it that way. I tell you, Ben, there's hundreds o' men and women and wee helpless bairns that's just clemming to death. Yo, don't see as much of it up i' Slowit nor on th' hill sides, though it's war there nor yo happen think. And now th' mesters are for doing th' work o' men an' women too wi' cunning contrivances that will make arms and legs o' no use, and water and steam in time will do the work that Natur' intended to be done by good honest muscle."

"Aw think yo' exaggerate, George," I said. "A little saving o' manual labour here an' there's one thing, th' displacement o' human agency altogether's what yo' prophesy."

"Aw've no patience wi' thee, Ben. Tha' cannot see farther nor thi own nose end. Aw tell yo unless the toilers of England rise and strike for their rights, there'll soon be neither rights nor toilers. Aw've looked into this thing further nor you, an' aw can see th' signs o' th' times. Th' tendency's all one way. There'll soon be no room for poor men in this country. Its part of a system aw tell yo'. There's a conspiracy on foot to improve and improve till th' working man that has nowt but his hands and his craft to feed him and his childer, will be improved off th' face o' creation. Aw've been reading aw tell you, an' aw've been listening an' aw've been seeing, an' aw've been thinking; an' what aw've read an' what aw've seen has burned into my soul. The natural rights of man are not thowt of in this country, th' unnatural rights o' property ha' swallowed 'em up. It's all property, property."

"Nay, George, yo're riding yo'r high horse again," I said; but I couldn't help admiring him, for he spoke well, and his face was all lit up with the glow of intellect and passion.

"It's God's truth aw'm speaking, Ben, and pity o't it 'tis true, as th' player says. What is it keeps folk so poor? Bad trade. What is it keeps trade so bad? Th' wars. Allus wars. For twenty years it's been war and war to it. What are we fighting for, I ask you?"

"To keep Boney out o' England," I said very promptly.

"Nowt o' th' sort, Ben—that's a bogey to frighten babbie's wi'—Boney axed nowt better nor to be friends wi' England. Th' French ha' more sense nor us. They saw all th' good things o' this life were grasped by th' nobles an' th' priests. They saw it were better to be born a beast of the field than a man child. They saw that the people made wealth by their toil; and the seigneurs, that's lords, and the church enjoyed the wealth they made, only leaving them bare enough to keep body and soul together. Aye, they're careful enough not to kill the goose that lays the golden eggs. That is, sometimes. Time's they over do it. But a trodden worm will turn, an' they turned in France. They sent their proud lords and ladies packing."

"To the guillotine," I interposed.

"Packing, I say, and the fat parsons, faithless shepherds of an abandoned flock, packing with them. Then the people begin to put things to rights."

"And a pretty mess they made of it," I put in.

"But all the kings and, emperors in Europe, an' all th' landlords an' all that had got rich by robbery, an' all th' bishops and clergy, little an' big, hangers on o' th' aristocrats to a man, took alarm. They thowt their turn would come next, an' they raised the cry of England in danger. It wasn't the people of England that wer' fleyed. Not they. They knew well enough nowt could make them waur off nor they were. Th' war were a put up job of th' king and th' nobles and th' squires. And who profited by it? The noble and the squire an' the sleek parson with his tithes. What has made corn as far beyond the poor man's reach as though a grain of wheat were a ruby or a pearl? The wars, always the wars. And the people, the thousands upon thousands of men and women who have no part nor parcel in this war, save to send their children to die on a gory bed, what voice or what part have they in all this? The part and the part of sheep driven to the slaughter"—

"But what has Horsfall to do with all this?" I asked, very naturally I think.

"He has this to do with it, Ben. Ever since th' bad times began, Englishmen ha' been told to stand together shoulder to shoulder agen a common enemy. Th' poor ha' borne their sufferings wi'out much murmuring as long as they saw th' rich suffer wi' themselves. Patriotism isn't a rich man's monopoly. Poor folk love th' owd country, though aw wonder sometimes what they love it for. But now what do we see? These new machines offer th' masters th' chance o' supplying their customers at a less cost to theirsen than they ha' done up to now. Aw'll give yo' an illustration of what aw mean. A lace frame such as they're putting up i' Nottingham costs £120. They say it'll save the work of four. Th' master saves in a year more than th' cost o' th' machine. He saves it, but who loses it? Why th' wage earners to be sure. And that's what they call standing shoulder to shoulder. Aw call it deserting your comrade and leaving him to shift for his–sen. Th' 'Leeds Mercury' only last week said there were twenty thousand stocking–makers out of employment in Notting-ham, and yo' may judge for yersen what that means."

"But what can yo' do, George? Yo' cannot fight agen th' law o' th' land. Th' masters ha' th' law at their backs—yo'll nobbut get yersen into trouble. It's waur nor kickin' agen th' pricks. Yo' surely wi'not ha' ought to do wi' machine breaking. That'll nobbut land thee i' towzer, an' happen waur nor towzer."

"It isn't towzer 'll stop me, Ben. Aw'm groping i' th' dark just now. Frame breaking and rick burning seems but spiteful work, but it is action, and action of some sort seems called for. If we submit like dumb cattle, our rulers say we are content and have no grievances; if we assemble in great numbers and proclaim our wrongs they hang us for sedition. What can we do, where shall we turn? Aw cannot see daylight which ever way aw turn."

"Cannot yo' let things bide, George? Happen things 'll shape theirsen. It's little such as us can do to mend things. If tha' were Lord Dartmouth na', tha' might do some good. But aw can see nowt but trouble for thee i' me'lling i' this wark, and what hurts thee tha' knows well will hurt me, George."

"Aw know that, Ben. And aw've more reason nor ever o' late for keeping out o' trouble. Is there ought between thee and Mary, Ben?"

"What, our Mary?" I asked, bewildered, somewhat by so sudden a change of subject, and not seeing the working of George's mind.

"Aye, your Mary," said George.

"What does ta' want to know for, George?" I asked; and I tried to ask as though I cared little for the answer, and yet I knew, all of a flash like, what the answer would be, and that somehow, and why I could scarce even myself say to myself, the answer would make me wince.

"Because, George, if ever aw wed, your Mary will be the lass."

"Yo'll happen ask her first," I said, nettled.

"P'raps tha's axed her already?"

"Tha' knows very well aw hannot, Ben. It only came into my head last neet when 'oo were singing 'Wild Shepherds.' 'Oo's a sweet voice, an' th' way she looks when 'oo sings makes yo' think a bit o' heaven's opened up, an' th' light inside is shinin' right down on her face—hasn't ta' noticed it, Ben?"

"Mary's ower young for courtin'," I said.

"But tha' hasn't told me, Ben, is there owt between yo' and her? But there cannot be. Tha'd ha' told me if there wor. Besides she's too near o' kin to thee an' browt up i' th' same house too. She'll be more sister like to thee, Ben, aw reckon. But is there owt?"

"Nay there's nowt, George. She's thine to win an' to wear for me. But 'oo's ovver young for courtin', George. An' if yo'r for our Mary, tha' mun put all thowts out o' thi yed but stickin' to work an' makin' her a good home. And that reminds me. It 'ad welly slipt mi mind. Soldier Jack was hinting summat t'other day. Tha' are'nt keeping owt back fra' me, are ta, George?"

"Can aw trust thee, Ben?"

"Tha' knows that best thissen, George." We had reached the very crest of Stanedge, and were looking down upon the Diggle side and over towards Pots an' Pans an' where the road leads to St. Chad's and winds round towards what is now called Bills o' Jack's. We came to a stand by common impulse. George stood right anent me.

"Can aw trust thee, Ben," he asked again, and looked at me as though he would search my very heart.

"Tha' knows best thissen," I replied once more; for I should have thought to lower myself by protesting to him who had been my dearest, almost my only friend, since we were boys together.

"With my life, Ben," he said very solemnly, and took my hand.

And then George told me something of what was afoot in Huddersfield. Steps were to be taken, he said, to dissuade the manufacturers from ousting manual labour in any of the various processes of the making and finishing of cloth, by the use of machinery. For this purpose the men were to bind themselves by solemn oath neither to work the new machines nor to work in any shop or mill into which they might be introduced. No violence of any sort was to be employed either against man or machine, at least not if the masters proved amenable to reason; and of that George thought there could be little question. "They cannot stand against us, if we are united," said George; "our weakness lies in action unconcerted and without method. If we set our faces resolutely against the use of these new fangled substitutes for human labour, we can at least compel the masters to wait till times are better and trade mends. It may be that when the wars are over and the market calls for a larger and a quicker output, machinery may be gradually introduced without hardship to those who have grown old in the old methods and who cannot use themselves to new ways. Meantime we shall have learned the secret and the value of combination and we may turn our organization to the protection and the improvement of the worker and to the wresting of those rights that are now withheld."

Now to this I could see no mariner of objection, and partly from curiosity, partly because my blood had been fired by George's words, but much more because it was George who urged it, I promised to attend a meeting of some of George's friends who were' like–minded with himself; and promised too, though not so readily, to keep my own counsel about what he had talked on.

The early evening of winter was falling, and we turned homewards. We did not speak much. My cousin was deep in thoughts of his own, and I, too, had enough to ponder on. I did not half like my new departure. I was not much of a politician, and had always thought my part in public affairs would be to ride to York once in a while and vote for the Whigs as my father had done before me. As for setting the world straight, I had no ambition that way. In time I had no doubt I should be either a deacon at the Powle or a churchwarden at the church, and probably constable of the manor if I thrived. To make fair goods, to sell them at a fair price, to live in peace with my neighbours, and in time to marry, such was the sum of my ambition.

And that sent my mind in a bound to Mary. The house would look strange and lonesome without Mary. I should miss her saucy greeting of a morning; I should miss her gentle bantering, the sunshine of her sweet face and the music of her voice. The more I tried to think of the old place without Mary, the less I liked the picture. And when I tried to console myself with thinking that there were as good fish in the sea as ever came out of it, I failed dismally.

When we reached home keen set for tea, there was the table laid all ready, and a scolding too for being late. But I turned away my mother's wrath by giving her Mr. Horsfall's greetings, and set her talking of him and his wife and all the family tree. For mother had a rare gift that way, knowing the relationship by blood and marriage of every family for miles around, and able, in a way you must hear to believe, to count up cousinships and half–cousins, and uncles and great uncles, till your brain turned round. Except my lord's family and the folk at the vicarage, who had come from the south, I think she made us akin to all the folk in Slaithwaite, Linthwaite and Lingards. As was natural, George took but little interest in this intimate pedigree, and about eight o'clock announced his resolve to take the road to the Brigg. He was greatly pressed to stay to supper, but would not, much to my mother's concern, who had a firm persuasion, that town bred lads never got enough to eat, and cherished a suspicion that George, though as hale and hearty a youth as ever went on two legs, and one as little likely as any to be put on, was starved as to his body and broken as to his spirit by his step–father.

It befell that night, whether by chance or that my mother schemed it so, that she and I sat up by the fireside after all the others had gone to bed. My mother had her eternal knitting, and I tried to settle my mind to a book; but could not, for thinking of matters not on the printed page. I gave up the effort after a while, and set my mind resolutely to think on my promise to join the plot against the masters; but all to no good, for do what I would, my thoughts strayed to what George had said of Mary, and I liked it less and less. It gave me a turn when my mother said—

"Mary grows a fine lass and noan ill–favoured, think'st ta, Ben? Not 'at aw set much store on good looks, for beauty's but skin deep, as is weel known. But Mary's one 'at 'll wear well, an' keep her looks to th' last," continued my mother, without waiting for the opinion she had asked from me. "Aw was just such another misen when yo'r father begun a courting me."

Now I opened my eyes at this, for it had never occurred to me to think of my mother as a beauty.

"Not but what there's points in Mary 'at could be mended," went on my mother serenely. "She's a notion o' keepin' things straight an' tidy, but 'oo's a bit too finickin' in her ways an' too mindful o' her hair an' careful o' her hands, an' happen too fond o' colour in her ribbons; but 'oo'l mend o' that when th' children come. An' she's mebbe too free o' her tongue."

Oh, mother! mother!

"But that comes o' your father encouragin' her an' laughin' at her answerin' back, when it would seem her better to hearken to what I have to say an' be thankful 'oo has a aunt to tak' pains wi' her."

"Aw dunnot doubt 'oo is," I cried.

"An' Mary's noan 'bout brass, an' though awst allus hold 'at it's better to ha' a fortin' in a wife nor wi' a wife, there's summat i' what th' owd Quaker said, 'at it wer' just as easy to fall i' love where brass was as where it wasn't. Ever sin' my sister died, an' Mary wer' left o' mi hands, her fortin' has been out at interest, an' we'n charged her nowt for her keep."

"Aw should think not, indeed," I cried, indignant at the very thought.

"There's them 'at would," said my mother tartly.

"We're not o' that breed, aw hope," I said. "Anyways we ha' not, so tha needn't fluster thissen, though aw'll tell thee, Ben, it's better to be a bit too keen about brass nor a lump too careless. So Mary 'll ha' more nor her smock to her back, wed who she will, an' a handy lass in a house, an' th' best of trainin, as all the country side will tell yo'. An' for my part, when th' parents is agreeable, an' plenty o' room i' th' house, an' there's th' spare bedroom, an' we could fit th' lumber hoil up for th' childer, an' when yo've made up yo'r mind, it's no good wastin' time; an' Easter'll soon be here, an' aw shouldn't like a weddin' 'atween Easter an' Whissunday. Tha'd better see what Mary says, an' aw'll speak to yo'r father afore th' week's out."

"But, mother," I cried, "Mary's nivver given me a thowt that way. Aw'm sure she just thinks o' me as a brother. Aw shud only fley her an' happen mak' it uneasy for her to live here, if aw said owt and she didn't like th' thowts on it."

"Who said she had given thee a thowt that way? Aw sud think she knows what becomes her better nor to be lettin' her mind things till th' man speaks. But Mary's a good lass, an' I'll go bail 'oll wed to please them as brought her up."

"Did yo, mother?" I asked with malice, for my father and mother had been married at Almondbury out of our parish, taking French leave of her folk. And as my mother rallied her thoughts for a reply, I made my escape to bed.

CHAPTER IV.

IN February of 1812, it was borne in upon our minds that something more than distress and disaffection were in our midst. These we were used to, and they had come to seem matters of course. It was painful to go to the Huddersfield Market these days. The old brick rotunda was opened as usual, and as usual the stalls were piled with cloth. The manufacturers stood by their wares, or gathered in anxious groupes in the alleys between the stalls. But buyers were rare, and prices ruinous. Shop–keepers in the New–street stood on their steps looking for a customer as eagerly as a becalmed captain for a cap of wind. Round the old market cross the famished workmen stood sullen and scowling. They had not much to say. They were too far gone even for anger. Their faces were now pinched and haggard. If a man had thrown a loaf among them they would have fought for it. It was said that at that time families had not twopence a head to live on each day. At the market dinners at the Cherry Tree and the Pack Horse the manufacturers dined together as usual but it was doleful work. We sat down to our meat as to funeral cakes.

Bad trade long drawn out had tired the staunchest of us, and there was not one ray of hope to brighten the outlook. War still dragged on, now a victory, now a defeat. But we had ceased to look for an issue from our troubles from the success of our arms. The contest seemed interminable, and meanwhile banks were breaking, credit was destroyed, old firms were failing; and men who had struggled on bravely, making goods to stock rather than close their mills and sack their old hands, saw no choice but to give up and own themselves beaten. Wheat was eight shillings a stone, and so bad at that, that it could not be baked; the poor rate was at twelve shillings in the pound, and worst of all, the poor were cursing their masters in their hearts and thinking their sufferings lay at their master's doors.

Now I cannot for my part think such a time was fitting for bringing in machinery. I know full well that water power and steam power and improved machinery have been of untold good to the poor; but those who were to reap the first profit should to my thinking have bided their time. But Mr. Cartwright, of Rawfold, Mr. Horsfall, of Ottiwells and some others, seemed callous to the sufferings round them. Perhaps it was they looked so intently at the distant object, that they could not see the things at their feet. They were both men impatient of obstacles; they resented interference; they pooh–poohed those who counselled delay.

In that month of February we had the first news of any violence in our neighbourhood. Late of a Saturday night a number of men with faces blacked and their dress disguised, some wearing women's gowns and others strange hood gear, broke into the dressing shop of Mr. Joseph Hirst, of Marsh, destroyed the dressing frames, the shears and other furniture of a gig–mill. The same evil fate befell Mr. James Balderson, of Crosland Moor, and Mr. William Hinchcliffe, of Leymoor. Then came the soldiers, the Scots Greys and the Second Dragoon Guards. They were billeted in the various hostelries of the town at free quarters, and it was not long before there was much scandal at their carrying on a drinking, swearing lot of men, a terror to decent girls, reeling on the streets in broad day with the loose women of the town, singing lewd songs, with no respect even to the gravest and most dignified magistrates in the town, paying heed only to their own officers, and that only when on guard or patrol. They were a bye–word and a reproach in the town, and of no sort of use at all.

Then, too, did the Head Constable of Huddersfield call upon all men over seventeen, and under fifty, paying rates to the poor, to enrol themselves as special constables, and among them was none other than John Wood, who looked mighty big with his constable's staff, and talked large to my aunt and George and to me, when I called at the Brigg about the valiant deeds he would do if ever Luddite fell into his hands. For by this time the name "Luddite" had crept into the district, how I know not. And at his step–father's big talk George Mellor smiled grimly.

I say I called at Mr. Wood's house at Longroyd Bridge. I had meant to have a talk with George about the smashing of the machines of which, and of nothing but which, the market talk had been. I was not easy in my mind about the matter. I thought, after my promises to George, it was but my due to know if he had any share in these doings. But I was let. My aunt had her ailments to talk of, and burdened me with messages to my mother. Then Mr. Wood was there whilst we took a dish of tea, and all his talk was of the dressing the Luds would get. I asked him if he intended to try the new machines in his own shop, to which, for my aunt's sake, we sent our own goods to be finished. But I gathered that my astute uncle deemed it safe to see how the cat jumped before committing himself. He was ever one for letting others do the fighting, and then coming softly in and reaping the spoils. So with one thing and another I got no talk with my cousin, and started off by my lone to walk to Slaithwaite over Crosland Moor. And near the Brigg itself I came on Soldier Jack, with a poke slung over his shoulder.

"Bide your time, Ben, and I'll be with you," he cried. "Good company makes short miles. I've a little errand o' my own to see to on Paddock Brow. Will ta come as far as th' Nag's Head and drink a glass and tarry there for me, or will ta company me to th' Brow? I'st noan be long, for it's not exactly a wedding I'm bahn to."

"Oh, I'll go with you," I said, willingly enough, for Jack was always well met.

"It's Tom Sykes I'm bahn to see. Yo' dunnot know him belike, a decent body but shiftless, and a ailing wife and a long family. There's a sight o' truth in what young Booth was reading to us th' other neet from a great writer, a Mr. Malthus, 'at a man who is born into a world already possessed, or if society does not want his labour, has no claim or right to the smallest portion of food; and, in fact, has no business to be where he is. At nature's mighty feast there is no cover for him. That's what you call pheelosophy. I'm bahn to comfort Tom Sykes wi' a bit o' pheelosophy."

"And is that philosophy you'n got i' your poke, Jack?" I asked "It seems weighty matter."

"Noa, this is a few crumbs o' arrant nonsense, fra' th' kitchen o' th' Cherry Tree. Th' cook there's a reight good sort, an' some day or other, aw don't say but I might—you know. But it's ill puttin' all yo'r eggs i' one basket. An' gi'ein' a shillin' to th' parson to tie you is a tighter job nor takin' th' king's shillin'. Yo' can't hop out o' th' holy estate as aw did aat o' th' army—on a gamey leg. But here we are at Tom's."

It was a low stone thatched house on the Lower Brow, and overlooked the river. Jack lifted the latch, and we walked into the living–room. It was bare of all furniture, save a round deal–topped table, three–legged, a low rocking chair by an empty fire–grate, a cradle and another, cane–bottomed chair, on which sat a man in his shirt sleeves, hushing a wailing child. The man was shock–headed. He had not been shaved for a week or more. His cheek bones stood out above shrunken cheeks. His eyes burned with an unnatural fire, and he had a hollow, hacking cough. He was trying to quiet the child, clumsily but patiently putting sips of a bluish fluid, milk and water, to its lips, with a crooked broken spoon. Another child, about seven years old, I judged, with neither clogs nor socks, all her covering a smock and a short frock scarce to her knees, was stretched on its face in a corner of the chimney, over a litter of sacks. And under the sacks lay—a something. We could see the straight outlines of a figure—I felt what it was, and my heart stood still. But Jack's eyes were not so young as mine.

"Where's yo'r missus, Tom?" he asked, swinging his bundle on to the ricketty table. "Th' cook at th' Cherry Tree has sent her a summat. See here's th' makin's o' a rare brew o' tea, screwed up i' this papper. Aw carried it i' my weskit pocket, for fear o' accidents. An' there's broken bread an' moat an'—but what's ta starin' at? Where is 'oo aw say?"

"'Oo's there, Jack—in th' corner there, under Milly. Yo' needn't fear to wakken her—'oo sleeps very sound. Gi' my compliments to Fat Ann at th' Cherry Tree an' tell her th' missus is much obliged. But 'oo isn't very hungry just now. Th' parson says 'oo's gone where there's nother hunger nor sorrow. But aw reckon if there is such a shop, there'll be no room there for my owd woman. Th' rich folk 'll ha' spokken for them parts, th' poor 'll be crowded out, same as they are here. An' yo', Ben Bamforth, an' yo' come to look on your handiwork? Yo' may lift th' cuvverin' for yersen. Novver mind Milly 'oo'll greet hersen to sleep agen, when yo're gone. Tak' a good look, man—it's nobbut a dead woman, improved off th' face o' th' earth—clemmed to death bi improvements. Nay dunna flinch, man, 'oo'll nother flyte thee nor bite thee" But I could not look, and I went silently out into the rutty, dirty lane and the murk night so cold and raw. For I had no words of comfort for the man—I could not speak in that silent presence—so I slipped away, only minding to pass a coin or two into the hands of Soldier Jack—"Light a fire and fetch a woman," I whispered, and Jack nodded and made no effort to have me stay.

I was in a distracted state of mind, drawn now this way and now that, as I made my way to Slaithwaite. My promise to George lay heavy on me, and I loved the lad. The scene of which I had been just now the witness filled me with an intense sorrow for the suffering I knew to be rife around us. But I shrunk from violence of any kind and from conflict with the law, of which I had a wholesome dread. I confess here, once and for all, I am not made of the stuff of which captains, heroes and martyrs are made—I asked nothing better of the world than to go my own way quietly and doucely, earning by honest toil sufficient for my daily needs, sustained by the affection of those I loved and safe in the esteem and goodwill of my little world. I was not therefore best pleased when Mary met me at the door and handed me a note which had been brought by an unknown messenger, who had been charged, he said, to give it into her own hands, and to impress upon her that she herself should convey it safely to me. It was addressed to me, and though I had had few letters from George Mellor I knew his handwriting, and I judged, too, that Mary knew it, and had all a woman's curiousness to know what the letter might say. It was brief enough, anyhow:

"Meet me on Thursday night at nine o'clock at the Inn at Buckstones.—George."

The inn at Buckstones stands, or then stood, almost alone on the road from Outlane to Manchester. All around were desolate reaches of moorland, with here and there patches won by hard toil from the waste and enclosed by dry walling whose solidity bespoke the rich abundance of good stone and the little worth of human labour. There were no neighbours to make custom for the inn. The coach never stopped there. An occasional wayfarer, or holiday makers from the town, at times would call there, but mine host of the Buck would have fared badly but for his pigs and poultry. It was a little inn, remote, unaccustomed, unobserved, and only those would chose it as a meeting place whose business was one that shunned the open day and the eye of man. I put the letter carefully in my breast pocket, putting aside Mary's questioning words and ignoring Mary's questioning looks as best I could. And at this, after a while, Mary choose to take offence, tossing her head, and surmising that folk who had letters they could not show to their own cousins were up to no good.

I was at the Buck punctual to my time. The night was pitch dark. There was neither moon nor stars to light one along the road, and the road was bad enough in broad noon. A feeble light shone from the low window of the inn. The outer door was shut, and did not yield to my push when I lifted the sneck. It was opened from within by George Mellor.

"Yo're to time, Ben," he said in a low voice as he grasped my hand. "I knew tha' wouldn't fail us."

"Who's us?" I asked.

"Tha'll know soon enough. They're waitin' for us i' th' room upstairs—but come into th' snug an' have a glass o' ale. Tha looks breathed and flustered, an' as if tha'd seen a boggart on th' road. There's a chap inside aw want thee to know—he's a rare 'un. He's a better scholard nor other thee nor me, Ben, and aw'se warrant tha'll like him, when tha knows him."

"Who is it, George?"

"They call him Booth, John Booth, th' parson's son at Lowmoor."

"Is he one on yo'?" I asked.

"As close as th' heft to th' blade," replied George. And I breathed more freely, for John Booth I had seen many a time at Mr. Wright's, the saddler's, in Huddersfield; and I, though I had had no speech with him, had heard much of his great learning and sweet temper. He was not one to harm a fly. His father was, I knew, the Vicar at Lowmoor Church, and a master cropper to boot. Surely the son of a parson and of a finisher was engaged in no enterprise that need daunt my father's son.

He was sat in the snug, a pot of ale before him, scarce tasted; a youth not more than twenty–one or two years old, with pale face, long lank dark hair that fell on either side a high and narrow brow. His eye was dark and melancholy, his lip's somewhat thin. His face was bare of beard, of an oval shape, and womanish. He had a low, soft voice, and spoke more town like than I was used to. But he had a sweet smile and a winning, caressing way that partly irritated me because I thought it out of place in a man. But it was very hard to stand against all the same.

"I am glad to see you, Mr. Bamforth," he said, placing a hand that, despite his trade, was small and white, in my own big, brawny fist. He looked very slim by the side of me as we stood hand in hand, for I am six feet and more and big built, and thanks be to God hard as nails and little bent even yet. But it is mind, my children, not matter, that rules the world.See how he tickled me at the very start, — "Mr. Bamforth" — there was a whole page of delicate flattery in the very words and way of breathing on it. It meant I was a man. It meant I was of some place and power in his reckoning of me. I felt myself flush, and I grew bigger to myself. Why, I do not think anyone had ever called me "Mr. Bamforth" before. Even 'Siah, our teamer, called me "Ben." The Vicar at the Church called me "Ben," and ruffled me not a little by the patronizing way he had. Mr. Webster, at the Powle, called me "Ben;" but that I did not mind, for he said it as though he loved me.

"I am glad to see you. Any friend of George Mellor's is welcome, but your father's son is thrice welcome. George, do you go in and prepare our friends to receive a new member. Set all things in order, and I will talk meanwhile with your cousin."

"And so, Mr. Bamforth," he continued.

"Nay, call me Bamforth, or plain Ben," I said. "Well, Ben be it then — And so, Ben, you, too, are willing to strike a blow for the poor and oppressed."

"I don't know about striking blows," I said. "To tell the truth I am here because I said I would be here; but what I am here for I do not know, except that I am here to learn why I am here. It's true enough my heart is heavy for the poor; but what I can do, and saving your presence what you can do, or George, or such as us, passes my wit."

"We can try, at least, the force of union," he made answer. "We can try what the force of numbers will do. We can entreat; we can threaten" —

"But what is a bark without a bite?" I asked. "And how can you bite without setting your own teeth on edge?"

"Ah! there's the rub," he said. "But we won't jump before we get to the stile. One step at a time and await developments, say I. But come, we will join our friends. It will be a comfort to me to have one cool head in our number. We have no lack of madcaps." The long low chamber which we now entered was in darkness, save for the light of two small lanthorns, placed on a long narrow table that ran down the centre of the room. Forms ran round three sides of the room. At the head of the table was an arm chair of ancient oak. In the centre of the table, flanked on either side by lanthorns, which turned their lights each to the other, was a human skull. In the chair sat one whom I felt rather than saw to be my cousin George. By his right hand was a Bible; on his left, one who acted as secretary and kept a roll of members, a precious document I would afterwards have given all I was worth to lay my hands on. The forms around the wall were close packed by masked men, in working dress, who rose as Booth led me into the room and placed me at the foot of the table confronting the president. All rose as we slowly made our way to that place, Booth holding me by the hand. I was in a cold sweat, and wished myself a thousand miles away. Booth left me standing there peering straight at him I knew to be my cousin.

"No. 20, I call upon you to explain to this candidate the principles of our order."

"We are banded together," said a voice from the line of figures on my right, a voice I knew at once to be Booth's; for no other man I ever knew, scarce any woman, had a voice so gentle, so plaintive. "We are banded together to assert the rights of labour, to resist the encroachments and the cruelty of capital. We seek to succour the needy and to solace the sorrowing. We aim to educate the toilers to a sense of their just rights, to amend the political, the social, and the economic condition of those whose only wealth is their labour, whose only birth–right is to toil. Our methods are persuasion, argument, united representation of our claims, and if need be, the removal of those mechanic rivals of human effort by which callous and heartless employers are bent on supplanting the labour of our hands. But this only in the last resort, all other means exhausted, our righteous claims flouted, our fair demands denied."

"Benjamin Bamforth," came my cousin's voice across the gloom.

"You have heard the statement of our aims. Are you willing to ally yourself with us and to aid us in our cause? If so, answer 'I am.'"

"I am."

"We are witnesses of your solemn obligation. Who vouches for Benjamin Bamforth?"

"That do I," said Booth.

"That, too, do I," said another voice that sounded familiar to my ears.

"Place before him the Book. Place your hands, Brother Bamforth, upon the Bible and fix your eyes upon these emblems of mortality. As they are, so be you, if you falter, or if you fail. Repeat after me the words of our oath."

Then, phrase by phrase, in a silence only broken by the voices of us twain and the heavy breathing of that grim group, I repeated after the playfellow of my boyhood and my manhood's friend the solemn words: "I, Benjamin Bamforth, of my own voluntary will, do declare and solemnly swear that I never will reveal to any person or persons under the canopy of heaven the names of the persons who comprise this secret committee their proceedings, meetings, places of abode, dress, features, complexion, or anything else that might lead to a discovery of the same, either by word, deed or sign, under the penalty of being sent out of the world by the first brother who shall meet me, and my name and character blotted out of existence, and never to be remembered but with contempt and abhorrence. And I further do swear, to use my best endeavours to punish by death any traitor or traitors, should any rise up among us, wherever I may find him or them, and though he should fry to the verge of nature I will pursue him with unceasing vengeance, so help me God and bless me, to keep this my oath inviolate."

"Kiss the Book."

I kissed the Bible.

"Show more light."

In each quarter of the room a light shone forth, its rays till now obscured.

"Brethren, unmask, and let our brother know his brethren."

I looked around me blinking in the sudden glare. There were many I knew not. More than one I knew. The voice that had haunted was the voice of Soldier Jack, who looked, I thought, somewhat foolish as my eye fell on him. There was William Thorpe, a cropper at Fisher's, of the Brigg, and Ben Walker and William Smith, who worked at my uncle Wood's. Thorpe, I knew, was a mate of my cousin George, and I was not much surprised to see him. Smith I knew only by sight, having seen him when I had taken work to be finished at the Brigg. Walker I knew somewhat better. His father was ever styled Buck Walker, having been somewhat of a gallant in his younger days, and even now fancying himself not a little. Ben o' Buck's was a young man of about my own age, dark and sallow, with deep set eyes and a sly fawning way. He had gone out of his way to be civil to me, and more than once in the summer–time had walked of a Sunday from Powle Chapel, where his father was a deacon, across the fields home with us. He was attentive in a quiet way to Mary to whom he spoke, I understood, chiefly about his sins, which troubled him greatly. Martha said it was his stomach that was wrong. She knew it by his pasty face and by his hands, cold and damp, like a fish tail. Martha was a lass of some prejudices. My father was rather partial to Ben, a quiet harmless lad, he judged, that would run steady and show no nonsense. I did not greatly care for him myself, but I wondered rather to see him where he was, not having given him credit for so much spunk. But most I marvelled, at Soldier Jack, yet did I gather courage from his presence, for I leaned on his stout heart and his worldly knowledge, gleaned in many strange scenes and lands.

But George was speaking to me again.

"There are signs in our Order, Brother Bamforth, and I will now communicate them to you. The first, the right hand passed behind the neck, thus, signifies 'Are you a Lud?' The party challenged should reply by placing two forefingers on his chin, thus. We have also a password which will admit you to our meetings, and to those of others in our movement. It is 'Work, Win.' You will now take your seat among the brethren and the business of the meeting will be resumed. 'Any reports?'"

"Enoch Taylors taken on six more men," said a Marsden man. "They're making frames as fast as they can. Orders are rolling in. Horsfall's putting them into Ottiwells as quick as they're made. Th' owd hands are told they're no use, an' young 'uns is being browt fra' no one knows where, to work th' shearing frames. Aw'n seen some cloth 'ats been finished on a frame, an' it welly broke my heart. Aw'n been a cropper, lad and man, for thirty year, an' aw nivver turned aht owt like it. It were as smooth as a babby's cheek. An' th' frame can do th' work of four men awn heerd th' mester tell. It's ruination, stark ruination, an' me wi' five childer an' yar Emma lying in."

"That's noan hauf o' th' tale—Horsfall's fair wild wi' joy. He says he'll feight Napoleon wi' a finishin' frame. He cries shame on th' Nottingham police. He says th' magistrates there owt to be drummed off th' bench. He says they're a pigeon–livered lot, an' if he'd been there, he'd a ridden up to th' saddle girths i' th' blood o' th' Luds before he'd ha' been baulked o' his way."

"Shame on him, shame on him!" broke out fierce voices.

"Reports come from Liversedge that Cartwright, of Rawfolds, has ordered a set of machines from Taylor. William Hall, have yo' owt to say?"

A man about thirty, dirty and slovenly, with a blotched face and slouching look, who it turned out lived at Hightown and had been dismissed from Mr. Jackson's there and had been taken on at Wood's, then rose. He had a great deal to say. He spoke of Mr. Cartwright: more of a foreigner nor an Englishmen, he called him. A quiet man with a cutting tongue. Had ne'er a civil word for a man an' down on him in a jiffy if he looked at a pot o' beer. Drank nowt himself, which Hall looked on as a bad sign and unEnglish. Was sacking th' owd hands and stocking Rawfolds with machines and Parson Roberson was worse nor him. I had a sight of that same fighting parson not many months after, and Bill Hall was not far off the mark.

"Has any brother owt more to say anent Horsfall or Cartwright?" asked Mellor.

"I move they're warned," cried one.

"I'll second it," said another.

"Give it 'em hot," cried a third. "Tell 'em plain we mean business. I'm sick o' letter writin'. They laugh at our letters." "Let them laugh," said George; "they'll laugh at wrong side o' their mouths afore we'n done wi' them. And now, lads, enough o' business. Th' landlord 'll be thinking we're poor customers. Let's have some ale and drive dull care away. A song, boys; who'll sing us a song?"

"That will I, George, but I mun drink first. My belly's beginnin' to think ahn cut mi throat."

A brother had left the room, and now appeared with an immense jug of ale, and tots were handed round. Cutty pipes were produced and coarse tobacco. Who paid the shot I do not know. But I have heard tell that some masters who were threatened paid quit money, and others even gave money that their neighbours' mills might be visited. But this I know not of a certainty, and only set it down as a thing that was said. This I know, there was no lack of ale among the lads, and money, too, came from somewhere.

"Now for your song, Soldier," said George, and the men settled themselves for a spree and a fuddle. The croppers were ever a free lot given to roystering and cock fighting and bull baiting and other vanities.

And thus sang Soldier Jack, and all that knew the song joined lustily in the chorus, for that wild moor there was no fear of intruders, and our host had not love enough for the justices to set them on good customers.

"Come cropper lads of high renown,
Who love to drink good ale that's brown,
And strike each haughty tyrant down,
With hatchet, pike, and gun!

Oh, the cropper lads for me,
The gallant lads for me,
Who with lusty stroke,
The shear frames broke,
The cropper lads for me!

What though the specials still advance,
And soldiers rightly round us prance,
The cropper lads still lead the dance,
With hatchet, pike, and gun!

Oh, the cropper lads for me,
The gallant lads for me,
Tho with lusty stroke
The shear frames broke,
The cropper lads for me!

And night by night when all is still
And the moon is hid behind the hill,
We forward march to do our will
With hatchet, pike, and gun!

Oh, the cropper lads for me,
The gallant lads for me,
Who with lusty stroke
The shear frames broke,
The cropper lads for me!

Great Enoch still shall lead the van.
Stop him who dare! Stop him who can!
Press forward every gallant man

With hatchet, pike, and gun!

Oh, the cropper lads for me,
The gallant lads for me,
Who with lusty stroke
The shear frames broke,
The cropper lads for me!"

The song was chorused with gusto by most there, and it was plain enough to see that the meeting had more hopes from great Enoch, as the Luds called the hammer used in machine smashing, after Enoch Taylor of Marsden, than they had from either persuasion or threats. That something more than words was in their minds was evident enough later on when we all turned out into a field at the back of the Buck. There was a watery moon in the sky that gave a ghostly sort of light. By this light Soldier Jack drew up the twenty or thirty men who left their cups and followed him into the fold. And there did Jack put us through our drill. One or two had muskets, a few had pikes. They had been fetched out of the mistal, where by day they lay concealed on the hay bowk. It was rare to see Jack at his drilling. We were formed in line fronting him, and Jack did gravely walk down the line, commenting on our appearance, and trying to bring us to some fashion of military time.

And this was the style of drill.

"Hold thi head up, man; thi breast's noan th' place for thi chin." This to No. 1.

"Dal thi, No. 2, will ta' square thi shoulders back or will ta' not? Hast ta' getten th' bellywark 'at tha' draws thissen in like that?"

"Turn th' toes 'aat, No. 3. I said heels together not toes, tha' gaumless idiot."

"Na' then, tenshun! Eyes front. Shoulder arms, right wheel. Mar— — —ch!" And away walked Jack with his head up and an old sabre over his shoulder, disguising his limp as best he could, at the head of his little column, as proud, I verily believe, as though he captained a company. It seemed to me poor fooling, then and always, but it gave such huge satisfaction to Soldier Jack, I never had the heart to tell him so, nor to shirk my drill.

"A poor shiftless lot," he complained to me as we walked near midnight across Cupwith Common, the three rough miles that lay between the Buck and Lower Holm. "A peer shiftless lot, but what could you expect from a lot of croppers?"

"What do you think to make of them, Jack?" I asked.

"Why, nowt," he answered. "Just nowt; but then yo' see they mun do something. It's all very well to go to th' Buck an' drink ale an' sing songs. I'll back th' croppers at drinkin' ale an' singing songs against th' best regiment the Duke has in Spain. But if all this meeting an' masking an' speechifyin' is to do any good and lead to owt, there must be action, sooner or later. And in that day it will be well for th' Luds if there is even one voice which they have learned to obey. Do you think it's the great generals that win battles?"

"Why, of course, it is?" I answered.

"That's just where yo're out," said Jack.

"It's th' sergeants and th' corporals. Yo' see in a feight yo' cannot see much further nor yo'r nose end. All yo'n got to do for th' most part is to keep your eye an' yo'r ear on th' sergeant that's drilled yo' sin' yon learned the goose step, an' do as he tells you. As long as he keeps his head an yo' hear his voice, calm an' cheerful, just as if yo' were in the barrack yard or on parade, yo'r all reight an' yo do as you're told, like Tommy Tun, whoever he wer."

"I never heard on him, Jack. Whose lad was he?"

"Aw don't rightly know, but aw reckon he were famous for keepin' in step. Howsomever, mark my words, George Mellor's a good lad, wi' fire enough for hauf a dozen. That lad o' Parson Booth's, 'at 'ud be better employed if he wer' at home helpin' his mother to rock th' craddle, is a rare 'un to talk. Thorpe's a good 'un if it comes to fisticuffs, but it'll be Soldier Jack they'll all look to when th' bullets is whizzing ovver their heads, an' what little wit they have is scattered an gone."

"But, surely, Jack, there'll be no whizzing of bullets?"

"Oh! won't there? Aye that an' waur. Do yo' know Horsfall, o' Ottiwell's, has got th' soldiers billetted in th' town, th' King's Bays. Aw've drunk wi' sum o' them, an' had a crack about old times. Oh! curses on this gamey heel o' mine that keeps me limping o'er Cupwith Common when I might be stepping out behind the colours to the merry music of fife an' drum. Yo'll never know, lad, the savage joy of battle. It is the wine o' life. When yo've once tasted it, even love an' liquor are flat beside it. But what can't be cured mun be endured. Well aw say, aw'n talked wi' a sergeant at th' Red Lion i' Marsden. They're patrolling th' district ivvery night. If we go to Ottiwell's, there'll be a warm welcome for us."

"But why are yo' in it, Jack, that's what caps me?" I said. "Yo're nawther a cropper nor th' son of a cropper."

"No. What o' thissen Ben?"

"Well, yo see, I promised George. I cannot run off mi word. An' George sees further, perhaps, nor I do. Then young Booth says its opposition or submission. Opposition may mean imprisonment or worse, but submission can only mean pining to death."

"Then yo'r in for George?" Jack asked.

"Well if you like to put it so, Soldier, yo'll none be so far off th' mark."

"Well then say aw'm in it for yo' an' for sport, an' cause an' its i' mi natur. But most, Ben Bamforth, it's for yo' an' another lad or two, 'at'll need a true friend an' a shrewd head an' a tricky tongue before this work's through. And so, good neet, an' wipe th' muck off thi boots, else that saucy Mary o' yours 'll be axing more questions nor yo'll care to answer."

CHAPTER V.

THE last day of March of that year of 1812 was a big day for me. I came of age. It would little seem me to say what mariner of man I was in the flush and vigour of my early manhood, but I was such a one as simple habits and plain fare and mountain air make of most. I was tall above the common, though even then not come to my full stature. And I was strong with a strength that frightened me. Folk marvelled at my height, for my father was but a small man, though wiry, and my mother matched my father. I had in those days ever to be careful of my head when I visited at folks' houses, for the doorways were low and there were joists in unexpected places, and many a rude knock did my poll sustain before I learned caution by hard dints. Many youths do overgrow their strength, but that did not I, and though I had not 'Siah's skill in wrestling, nor knew the tricks of the fall, 'Siah could not throw me, and once I got him in my arms, though he was thick set and solid, I could strain him in my hug till his very bones could crack. But my inches, three Score and fourteen, were much mocked by the lads about, who would make a spy–glass of their hands, and fixing an earnest gaze upon the crown of my head, would ask with mock concern if it were warm up there.

Now on this, my birthday, nought would satisfy my mother but that we should have a tea–drinking. I was in no great mood for such doings, but my mother must ever have her way. She said it was no, ordinary birthday. A man became a man but once in a life–time, and moreover, and this settled the matter with her, in no decent family was such an event allowed to pass unmarked. Times were bad she granted, but it was not as though we were bound to live from hand to mouth. So I bid my friends. Of course, George must come, and a handsomer, brighter lad never set foot in Lower Holme than George looked that night, all fun and laughter, with a jest for everyone. And he brought with him Ben Walker, whom I made welcome, as I should have made welcome the Evil One himself had George brought him. And I liked Walker as little. From the very first I misdoubted that man. I disliked his toad's hand, his shifty eye, his low speech. There was something sly in his very tread, and his laugh had no heartiness in it. Then he was so cursedly civil to everybody. He praised my mother's cakes: never were such cakes, and though, God knows he was welcome enough to eat his fill, he did not praise them without fair trial. He praised the tea, he praised the pig–cheek, he set little Mr. Webster all of a glow by telling him how edified he was by his last discourse at Powle Moor, but he had like to have come to grief with Soldier Jack by belittling the great Duke. Then he fell to praising Mary, and here he had like to have spoiled all, for as he spoke of her good looks he let his eye dwell upon her features with a look so gross that Mary coloured red with wrath, and my mother told him sharply Mary was not a slave for sale in the market, and we needed no inventory of her charms. So he at Mr. Webster again on religion, and as Buck Walker, his father, had turned pious in his latter days, and was now a leader at the Powle, the good man and Ben hit it rarely together. But his eye, I noted, ever wandered to Mary, and it liked me not.

I had asked, too, John Booth and his sister Faith, a demure young maid as ever made a courtesy. She was just all that Mary was not, and yet she pleased, which, when you think of it, should set us marvelling at the great goodness of God that hath so fashioned our maids that even their very extremes are admirable. For Mary was rosy and plump, with auburn curling hair, that would never be kept by net or string, but would escape and wanton over her face and neck, and had a laughing eye of blue, with rosy lips, and a saucy tongue. A very ray of warm sunshine was Mary.

But Faith was dark as a sloe as to hair and eye, with a skin of delicate white, and slender as a lily's stalk, and gentle of speech and somewhat shy of manner, yet with no awkwardness withal. My heart, did warm to her from the first, and I think too she favoured me from the very day her brother made us acquaint at his master's shop in Huddersfield. Perhaps because I was so big and strong, whilst her brother, though wonderful far learned in books, and with as big a soul as was ever put in man's body, was only a short remove from a woman in those things which women love in man. And strange as it is that two maids so unlike should both be so sweet to live with and to think upon, is it not stranger still that two men so unlike as Soldier Jack and myself should be at one about Faith's sweetness and loveableness.

Jack, if we might credit his own word in the matter, had a wide experience in the lists of love, but chiefly, I fear, among the hussies that followed the camp and the warm and yielding beauties of sunny Spain. Yet did this tried veteran surrender the garrison of his heart without parley and without terms to the gentle assault of this pure and modest lass, but with no thought of other love than a father's or a brother's, for Jack was well into the forties, and had had his fill of the burnings of a warmer flame.

Now after our tea–drinking was done, my father and Mr. Webster settled down by the fireside to smoke their pipes and talk of town's affairs and the ever pressing sufferings of the poor. Mr. Webster's talk was heavy hearing. He knew every family on that hill–side, and scarce one was free from griping want. The parson's voice would falter and tears come to his eyes as he told his tale, and I could see my father shift uneasily in his chair and his hand wander to his pocket, and my mother would break in with "Hear to him, now!" "The likes o' that," "God save us," and so on. And presently she went into the outer kitchen where leavings of our feast were spread, and when Mr. Webster went home that night Josiah trudged by his side with a hamper of good things. Not, be sure, for Mr. Webster himself, for of his own needs, though these were rather suspected than known for sure, the good man spoke not at all; and I will go bail he proved a trusty steward of the comforts borne on 'Siah's broad shoulders.

For us younger ones there was no lack of sport, Postman's Knock and Forfeits and other games in which there is overmuch kissing to my present thinking though I did not think so then. And if, whenever the rules of the game did give me occasion, I chose Faith rather than Mary, had I not reason in that Faith was the greater stranger to our house, and I was ever taught to be civil to our guests. And I was no little nettled by the carryings on of Mary and George. In my heart I cried shame on Mary, and said to myself it was unseemly that a maiden of a respectable family should so set herself at any man. It was "George" here and "George" there, and "Cousin Mellor" and "Cousin Mary," though what kinship of blood there was between them was so slight it was a manifest pretence and cloak to make so much of it. I do hate a forward girl, and it was not like our Mary to make herself so sheap. Why, but the week before, being moved thereto on seeing her more tantalizingly pretty than common, I had made to give her a cousinly salute, and she had smacked me smartly on the cheek and started away in a rare pet. But I took care this night she should see I could play the swain as well as any George among them, and Faith seemed nothing loth. Not that she was over–bold. When I would kiss her she would turn her cheek to me with a pretty readiness, and seemed in no wise to mind it; but when George could spare a thought for any but Mary, and choose Faith, the colour would crimson her cheeks and brow, and she would turn her face away, and then, lo! all her flush would fade and leave her pale and trembling.

But we were perhaps getting over old for such games not yet old enough for the whist to which our elders had betaken themselves. So Mary, after no little urging thereto, did seat herself at the spinnet, which was a new joy in our house and had been the occasion of some bitterness to our friends. And touching the keys softly thus she sang very roguishly:—

> "Love was once a little boy,
> Heigh ho! heigh ho!
> Then with him 'twas sweet to toy
> Heigh ho! heigh ho!
>
> He was then so innocent,
> Not as now on mischief bent;
> Free he came; and harmless went,
> Heigh ho! heigh ho!
>
> Love is now a little man,
> Heigh ho! heigh ho!
> And a very saucy one,
> Heigh ho! heigh ho!
>
> He walks so gay and looks so smart,
> As if he owned each maiden's heart
> I wish he felt his own keen dart,
> Heigh ho! heigh ho'!
>
> Love, they say, is growing old,
> Heigh ho! heigh ho!
> Half his life's already told,

Heigh ho! heigh ho!

When, he's dead and buried too.
What shall we poor maidens do?
I'm sure I cannot tell—can you?
Heigh ho! heigh ho!"

Whereat my father and Soldier Jack shouted lustily "Heigh ho'! heigh ho!" and my mother shook her head but with a smile, and Mr. Webster must confess it was a pretty air and taking one, and trusted the singing thereof was not a holding of the candle to the Evil One. But Mary made a mouth at him and said, 'twould be time enough to be sad when she was too old to be merry.

Now after the singing of this catch it so befell that my mother had some occasion to desire from the village some small matter for the supper table, and Martha being intent upon getting ready the supper she bid Mary privily slip away and fetch the things she needed. This did Ben Walker overhear, though it was no business of his, and when Mary, watching her chance, had gone softly out of the one door, Ben, making some excuse, did steal away by the other, a thing we thought nothing of, deeming it but natural that a young man should seek to company a maid, and I not uneasy on Mary's account, the night being fine and clear, and decent women being not molested in our parts, where strangers came little, and all were as friends and neighbours.

Now she had been gone some three parts of an hour, when I heard the front door open hurriedly and then slam to. My mother rose quickly and went into the parlour. It was in darkness, for we seldom used it save for company, and for our company of this night it was not large enough. But despite the gloom I knew it was Mary. My mother drew her into the house and placed her in her own rocking–chair. All had risen to their feet. Mary's hat was hanging by its strings down her back. Her decent neckerchief that covered her neck and bosom had been torn aside, and some of the fastenings of her dress undone. She was panting hard for breath, and for a time could form no word.

"Where's Ben Walker?" I said, and then Mary found her voice.

"Aye," she cried, "where is he? Oh! the coward, the coward!" and then she sobbed and cried again "Oh! the coward, the coward." And just then the sneck was lifted and Ben Walker walked in.

He stood in the door way; but I banged the door behind him; and Soldier Jack took him by the arm and drew him into the room, whilst Faith soothed Mary and straightened her dress.

"And now, Ben Walker, give an account o' thissen," said George, standing before the shrinking man, with clenched fist and a flashing eye.

And Walker shamed and faltered. His eye wandered from one face to another, and found no comfort anywhere.

"It's noan o' my doing, George. Tha' needn't look so fierce. Awn laid no hand on her, han aw Mary? Speak th' truth, choose what tha' does, it goes th' furthest."

"Oh! you coward, you pitiful coward!" was all that Mary could say; but she was calmer now.

"It wer' this way," continued Walker reluctantly. "We'd done th' shopping at Ned o' Bill's, an' had passed th' church an' got well into th' lane comin' back. Aw wer' carryin' th' basket."

"Where is th' basket?" cried my mother.

"By gow, I reckon aw mun ha' dropped it. Aw nivver gav' it a thowt', an' aw nivver missed it till nah. As aw wer' saying', aw wer' huggin' th' basket wi' one arm, an' aw'd axed Mary to hold on to th' other."

"As if aw'd link wi' sich as thee," said Mary, bridling again.

"An all at onst, about half–way up th' broo' a felly lope ovver th' wall. He wer' a big un, aw tell yo', an' ther' wer' more behind, aw heard 'em eggin' 'im on. If he'd been by hissen aw'd ha stood up to him if he'd been as big as a steeple. He said nowt to me, but he gate hold o' Mary an 'oo started to scream an' struggle, an' aw heerd him say he'd have a kiss if he died for it. Aw wer' for parting on 'em, but he gav' me such a look, an' aw thowt aw heerd others comin, so aw just made off across th' fields. Tha' knows, George, duty afore everything, an' if th' soldiers is about they're happen comin' here an' tha' knows best whether tha' wants to see 'em."

"A soldier was it," I cried. "What mak' o' man wor he?"

"Aw tell thee bigger nor thissen, wi' a black poll an' a eye like a dagger blade for keen, an' ther' were a scar across his face."

"It were one o' them chaps 'at's stayin' at John Race's at th' Red Lion i' Marsden," said Mary. "He stopped me once afore a week back, when aw wer' walkin' out that way on. But he spoke me civil then, an' aw thowt nowt on it. But he's been drinkin' to–neet an' used me rough an' fleyed me. But aw reckon he'll keep his distance another time. It'll be a lesson to him."

"How does ta mean, Mary?" said my mother. "Aw got one o' his fingers between my teeth an' aw bit him, an' bit him, an' bit him, an' he had hard to do to throw me off. Then he called me a vicious little devil, an' aw tucked up my skirts an' ran for it. Aw wer' more fleyed nor hurt. But thee! Ben Walker, thee!" and she turned from him, with a look of such contempt and scorn that Ben hung his head with a hang–dog look and mumbling something about outstaying his welcome and making his way shorter, he slunk off, no one staying him.

And thus was my birthday party dashed. We could settle down to nought after that. Mary was feverish, and laughed over much. My father talked of going down on the morrow to Milnsbridge and laying complaint to Justice Radcliffe. Little Mr. Webster said something, in a very half–hearted way, about praying for those that despitefully use us, and my mother flighted Mary, most unjustly I thought, for having ever spoken to the man at all, and so encouraged him. Soldier Jack said little, but I know he resented the outrage, for it is one thing for soldiers to make light with other folks' women–kind and another guess sort of thing to have your own friends fall into their clutches. But George was warmest of all. He made us a grand speech agen the army and officers and men, which Soldier Jack swallowed with an ill grace. Hetty listened to him with all her ears, and you could see she liked to hear him rave on. And Mary, too, when first he began, harkened keen enough, but soon she turned away impatiently and busied herself with setting the supper, and I thought she had looked for something from George which did not come.

For me, I am slow of speech, stupid, Mary ever said. But I thought to myself: "A long, tall man, as big as a steeple, with a black poll, and a scar on his cheek," and long after George and John Booth and pretty prim Faith had started for Huddersfield, and Soldier Jack and Mr. Webster had gone Powle way, I lay awake in bed thinking of a thing. The next morning I was up betimes. My father was away after the forenoon drinking, to try to sell a piece or two, a thing that every week became more difficult. There was no work to be done after the cattle had been foddered. We had almost given up work at our trade. We bad as many pieces in stock as we had room for it had gone hard with us to stop the output of country work, but what would you with the best mind in the world, you cannot go on forever making to stock. So our looms were still and time hung heavy on our bands. In the shippon I had had a word with 'Siah and when, dressed in my Sunday best, I struck off towards Marsden. I found him waiting for me on the road. "Yo' mun keep' yo're head, Ben," he said, "Watch his een. Face him square an' watch his een. He's a big 'un wi' a long reach. He'll likely come: at thee like a mad bull. Keep out on his way when he rushes. Let him tire hissen. Keep thi' wind. Dunnot let him blow thee, let him blow hissen. He'll be in bad fettle, wi' no stay in him. Th' way these sogers ha' been living lately, he'll ha' more water nor wind in him, an' more ale nor water. Then, when he shows signals o' distress, work slowly in, and when tha' gets a fair chance, hug him, break his ribs, squeeze th' guts out on him. Glory hallelujah, he'll gasp like a cod!" Then would 'Siah, after looking carefully round to see we were not observed, stop in his walk and feel my arms and legs as if I were a horse he wished to buy; then at it again with more advice. Once, with a wistful air, he surmised it might be better to fight by proxy, to let him pick a quarrel with Long Tom, as he said they called the soldier who had misused our Mary so. But he did not try long on that tack and had to content himself with hoping that some day or night, one of the red coats would try his game on with Martha and then—Glory Hallelujah! I smiled and 'Siah read my thoughts but he only said: "Oh! them sort's noan particular. An' there's points about Martha, mind you, there's points about Martha."

At the Red Lion we found John Race, the little, round, red faced landlord in no very good humour. It was early in the day for drinking, to my taste, but 'Siah having a nice sense of honour in these matters, declared we must have some thing for the good of the house and offered, if I could not stomach a pint myself, to drink my share. So I called for a quart for 'Siah. Race handled my money very lovingly and then spit over it for luck.

"It's little of the ready comes my way now, Ben," he said.

"What! and a houseful of soldiers, John?"

"Oh! dun–not speak on it, Ben," he cried. "It's a ruined man I shall be if this goes on another month. It's 'John' here and 'landlord' there from morning till night or till next morning rather. And paying for their drink is just the last thing they think of. Th' kitchen door is white wi' chalk, and, well I know it's no use keeping the scores. It's just force of habit.

"But surely, John, you need not serve them unless they pay."

"It's easy talking, Ben. Th' law's one thing, but a house full o' soldiers is another. And aw cannot be everywhere an' my dowter an' th' servant, an' for owt aw know th' missus hersen are all just in a league to ruin me. Their heads are all turned wi' th' soldiers an' such carryin's on in a decent man's house wer nivver seen before or since."

"But what about the officer in command?"

"What, him! Complaining to him is just like falling out with the devil an' going to hell for justice. Sometimes he laughs at me, sometimes he swears at me, sometimes he sneers at me, and to cap all, when I turn, as a trodden worm will turn at times, he just tells me to go clean the pewters, and send mi dowter to amuse him. An' th' warst on it is 'oo's willin' enough to go. What will be th' end of it all, is fair beyond me. But nine months 'll tell a tale i' Marsden, or my name's not John Race."

John would have run on for ever, but I was anxious to get my own business done so I bade him show me up to the Captain's room. The landlord's own private sitting room and an adjoining bedroom had been appropriated by the officer, and I followed John up the narrow, creaking, stairs. At a door on the landing he knocked, and a thin voice within called on us to enter and be damned to us.

The room was small and low and packed with furniture of all styles and ages, more like a dealer's shop than an ordinary room. Folk said that many a quaint and costly ornament had found its way to John Race's in settlement of ale shots and gone to deck the room which was his wife's delight. But Captain Northman or his friends had treated it with scant reverence. On a table in the centre were a pack or two of cards and a couple of candles, that had guttered in the socket. A decanter half full of brandy stood by their side, whilst another, empty, and the fragments of a glass, lay on the floor. Boots, spurs, gloves, swords canes, were strewn about on the chairs, and the scent of stale tobacco reek and fumes of strong waters filled the room. A table, with an untasted breakfast set upon it, was drawn to the window, and by it, in a cushioned chair, sat a young man of some five and twenty years, dressed in his small clothes and a gaudy dressing–gown, yawning wofully and raising with unsteady hand a morning draught to his tremulous lips. He had evidently had a night of it and his temper was none the better for it. I raised my hand respectfully to my forehead as I had seen soldiers do, but he only stretched out his legs and stared me rudely in the face.

"Well, fellow," he said at length, "what's your pleasure of me that you must break in on my breakfast?"

"My name, sir, is Benjamin Bamforth."

"Ben o' Bill's o' Holme," said the landlord.

"Well, why the devil can't he stop at home?" said my lord. "Come, sir, your business."

"Captain Northman," I said civilly, and speaking my finest, nothing daunted by his captaincy, but nettled by his slack manners, for even Mr. Chew, the vicar, treated me with civility as my father's son; "Captain Northman, you have in your Company, a soldier known as Long Tom, his proper name I know not, nor his rank."

"Corporal Tom, well, what of him?"

"Sir, I complain that last night he did wantonly and without enticement or other warrant insult my own cousin Mary, as she was returning home late in the evening."

"Well, sir?"

"And I lay this complaint that he may be punished as he deserves."

"And is that all?"

"And enough too, it seems to me, Captain Northman."

"Good God! was ever the like heard!" exclaimed the Captain. "Here I am half pulled out of my bed in the small hours by a giant boor, my head all splitting with this vile liquor not fit for hog wash, and all because Long Tom chooses to kiss a pretty girl, who ten to one was nothing loth."

"Captain Northman," I said, very quietly, "I may be a boor, but I am one of the boors that pay your wages. Neither is it the part of a gentleman to meet a request for redress by an added insult. But I see I mistook my man and now I shall take my own course." So I turned on my heels and strode down the steps.

"Long Tom's in the kitchen," whispered 'Siah, and to the kitchen I strode.

Here were about a dozen men in shirt sleeves, lounging and lolling about, some smoking, some pipe–claying their belts and polishing their arms, others drinking and at cards even thus early. It was not difficult to pick out my man. He was stood with legs outstretched before the fire. I made straight to him, and by the look he gave I knew he guessed my errand. I strode straight to him and without a word I smote him with the back of my hand across the face. The angry blood rushed to his cheeks, and he clenched his fist. The other soldiers jumped to their feet. "Fair play" cried 'Siah. "Man to man and fair play."

"A fight, a fight."

"A ring, a ring."

"Into the yard with you my bully boys" said one who seemed to have authority, and into the yard we went, the whole company behind us, in great good humour at anything that promised sport.

"Two cans to one on Long Tom," I heard. "I lay even on the bumpkin," said another, and I was grateful even for that bit of backing.

"Keep thi' temper an' bide your chance," whispered 'Siah, anxious to the last.

And then we faced each other, Long Tom and I. He was stripped to the shirt and I stripped too. He was as big a man as I with more flesh and more skill. But all the loose living had told on him and he soon began to blow. He hammered at me lustily and I took it smiling. If he brayed my face to a pulp I meant to get one in at him. My chance came at last. I put all my force and all my weight into one blow full at his mouth. He guarded and made as tho' to counter. But his guard went back on himself, and my fist went plumb on his month. He went down like a felled ox and rolled on the ground kicking his heels and spitting out blood and his teeth. Then 'Siah raised a great shout and even some of the soldiers seemed not sorry to see the mighty fallen. And 'Siah led me off, feeling dazed and weak as a woman, and with a strong bent to blubber like a baby, now it was all over, for I am not used to fighting, and would any day rather give a point or two than fratch.

John Race, in a quiet way, was as rejoiced as 'Siah, but dare not show it too openly, for fear of angering the soldiers, of whom he was in great dread. But as I put my head under the pump and swilled my face he brought me a stiff runner of brandy and would take no pay. And presently others of the company came a round me and pressed me to drink, and the little captain, who had watched us from the window, came down and urged me to take the King's shilling. "Faith," said he, "there's blood in you, man. I thought they put sizing in your veins, but it's blood after all." "Aye, my little tom tit," said 'Siah who had no reverence for dignities. "It's blood 'at wouldn't stand mastering by sich as thee. Tha' need'nt fluster thissen. Aw'm noan bahn to hurt thee. But if tha' can get any o' these felly's to back thee, aw'll be glad to feight the two on you. Will'nt one on yo' oblige me? Noa? Weel nivver mind, cap'n, aw'll happen come across thee in a year or twi when th'art full grown, an' if thi' mother 'll let thee, tha' may happen ha' a bang at me. Come, Ben, let's go back to yar wark. This is nobbut babby lakin!" And so, 'Siah bore me off, with colours flying.

On our homeward way we had much scheming as to how I should account for my face, which began to puff and show divers colours.

'Siah was for telling the story as it was, but I had no mind that Mary's name should be mixed up in it. So we kept abroad the whole day and to my mother's great grief and my father's anger we presented ourselves late at night; 'Siah really, and myself feigning to be drunk. And Mary was so disgusted that she would scarce look at me, saying the sight of my face set her against her food. But towards the week end, Martha musts have got the secret from 'Siah and passed it on, for one night when I sat brooding by the fire, with no light but the glow of the embers, a light form stole softly behind my chair, and a pair of warm arms went round my neck and a tearful voice sobbed.

"O! Ben, yo' mun forgive me. But aw'll never forgive missen."

What is the magic of a woman's kiss and how comes it that under some conditions the touch of her lips will stir you not at all, and under others will kindle in your heart a flame that lasts your life–time. Till that moment I vow I had had no love for my cousin Mary, save such as a brother may have for his sister, between which and a lover's love is, I take it, the difference between the light of the moon, and the light of the sun. I had sometimes kissed her and she had submitted as not minding. But of late she had eluded me when I had sought to salute her, which skittishness I had put down to what was going on between her and George. And now, unsought, she had put her arms about my neck and drawn back my head to the warm cushion of her breast and pressed a kiss upon my brow. And lo! love, glorious love, full grown and lusty, leaped into the ocean of my being and ruled it thenceforth for even. And yet when I sprung to my feet and held out my arms and would have taken Mary to my heart, she sprung away and bade me keep my distance, and when I made to take what she would not grant, she grew angered, so that my heart fell and I was sick with doubts and sadness. And here, tho' little given to preaching, I would deliver my homily anent all shams and make–believes. Here was Mary setting my thoughts once more on a wrong tack so that I had no choice but return to what I had taken for granted, that it was a made up thing between her and George Mellor. And but for that belief many things that happened might not have befallen. Then, too, after my fight with Long Tom, my father gave me a talking to on my loose and raffish ways, and yet the very next market day, I heard of his boasting to all and sundry of my deeds, and the rumour thereof grew so much beyond the simple truth that I should not have some day been surprised to hear that I had routed a whole regiment. My mother, too, scolded me not a little and wept over my bruised skin, but among the women folk of our parish she bragged so much of my strength and my courage that I had like to become a laughing stock among the men. Even little Mr. Webster, who spoke to me at nigh an hour's length on the sinfulness of brawling and on the Christian duty of turning, the other cheek to the smiter, did ever after that honour me by asking the support of my arm when he returned late home, saying no one would molest him while I was by. Only Martha, among them all, was honest, for she made no secret of her delight in me, loading me with praises so that 'Siah began to look at me with an evil eye, and she insisted on giving me each day to breakfast a double portion of porridge and piling up blankets on my bed till I was like to be smothered.

But Mary spoke of my doings not at all, whilst Faith, when she heard of the fray, prattled prettily a whole afternoon, and said so many sweet things to me that Mary became waspish and told her I was set up enough by nature without folk going out of their way to spoil me by soft sawder. Then Faith must unsay half she had said and finished by opining that, after all, the proper course would have been to horse–whip Captain Northman before his own Company.

And this, she thought, was what George would have done.

CHAPTER VI.

It must not be supposed, because I have turned aside to tell of my own poor affairs, that the Luddites were idle all this while. Indeed it is very difficult for me to give any notion of the state of this part of the country at that time. Trade was as bad as bad could be. Nobody seemed to have any money to spend on clothes. It took most folk all their time to line the inside, and the outside had to make shift as best it could. It was cruel to see the homes of those who had no back set and depended on their daily toil for their daily bread. And yet some manufacturers persisted in putting in machines that could have but one effect, to turn adrift many of those who still had work. And with it all arose in the minds not only of the croppers but of all the working people for miles around a feeling of injustice, of oppression, a rankling sense of wrong. And the poor felt for the poor. They got it into their heads that the rich cared nought about them, that their only thought was to look after themselves, to fill their own pockets, and the working folk might rot in their rags for ought they cared. And added to this was a chafing sense of their own helplessness. They felt like prisoned birds dashing against the bars of a cage. You see they had no say in anything at all. They were Englishmen only in name their lives, even when times were fairly good, were none of the brightest. It was mostly work and bed and not too much bed. Hard work and scant fare and little pleasure. They had love and friendship, for these come by nature, but they had little else to bring a ray or two of sunshine into their lives. When people in those days met together to set forth their grievances they were persecuted for sedition; when they didn't meet and were quiet and law–abiding our betters said we had no grievances. Nay, if there was no violence both of speech and action the wise–acres in London said and thought all things were for the best in the best of all possible worlds. You couldn't talk sense into them, you just had to poise it into them. So what would you?

Anyway, before the Luddites had been banded together many weeks it was well understood that we existed for bigger things than to break shears and crop-ping frames. Booth was always dinning this into me when I hinted at the waste-fulness of smashing costly frames and other such like mischief. "We must arouse the conscience of our rulers," he said. "They cannot, or will not, see how desper-ate is our plight. Besides, nine tenths of them have a personal interest in war, in prolonging shutting our ports. Their sense of right will not move them: we must frighten them." Then he would smile in his sweet, sad way and say something in the French which he explained to mean that folk cannot have pancakes without breaking eggs, and after that I never lifted a hammer to smash a frame but my mind went to Shrove Tuesday and I had a vision of Mary with sleeves rolled up and face flushed by the heat of the fire, her dress tucked between her knees, tossing pancakes up the big chimney, and catching them sissing as they fell with the browned side up into the spurting fat.

Not that I did much machine breaking myself. There is a canny thriftiness in my nature that made me dislike such wantonness. Besides George Mellor was really the soul of the whole affair: and where George was there was no peace. He seemed like one possessed. From the Shears Inn at Hightown to the Nag's Head at Paddock, from the Nag's Head to the Buck, night after night, swearing in men, arranging midnight visits, dropping into this shop, loitering by that, counselling one man, winning another, he seemed to be everywhere at once, to know every man's wants and every man's grievance. What master to leave alone, what to fley. How he did it all and when he slept is a mystery to me. And he never lost heart never wavered from his purpose and there never was a moment when we didn't, all trust him and all love him —save only one.

I say I didn't handle Enoch much myself. We called the big sledge hammer that we battered the frames with, Enoch, after Mr. Taylor of Marsden. George saw I did not like the work, and the distance of my home from Longroyd Bridge made a good excuse for me. But 'Siah gloried in the work and when I saw him of a morning dull–eyed and weary and his clogs dirty with fresh clay I guessed what he had been at, and so in time did Martha too. But I could not always shirk my share of this midnight work, little, as it was to my liking. 'Siah had brought an earnest, message to me from George. "Yo' mun go, Ben. Th' lads are talking," 'Siah had said.

And so, after milking time one night in the first week in April I told my mother I must go down to th' Brigg, and she must not be uneasy if I did not come home that night, as I should probably stay at my aunt's; and my mother must needs send by me a basket of eggs and a cream cheese for her sister, and a rubbing bottle for her rheumatism with full directions for its use. I saw a look pass between Martha and Mary when I said I was going to th' Brigg, and Mary said:

"Mind yo' don't bring a black eye home wi' thee, i' th' mornin', Ben. But if th' art so set up wi' thissen for feightin', do it by daylight. It's ill wark that winnot bear th' sun's face," and then I knew Martha had been talking. But I reckoned not to understand her, and off I set with as poor a heart for my job as if I were going to be hanged.

Up by Kitchen Fold I came up with 'Siah and Soldier Jack. It was a darkish night, wet, drizzling and cold. We made off over by Crosland Moor, and never a soul did we meet till we were falling into Milnsbridge where Justice Radcliffe's house was. Then we passed a patrol of horse. They challenged us, and each of us had to tell a different lie. But they had no ground for stopping us, and they went their way over the moor, their horses pacing slowly and the riders peering on either side into the darkness of the night. I never knew those horse soldiers one bit of use all the time, and with their loose ways they did much harm. Those that had a tale which could pass muster would walk past them bold as brass. Those that couldn't face them just avoided them, which was easy enough whether by day or night, for stone fences are good for men to hide behind, and at the best it is a hard country for men on cavalry horses.

At the Nag's Head, at Paddock, we found George Mellor, William Smith, Thorpe, Ben o' Buck's, his brother John, Tom Brooke, Bill Hall, and two or three others who worked at Wood's. We had a glass apiece, and we needed it, or thought we did, which comes to the same thing in the end. These new–fangled teetotal fads hadn't come in then, and when folk didn't drink it was because they couldn't get it. Anyhow a glass of hot rum and water, on a perishing night, warms the cockles of your heart, and for my part I should have been well content to stretch my legs before the big kitchen fire at the Nag's Head and caress my stomach with another glass. But George was impatient for us to be off. So we up Paddock, by Jim–lane to the bottom of Marsh. There is a two–storied stone house there looking over to Gledholt, with a mill at the back of it. I knew the owner by sight well enough, a little spindle–shanked man, with a squeaky voice. I had seen him many's the time at the Cherry Tree. Fond of his glass he was, and a great braggart when warmed with liquor. He was a foremost man in the Watch and Ward, and I had heard him boast oft enough of what he would do if the Luddites ever came his way. So I sniggered a bit to myself when we came on to the road in front of the house. The windows were all dark in front. We went up the house side to the mill yard. Here was a door barring the way into the yard.

"Give us a leg up, Ben," whispered Thorpe, and over the top of the door he went, dropping heavily, and with a curse, on the other side.

"Did ta think aw were a cricket ball?" we heard him say. "Throw us a hammer."

Then there was a sharp blow or two, the rattle of a chain, the angry yapping of the yard dog. The door fell open on one lunge, and in we pushed pell mell. We could see a light spring out of the darkness in the chamber window, and we began to bray at the kitchen door. Someone had fetched the dog a crack with a stick, and it had limped whining and growling into its kennel.

"Open the door," cried George.

A bedroom window was opened about half–an–inch, and a piping voice, all tremulous, faltered, "What mean you, good gentlemen? What is your will? For heaven's sake go away quietly. The Ward are on their rounds. They may be here any minute. My missus is shouting for them out o' th' front window. Go home to bed, good masters, and I'll never tell."

"Go stop her mouth, and come down and let us in. Quick now, or it will be worse for you," said George, sternly.

We waited a while, only giving a reminder by a hammer tap on the door panels and breaking a window or two out of sheer mischief. Then there was the fumbling at a chain, the bolt shot in its socket, and the kitchen door was opened. And there in the kitchen, where the embers of the fire were still glowing, stood little Mr. — — —(I won't tell his name, for he was a worthy man, only with words bigger nor his heart) in his shirt, his pipe shanks all bare, and his knees knocking together quite audibly. Well! it was a cold night. Say it was the cold. And his hand that held the metal candlestick shook so, the tallow guttered all down the candle side, making winding sheets. At the bottom of the steps leading upstairs, I caught a sight of a vinegar–faced woman in night–dress and a filled cap.

The remains of the supper were on the table, a very frugal supper, some cheese and haver bread. An empty pitcher was on the table. George Thorpe got another candlestick from the high mantlepiece and went down the cellar steps, and we heard him blowing up a spigot and coaxing a barrel, and the ale coming into the pitcher with a gurgle, like you may fancy a man would swallow if he were half–throttled. It was a lean shop, I warrant you.

There was an old oak armchair by the Dutch clock, and George drew it to the fire.

"Sit down, Mr. S——," he said. "And you, Mrs. S——, go back to bed and keep warm and quiet. It's no use shouting. Th' soldiers are away over bi Crosland Moor, th' constables are over Lindley way. You'll only catch a cold and spoil your sweet voice. But mind you, no noise, or I'll send a man to keep you company. And now, Mr. S our business is with you."

Poor Mr. S——. I smile even yet as I write of him. He trembled so, the rails rattled in the chair, and kept looking this way and that, and jumping at every movement. And yet how he used to strut about the Cherry Tree yard, cursing the ostler, and cuffing the boys that pestered him for pence.

"You have some of the finishing frames in the shed there?" said George.

"Y–e–e–s, good Mr. Ludd, y–e–e–s, but only little ones."

"How many?"

"One, or mebbe two."

"How many more?"

"Well, mebbe three or four."

"How many men have you sacked lately?"

"A two or three."

"And how many more?"

"Well, mebbe a score."

"And how are they living?"

"I dunnot know."

"And their families?"

"My missus gi'es 'em summot to eit whenever we'n more nor we can eit ours-en?"

"Haven't yo' a pig?"

"Ay, well when th' pig's fed of course."

"Yo're one o' th' Watch an' Ward. Where's your staff?"

"By th' looking glass there, with th' lash an' comb; oh! dear, oh! dear."

John Walker pocketed the constable's staff. "Where's your gun?"

"I' th' chamber."

"Fetch it, No. 20."

And Soldier Jack hopped up the stairs, and we heard a shrill shriek and a cry of "Murder! Thieves!" and then Jack limped down again, whilst Mrs. S——— stood at the stair–head and hurled threats and bad language at his back.

"Where's th' key o' th' mill door," went on George, as cool as if he were eating his dinner.

"Oh! dear, oh! dear, you surely winnot harm th' frame's. They'n cost me a hundred and fifty pound apiece, an' I owe to th' bank for 'em yet."

"The key, the key."

Then from a drawer in the dresser he drew the big, heavy key.

"No. 22, 23, 25. Do your duty."

And John Walker, Thorpe and Bill Smith stalked across the mill yard with a lantern. The dog sprung at his chain again, poor animal. There was the creaking of the lock. Then after a pause a voice from the dark sounded:

"Stand clear, Bill," and bang, came the hammer, crash went wood and iron, and the costly frames were wrecked beyond repair. Poor Mr. S— groaned as if his heart were breaking, and his wife at the stair head gave a shriek every time the hammer fell.

"And now," said George, producing a horse–pistol, "but one thing remains. Here is a Bible. You must swear never to make complaint of what has been said or done this night, lest worse befall you."

"Oh, yes, Mr. Ludd, I'll swear. I'll swear anything only go leave us. Oh! my poor frame's! And if I don't die of rheumatism after this night, it'll be a miracle."

"And to take back the men you have sacked?"

"Yes, yes."

"And never more to put up machines to take the bread out of honest men's mouths?"

"Never, never, so help me God. Oh! do go, good Mr. Ludd."

And go we did; but not before George had very politely gone to the foot of the stairs and drunk out of the pitcher to Mrs. S———'s health, and said how sorry he was that business had compelled him to pay his respects to so worthy a lady so late at night. Then we hurried off, over the fields, into Gledholt Wood, where we took off our masks, and went by different ways to the Nag's Head.

Now could you believe that the very next Market Day I saw Mr. S ——— at the market dinner. He was telling to a group of listeners how he had been roused in the night by the crash of machines, how he had jumped out of bed, seized his flint lock carbine, rushed down the steps into the mill yard, laid low one of the gang with the stock of his weapon, being anxious to avoid bloodshed, and the whole thirty or forty had fled before him carrying off their wounded, but not alas! till his machines had been broken.

It must have been some other night.

But Mr. S——— kept his promise. He put up no more frames, even when the troubled times were half forgotten and the Luddites no more a terror. Perhaps he had difficulties with the bank.

But that is ahead of my tale, for I have not done yet with the night we broke the poor man's frames. Going down from Marsh to the foot of Paddock, Ben Walker must need fasten himself on to me, though with half an eye he might have seen, even in the dark, that I wanted none of his company. But he linked his arm in mine, and put on that fawning way of his that fair made my flesh creep.

"And how's thi father, Ben, and yor good mother an' all the friends at Holme?"

It was in my mind to tell him none the better for his asking, but remembered in time that civility costs nought, and so made him as civil an answer as I could fashion.

"And how's Mary, sweet sonsy Mary?" he went on, taking no note of what I was saying about my father's touch of asthma, which was plaguey bad at the back end of the year.

It was just sickening to have him mouthing her name as if he were turning a piece of good stuff on his tongue, so I answered him short enough.

"Yo cannot tell, Ben, how my heart warms to Mary and to you, Ben, for Mary's sake, and to all that's kin to her, even to the third and fourth generation," he added, after a pause, to make it more solemn and convincing like.

"Aw'm sure we're much obliged to you," I said; "but yo'n a queer way o' showing your liking."

"Yo mean leaving her when Long Tom was so unmannerly. It isn't like thee, Ben, to bear malice nor to cast up things in a friend's face. Let byegones be byegones. Aw know aw'm not a warrior, Ben. Aw'st never set up to be a man o' wrath. We'n all our failings, Ben, an' feightin's noan my vocation, that's flat."

"Well, say no more about it," I said. "Let's talk o' summot else. It's lucky for Mary she's got somebody to stick up for her that'll noan turn tail an' leave her to do her own feightin'."

"Meaning thissen, Ben; aw heard about th' setting down tha gave Long Tom."

"Nay, aw weren't thinking o' missen," I said, "tho' yo' may count me in. But it's no business o' thine. Talk o' summot else, aw say."

"But it is a concern o' mine, Ben. It touches me quick does ought 'at touches Mary. How would ta' like me for a cousin–i'–law?"

"A what?" I said.

"A cousin–i'–law. Aw reckon that's what aw should be if aw wed Mary."

"Thee wed Mary!" I cried, half vexed but tickled withal "Thee! Why, Ben, lad, if aw know ought of a woman she wouldn't look th' side o' th' road tha'rt on. Besides she's noan for thee, Ben."

"Happen she's bespoke nearer home?" he said.

"Aye, nearer thi own home," I said, for George and Walker lived not so far off each other.

"What, George Mellor?" he cried.

"Aye, George Mellor," I said, and strode on faster and would have said no more. And if I said more than my knowledge warranted me, I spoke no more than I deemed to be true.

"Nay, Ben, dunnot be angered wi' me. It's no shame to anyone to lose his heart to such a lass as Mary. Aw know tha's set agen me, Ben. Aw know aw'm noan fit for her; an' if it comes to that where will ta find th' man that is?"

I never liked Ben Walker half so much in my life, or I'd better say I never disliked him half so little as just at that moment, for false as he was and mean, one glimmer of truth and nobleness he had about him, and that was his love for Mary. And yet it galled me to have him speak of Mary at all. But he would not have done.

"Aw could do well by her," he said. "Better nor yon fine spark we call General. Why, man, his head's full of nonsense, just pack full. All about the rights o' man, and reform and striking down the oppressors of the poor. As if such as him can do owt! We're all melling wi' things too big for the likes o' us, Ben, an' fools as we all are, George is the biggest o' th' lot, for he hasn't sense enough to know he is a fool."

Now there was just enough in this to make it sting the keener. So I pulled up short and said:

"If that's your opinion about George, go tell him so thissen. An' if yo've ought more to say about our Mary go say it to hersen. Yo'll get your answer straight." And I spoke so rough any other man would have flared up; but Ben Walker could swallow more dirt when it suited his purpose nor any man I ever came across.

"Oh! it's easy enough for thee to talk, Ben Bamforth," he said. "Tha cares nowt about her. Aw thowt happen tha did. An' yet aw might ha known different. Come to think on it, yo'd eyes t'other neet for nobbudy but Faith Booth. An' yo'll find her willing enough, an' one man's meat's another man's poison. A pawky ailing wench, but if yo' fancy her it's everything. Aw wish yo' luck, Ben, aw do indeed."

"Ha' done with yo," I cried in anger. "Faith Booth's as much aboon me as our Mary is aboon you. And never speak again to me about such things as this. I want no secrets from you, and I'll tell none to you. We're in th' same boat as far as this business we're on to–night goes, but beyond that we've nought in common; and so, Ben Walker, without offence, give me as wide a berth as I'll give thee." And I fairly ran off and left him.

In the kitchen of the Nag's Head, George Mellor and Soldier Jack and some score or more of those who had joined the brotherhood, mostly men of the neighbourhood, but some from Heckmondwike and Liversedge way, others from Outlane and the Nook, were already in warm debate. The fire was roaring in the grate, pipes had been lighted, pewters filled, and the buzz of conversation and bursts of laughter filled the low room. George was in great fettle that night. He was always best and brightest in action. Indeed he had much to put his head up. He was obeyed, without question, by many a hundred men; all bound together by a solemn oath, who had implicit trust in him. The military and the special constables were only our sport. They were never any serious hindrance, at first, to anything we took in hand. The mill owners were in fear for their machines, and would rather any night pay than fight. And for the great mass of the people, those who had to work for their living, they believed in General Ludd. In some way they could not fathom nor explain the Luddites were to bring back the good times, to mend trade, to stock the cupboard, to brighten the grate, to put warm clothes on the poor shivering little children. It is not much the poor ask, only warmth and food and shelter, and a little joy now and then. They are very ready to listen to anyone who will promise them this, and if they do not see exactly how it is all to come about, are they the only ones who mistake hope for belief? And George liked the people's trust. When an old hag stopped him in the road and praised his bonny face and bid him be true to the poor, anyone could see the words were sweet to him, and he would empty his pocket into her skinny, eager hand. And he liked too the sense of powers. To command, to be obeyed, to be trusted, to be feared—by your enemies who does not like it? Find me the man who says he doesn't and I'll find you a liar.

Where George got his money from to treat as he did I don't know. He nearly always had money with him, and when he hadn't he had credit with the landlord. We never stinted for ale on the nights we were out on such jobs as that at Marsh, and this night was no exception. And his good humour was shared by all of us. Those who had been up to Marsh had to tell the tale to those who hadn't, and there were roars of laughter as Soldier Jack showed the scratches left on his face by the sharp nails of Mrs. S———.

"We're winning all along the line," George cried. Th' specials is fleyed on us. They take care to watch an' ward just where they know we're not. Th' soldiers don't like their job. It's poor work for lads o' mettle hunting starving croppers. Th' people are with us. But we must strike a decisive blow that will once and for all show our purpose and our power. Every frame in the West Riding must be broken into matchwood; every master must learn that he has resolute and united men to reckon with. Let us once show our strength, and we will not rest till things are bettered for all of us. But we must strike a blow that will be felt the length and breadth of the land. It is baby work that we have been on to–night. We must go for the leaders of the masters, for those who hearten up such men as S———, of Marsh, the men who have both the brains and the pluck, curse 'em, not for the sheep who follow the bell–wether.

"Cartwright, of Rawfolds," cried a Liversedge man.

"Horsfall, of Ottiwell's," said a Marsden cropper.

And then men laid aside their pipes and drained their pewters. And a man was set at the door to see no strangers entered, and we saw to the fastening of the shutters, and that no clink made a spy–hole into the room. And those who spoke hushed their voice, and those who listened strained an anxious ear. It was no child's play now.

"Taylor's have sent out a big order of finishing frames for Cartwright," said one Marsden man.

"Aye, and Cartwright swears he'll work them if not another mill owner in England dare," said William Hall, of Parking Hole.

"I like his mettle," said George. "That Cartwright is a game cock, and we must cut his comb or he'll crow over th' lot on us. If we can only settle such as him, we'st have no bother wi' th' others. Na, lads, my mind's made up. Yo' all know what this Cartwright is doing. Aw've nowt agen him except th' machines. If we let him put up those frames he's ordered, and work 'em, we might as well chuck up. One encourages t' other, and if one succeed another will, nay must, follow suit."

"There's nowt to choose between him an' Horsfall," said the Marsden man. "Aw cannot tell what's come over Horsfall. He allus used to be a decent master till this new craze came up. But naa' he talks o' nowt but machines, machines. An' th' way he raves on about th' Luddites is enough to mak' a worm turn. If he's not lied on he said t' other day at th' market that he'd ha' his own way i' th' mill if he had to ride up to his saddle girths i' Luddite blood."

"Well, well," said George with an ugly gleam in his eye; "Horsfall can wait. What do you say, Ben?"

"Aye, Horsfall can wait," I said, and would have said more if need were, for I shrunk from having part or parcel in any attack on Ottiwell's.

"Well there's an easy way to settle it," said William Hall. "Let's toss up."

"Aye, that's fair enough," said several voices. "Heads for Horsfall, tails for Cartwright." And so it was settled. I live again that moment of my life. Forty years roll away as though they had not been, and clear and vivid I see the group of eager men gathered round the hearth, with George erect and masterful in the centre.

"Who'll call for Cartwright?" said George.

"That will I," said Hall.

"Then here goes," and George balanced a penny on his thumb and forefinger.

"Cry before it drops," he said, and span the coin in the air.

"Tail," said Hall, and every man held his breath as George tossed the coin and caught it. He had to stoop over the fire to see the face of the coin after he caught it.

"Tail it is," he said, and thrust the penny into his fob.

"By jinks I'm fain," said Hall. "Aw owe the b——— one, and now aw'll straighten wi' him. He'll rue the day he sacked Bill Hall for drinking."

And for me I too was fain. For Rawfolds seemed a long way off, but Ottiwell's was close by home.

"We'n got our work set," said George. "It mun be a reight do. Cartwright sleeps in his mill every night. He has soldiers there, too, in the mill with him. The gates and doors have been strengthened. There are other soldiers billeted in the village. Th' mill bell will alarm the country. But we can do it, lads, if yo' are the men I take yo' for. No flinching and we'll strike such a blow at Rawfolds as will make old England ring again. And now, lads, to business."

It were quite beyond me to tell all the plans we made that night. We fixed Saturday the 11th of April for the job, and a man called Dickenson promised to let his mates on that side know our arrangements. We were to meet at the Dumb Steeple by the Three Nuns at eleven of the night. There were to be men from Liversedge, Heckmondwike, Gomersall, Birstall, Cleckheaton, and even from Leeds; and on our side we promised a full muster. Soldier Jack was to see that everyone was warned, and such arms as could be begged, borrowed or stolen were to be got together. The boys were keen enough for work, and nothing doubted of success. We had had it all our own way up to now, and who was Cartwright that he should check us?

It was in the small hours when we stole out into the raw morning air, taking our several ways homewards.

I had not far to go, for I was to sleep with George at the Brigg.

"I'm glad it fell on Cartwright," I said to my cousin, as we doffed our things that night.

"Aw thought tha would be," said George.

"It wer' a weight off me when it fell tails," I added.

"But it were a head," said George with a quiet smile.

"A head!"

"Aye, a head. But I knew tha wanted tails, so I turned it i' my palm when I stooped o'er th' fire."

And yet men talk about fate.

CHAPTER VII.

YOU may be sure such doings as those of which I have written were country's talk. People talked about nothing else. Wherever you sent you heard of misery and want and of the men who were banded together to fight the masters. And the Luddites had the approval of the people. I mean the general run of the people. Not, of course, everybody. Mr. Chew, the church parson, was very bitter against them, and warned his congregation against them, and all those who loved darkness rather than light. But the working men, even those whose own handicraft was not threatened by the new frames, favoured the Luddites. I remember that in May of that year a poor woman at Berry Brow, that was thought to have given some information to Mr. Radcliffe, was nearly torn to pieces by her neighbours. Her skull was fractured by a stone. Perhaps because the Luddites felt secure in the general approval their secrets were ill kept.

I do not know how it came about, but at Holme I was soon made aware that I was well regarded. When I went to chapel at the Powle, people made way for me as though I were somebody, and the women folk, in particular, took care I should know I stood well with them. If my father and I stopped to swap the news of the day with our friends and neighbours, and the talk turned on the great questions of the time, men would look to me to know what I had to say, and my words would be quoted from house to house as they had never been quoted before.

Who blabbed? I don't know. Not I, in very truth. 'Siah, I suspect, to Martha. For me, I hated most genuinely the secrecy and underhandedness of the thing. I hated to slink about in the dark, to drop behind a hedge when I heard the fall of a horse's foot, the rattle of a scabbard, or the champing of a bit. I hated to put on a mask and a smock, and to steal about with my heart in my mouth, and I hated more than all to turn aside my face from the mute questioning of my mother's eyes.

Once there was questioning that was not mute. It was a Sunday evening, about the time of the meeting at the Nag's Head. We had been to chapel, and Mr. Webster was home with us to supper. John Booth and Faith were there. The nights were lengthening, and there was a warmer breath in the air, and the cuckoo had been heard on Wimberlee. After supper I had set myself to walk towards Huddersfield with John and Faith, and before we must start Faith had said she would like me to show her the roan calf, new come, whilst Martha made up a bottle of the beestings to carry home with her, so we went together into the shippon. The little straddling thing was in a corner by itself, warded off, and Faith bent over it and let the ruddy little thing suck and slobber over her hand, whilst the mother with patient wistful eyes looked over her shoulder and lowed lovingly. Then I must wipe Faith's little hand with a wisp of hay, and I vow it was a monstrous pretty hand, white and thin, not like Mary's, brown and firm and plump. And whilst I held her hand in my big palm, Faith looked up to my face in the obscure light of the mistal and said very softly:

"Ben, you know our John is soft and easy led, not big and strong as your are. And oh! if harm come to John it would kill my father and go nigh to break my heart. And now he has secrets from me. He is anxious and ill at ease. He is no longer frank and glad, and he tells me nothing. And Mrs. Wright, the saddler's wife, where you know he is serving his time, tells me he is sore changed of late—stopping out to all hours, and strange men coming to their shop with letters and messages, and John whispering in corners with them as if he were plotting a murder. She says she cannot sleep o' nights for thinking of it all. And oh! Ben, my heart tells me he is in danger, and what shall I do if harm befall him?"

"Nay, Faith, lass," I said, stooping down to get a fresh wisp of hay, and maybe to hide my face from that gaze that seemed to read my thoughts too plain, "Nay, Faith, what harm should befall your John? You mustn't set too much store by what Mrs. Wright says. What if John does stop out a bit late at nights? Saddlering's a confining job, and most like John needs a long walk to straighten his limbs after being at th' bench all day with his legs twisted all shapes like a Turk. An' yo're never sure, yo' know, Faith, o' young folk, even th' quiet 'uns. Perhaps your John's doing a bit o' courting."

"Ah! Ben, if I could think it were only that. For well I know if John were cour—; were doing what you say, you'd be like enough to know of it."

Now how should that be I wondered, but said nothing, only too glad to think I had set her thoughts on a false scent.

"But it isn't that, Ben. Speak low. No one must hear us. I know John has a warm heart, and one that feels for the poor. And he is always reading and talking and thinking of politics and the doings of the Parliament men, and sometimes the things he says take my breath away. And Mrs. Wright says—oh! Ben, how can I tell it you?—that she sadly fears our John has taken up with th' Luddites an' is going about the country with th' constables on his track, an' maybe th' soldiers watching him, an' some night he'll never come back and my father's grey hairs will be brought with sorrow to the grave."

"Mrs. Wright's a cackling old fool," I said; but Faith went on.

"And, oh, Ben, she says that it's all George Mellor's doing. She says George will lead him to the gallows, and many a mother's son beside. It's awful to hear the things she says about George. I'm sure they aren't true. I'm sure George would never do anything that wasn't noble and good and true. I've always comforted myself with that. Whatever it is, I've said to myself, if George has ought to do with it, it must be right. If it's right for George, it's right for John. I told Mrs. Wright so, though I don't like talking of these things, but she angered me so."

"Well, and what did the old beldame say to that?"

"Oh, shocking things. Th' best she could find to say for him was that he wer' a conceited puppy that thowt he could set th' world to rights by talking big. But she thinks the world o' thee, Ben—a steady, proper, young man, she called yo', wi' his head screwed on right, and not stuck full o' stuff an' nonsense, like George. She said she'd warrant yo'd sense enough to mind your own business, and those that had more had no sense. So, Ben, I want yo' to promise me to say a word to John. He'll mind yo' if he won't me. He's all th' brother I have, Ben, and oh! my heart mistrusts me, there's trouble coming, and I know not whence nor how."

I had put the lanthorn on the bin and Faith had both her hands in mine, and her pale, sweet face was turned up to mine, and she looked at me with eyes that were wet with tears, and her low sweet voice trembled and caught in a sob. I never was in such a fix in my life, and I found no way out of it by cursing Mrs. Wright in my mind for a meddlesome old harridan, though as decent a woman as ever lived.

"And now, Ben," pleaded Faith, "you see what trust we all have in you. Not but what I have trust in George, too, and I can't think what has set Mrs. Wright against him so. But perhaps he has overmuch spirit and pride, and it's no great fault in a man, is it? But you will speak to John, won't you, Ben, and warn him not to break his father's heart, and to mind what he does and says."

And just then, the mistal door flung open and Mary came in, and I still had Faith's hand in mine.

"Oh! I'm sure, I'm sorry if I intrude," said Mary, "but I thought you'd come to show Faith th' new calf."

"And so I did."

"It seems to me more like you were telling her her fortune," said Mary in a very waspish way which she could put on very quick when she was not pleased. "But John's waiting for yo', and mi uncle says yo're to excuse Ben setting yo' home tonight, he has summot to say to him while Mr. Webster's here. It's a pity, for happen if he walked home wi' yo' by moonlight, he might ha' seen to your fortin coming true."

"For shame o' thissen, Mary," I said angrily. "Nay dunnot take on, Faith; it's only Mary's spiteful way. Nobody heeds her." And I turned to go into the house.

"And you promise, Ben," cried Faith, after me.

"Aye, I'll mind me, Faith; I'll mind me."

"I declare, Faith," I heard Mary say, "These may be town ways, colloguing wi' strangers i' th' dark. But we're none used to 'em at Holme. Yo' might be a pair o' Luddites, such carryings on."

It was easy enough to see something more than common was troubling our folk. My father was sat in his chair by the fireside, but his pipe lay discarded on the table, and his ale was untasted in the pewter. My mother was rocking nervously in her chair, and she was creasing and smoothing her silk apron as she only did when she was what she called "worked up," and little Mr. Webster first crossed his left leg over his right knee, and then his right leg over his left knee, and mopped his brow with his handkerchief as though it were the dog days. "The murther's out," I thought, for something told me what was coming.

"Sit you down, Ben," said my father.

"And put th' sneck on the door," said my mother. "I declare what wi' folk fra Huthersfelt an' what wi' folk fra Low Moor, this house is getting waur nor Lee Gap, an' yo' never know who'll come next, nor when to call your house your own."

Now this was unlike my mother, who was not one to welcome people to their face and back–bite them when they were gone, like I have known some do.

I put down the sneck and sat me down on the settle and waited.

"Mr. Webster's been talking, to us, Ben," said my father very gravely.

"And blind as a bat I've been not to see it misen," snapped my mother.

"Talking to us about yo', Ben," father went on, "and very kind and friendly of him we take it, and it explains a many things I've wondered at more nor a little. Only last market day I met Mr. Horsfall i' th' Cloth Hall, and I said 'Any more news o' th' Luddites, Mr. Horsfall,' and he snapped out summot about it not being his way to carry coals to Newcastle. Aw wondered what he meant, but it's plain enough now what he were driving at."

Plain enough. But I must make a show of some sort, so I said:

"Perhaps yo'll make it plainer, father."

"Well, Mr. Webster, and I'm sure we thank you kindly and know it's well and neighbourly meant, and only what we should have looked for from you, Mr. Webster,—Mr. Webster says folk are talking about you, Ben, and that our house, this very house I were born an' bred in, is known an' watched for a meeting place of th' Luddites. Mr. Webster says he's had a hint or two from more nor one that's like to know 'at would be sorry to see a decent family that always held its head up an' paid its way, brought to trouble and maybe disgrace by carryings on that's agen the law an' cannot be justified. But there, Mr. Webster, aw'm a poor talker, tell him yersen, an' let him answer yo' if he can."

"I'm' not at liberty to say who my informant was, Ben," said Mr. Webster. "But briefly the matter is this. One of my deacons"...

My thoughts flew, I know not why, to Buck Walker, Ben's father—"asked me privately this morning if I knew whether it was true, that you and George Mellor were strongly suspected of being of the party that broke into Mr. S———'s mill at Marsh. And others, too, have hinted at the same thing, and one of my brothers who labours in the Lord's vineyard at Milnsbridge says that it is common talk in those parts that George Mellor and his cousin from Slaithwaite way are the head and front of the grave doings that now distract the country and add crime and violence to poverty and hunger."

"Drat that George Mellor, that ever I should live to say so of my sister's son. And him coming here so much of late and making him welcome to the best of everything, nothing too good for him, and couldn't be more done by if he were my own son. As is nothing but right by your own sister's son, and him wi' a step-father that would aggravate a saint. Who'd ha thowt it o' George, leading yar Ben, that wouldn't harm a flea an' scarce pluck to say boo to a goose, into all maks o' mullock, an' dragging decent women out of their bed by th' hair o' th' head, an' goodness only knows what beside. But I'll lock thee in this very night wi' mi own hands, and out o' this house tha doesn't stir fra sunset to sunrise, or my name's not Sarah Bamforth. An' let George show his face here again if he dare. An' so nicely as I had it all planned out too. Aw made no doubt he wer' companying that pale faced lass o' Parson Booth's, an' a rare catch for her aw thowt it would be to have a fine, handsome, well–set–up young man i' th' family that would bring some blood an' bone into th' breed, as it's easy to see their father's had all run to furin gibberish an' book learning, so at he'd none to give his own childer, poor warmly things." Thus my mother.

"Well, Ben, has ta nowt to say for thissen?" said my father, not angrily, but with an unspoken reproach in his voice: and my conscience smote me sore.

"You see, Ben," said Mr. Webster, perhaps noticing my silence and to give me time to gather my thoughts. "You see, Ben, a young man like you is scarcely his own master. If you had been 'Siah, now, it would have been different. A decent man is your servant, Brother Bamforth, and helps my infirmity mightily when he lights me home of a dark night, a decent man though with still a strong leaven of the old Adam and much given to the vanities of the flesh and idle conversation. But 'Siah is his own master though your man. His family is under his own hat. He has neither kith nor kin, that he knows of, and he stands, so to speak, on his own bottom. But you, Ben, are your father's son, and what you may do, be it for good or be it for evil, must reflect on your father's name and on this honoured house."

Ah! there was the rub. It was the thought of that had given me many a sleep-less night, and made black care walk daily by my side.

"Cannot ta speak, man?" my mother cried. "Are ta going to sit theer as gaum-less as th' town fool, wi niver a word to throw at a dog. Who yo' breed on aw cannot tell, not o' my side. It's not his bringing up, Mr. Webster, it's the company he's fallen into lately."

But what to say I could not think. All sorts of old proverbs came into my head—"a little word's a bonny word," "least said, soonest mended," and so on. I loved my mother. I honoured my father. I revered Mr. Webster. But my secret was not my own; there was, too, that terrible oath. I wished for the thousandth time that I had had nought to do with the Luds: and there were the three faces turned to me, all question, and waiting for me to find speech to answer.

"Father," I said at length, "Have you ever known me tell you a lie?"

"Never, Ben," he said with hearty emphasis.

"Would you have me begin now?"

"Tha knows better."

"Then ask me no questions, father, for the truth I may not tell, and lies I would not. That I am in great trouble you all can see. That I will seek to so bear my trouble that it shall touch only myself, you must trust me. God knows it grieves me to seem wanting in respect or confidence where respect and confidence should need no asking, but in this matter I must tread my own path, for I cannot turn back and yet I dread to go forward. Press me no more, for if you do, I must leave home and that now. I thank you, Mr. Webster, that you have spoken to my parents. This was bound to come, and I have feared it more than ought either Mr. Radcliffe or any on 'em can do. And now, my say's said, an' with your good leave, I'll bid you a fair good night."

And I lit my candle, and stooping over, kissed the cheek which my mother for the first time in my life did not offer to me, and went slowly and heavily to bed. Long after I had drawn the clothes over me, I heard the murmur of conversation below, and when the morrow came I had not long to wait before I knew the upshot of the anxious debate that had lasted long after the usual time for bed.

I had gone into the mistal, where I knew I should find 'Siah. My father it seemed had risen earlier than usual. 'Siah was grooming old Bess, sissing over her flanks with much vigour, and prodding her loins with the comb with many a "stand over, lass," "whoa," "will ta?" and much make–believe that the old mare was a mettlesome beast, full of fire and vice, whereas in sooth a quieter animal never was shod.

"Yo're agate early this morning, 'Siah," I said; "what's up?"

"Nay that's what caps me, Ben Summut's up, certain sure. Thi father fot me out o' bed awmost afore aw'd shut mi een. 'Tha mum fettle Bess up an' see to th' gears' he said, 'we'st be off for Macclesfilt as soon as we can mak' a load.'"

"To Macclesfilt? Why there's no fair on this time o'th' year, 'Si. Tha must ha' been dreamin'."

"It's a dream at's fetched th' sweat on me, if it were a dream. Aw'm noan gi'en to dreams 'at fetch me out o' bed i' th' middle o' th' neet. But dream or no dream we're off in a day or two, choose how. Tha'll be going too, Ben."

"What do yo' make on it, 'Si?"

"Why it's plain as th' nose on thi face. We're none bahn to sell pieces, for there's nobody got any brass to wear. An' aw reckon thi father's noan so weel off 'at he can afford to give 'em away. So if it isn't for business it mun be for pleasure or happen for health. P'r'aps it's for thy health, Ben. Tha looks delikit, tha great six feet o' beef an' bacon. A change o' air will do thee good."

"Tha knows well enough, 'Si, I cannot go away just now, not before next Saturday. Yo' know what's fixed for next Saturday."

"Aw know weel enough, an' more the reason for a change o' air, say I."

"What 'Si, turn traitor and leave our comrades in the lurch?"

"Hard words break no bones, Ben, an' I, for one, am sick o' this trolloping about hauf th' neet through; often as not weet to th' skin; an' nawther beef nor beer, nor brass nor fun in it. Aw'd rayther list for a sodger gradely. It's wearin' me to skin an' bone, an' all for what aw'd like to know?"

"For th' cause 'Si."

"Damn th' cause. Let th' cause shift for itsen. Aw'm noan a cropper nor a weaver, nor owt but a plain teamer, an' aw tell yo' Ben, we'd both be a darn sight better out o' this job nor in it."

"But our oath, 'Si."

"Promises an' pie crusts wer' made to be broken aw'n heerd yo'r mother say."

"But our honour, 'Si."

"Fine words butter no parsnips, aw'n heard Mary say. Besides honour's for gentlefolk. It's too fine a thing for a teamer. Stand ovver, tha brussen owd wastrel!"

"When do we start for Macclesfield?"

"Happen. Wednesday, happen Thursday. Not o' Friday if aw can help, for luck. Any road as soon after next market day as we can load, bi what thi father says."

"Well, 'Si, listen to me. I've promised George I would bear a hand i' this Cartwright job, an' I cannot go back o' my word. Besides I've promised more nor George. I cannot tell you all, 'Si, but my word's passed to stand by John Booth, an' see him safe out o' this muddle; an' see him safe out of it I will if I can."

"Petticoats again," muttered 'Siah.

"After that, I promise yo, 'Si, I'll be main glad to be clear of the whole business, and so I'll tell my cousin George. If machinery's to come we must find some better way of meeting it than with a sledge hammer."

"Ah! that's th' sensiblest word tha ever spoke, Ben Bamforth."

"But mark, 'Si, Bess must not be ready to start till after Saturday. Yo' understand: a nail in her hoof or a looseness i' th' bowels, I leave it to thee, 'Si. But leave here till after Saturday I won't, an' neither will yo', if yo're th' man I take thee for!"

"A wilful man mun have his way. Go to thi baggin', Ben. Don't let 'em see us talkin' together. Aw understand thee, an' tha'st have thi way; but after Saturday a team o' horses shan't drag me a foot after George Mellor, an' there's my davy on it."

And 'Siah crossed two fingers and spat over them, and that I knew to be more binding on 'Si than any Bible oath. So I turned to go, much relieved and easier in my mind now I had shaped a clear course. But 'Siah had not quite done.

"Hauf a minnit, Ben. It had welly slipped mi mind. Has Mary said owt to thee about yon Ben Walker?"

"No, what about him? Ben o' Buck's yo' mean?"

"Aye, t' same felly, him at run away fra Long Tom."

"Well, what on him?"

"He's been after her agen."

"Who? Tom?"

"No', guise ang thee, Ben o' Buck's. Martha tell'd me. But aw reckon he'll noan come agen in a hurry. 'Oo sent him away wi' a flea in his yer 'oil, bi all accounts."

"Aye?"

"Aw cannot tell what t' ar' thinkin, on, Ben. It's no bizzness o' mine, but there 'oo is, ripe an' bloomin' an' ready to be plucked. 'As ta no een i' thi yed, at tha leaves her for all th' gallus birds i' th' country to pluck at when 'oo's thine for th' askin'?"

"Stuff an' nonsense, 'Si. We winnot talk about it. But what about Walker?"

"Nay, aw dunnot know all th' tale. Martha's ready enough to talk about some things, particular about th' iniquity o' a pint o' ale. But 'oo just gave me to understand 'at Walker's popped to Mary, an' Mary's as cross as a bear wi' a sore ear."

"Tha doesn't know what she said to him, 'Si? But theer aw've no right to ask, an' tha's noan to tell. Maids' secrets are not for us to talk about."

"Aw didn't gather 'at 'oo said much. But Martha said 'oo heard a smack, an' it didn't sound like th' smack o' a kiss, an' 'oo saw Ben goin' down th' broo very white i' one cheek an' very red o' th' other, an' lookin as ugly as a cur that's lost a bone. So tha can draw thi own conclusions, Ben, that is if thi, what d'ye call it, oh, thi honour, will let thee."

And with this sarcasm, 'Siah dug his head into Bess's ribs and began a vigorous scrubbing that set the old mare dancing and stamping, and put an effective end to further confidences.

That was a gloomy week at our house. Mary was as contrary as contrary could be, my mother was sad and tearful, my father glum and stern. He told me that if it was all the same to me he intended going to Macclesfield in a day or two, and bade me write to some of our customers there and by the way. But I knew that it was a needless journey, and taken only to get me out of harm's way. I dared not say I would go after Saturday, for fear of starting enquiries as to my reasons for delay. So I merely said I should be ready when he was, and that seemed to cheer him a bit.

I dreaded meeting my cousin George, but I knew it had to be done. My mind was fully made up to tell him I could not continue by his side in this organized attack on machines I had been busy thinking the matter out. The objection to machinery was that, it displaced human labour. Well, I argued, a scythe is a machine, so is a pair of scissors. If I proposed to do away with the scythe at hay time and clip our three acre field with my mother's scissors, everyone would think me a lunatic. The more I thought of that illustration the more I liked it, and I wondered how George would get over it. But, somehow, as I walked down, to the Brigg to have my talk with George, I got less and less comfort from my logic the nearer I drew to Huddersfield. George was at home and fortunately we were not interrupted. He was in a towering rage, and I could not have found a worse time for my errand.

"Yo're just the man I wanted to see, Ben," he said. "I feel I must talk to somebody and let th' steam off a bit. But somebody'st smart for this. An eye for an eye and a tooth for a tooth th' old Book says, an' a blow for a blow too, say I. Aye, by

God, a blow for a blow, a hundred blows for one, insult for insult, outrage for outrage, and ruin for oppression. The proud insolence of the man! Am I a dog that I should bear this thing? Answer me that, Ben Bamforth."

"Whatever's up, George?" I asked. "Do sit thee down and talk quiet and sensible. An' quit walking an' tearing up an' down like a tiger in a cage. One would think th'd lost thi wits, an' I particler wanted a quiet talk."

"Quiet, aye, yo'd be quiet if somebody cut thee across th' face wi' a whip. Listen here. Aw'd been up to Linfit, an' were comin' quiet as a lamb along th' road back to th' cropping shop. An' just above th' Warren House, by Radcliffe's plantation, tha' knows, wer' a woman about thirty year old, crouched agen th' wall. I could see a pair o' men's shooin sticking out fra underneath her skirt, and it's my belief 'oo'd nowt on her but just that skirt an' an old thin black shawl. Neither sock nor shift, an' it's none too warm o' neets yet. She wer' crying and moanin' an' rocking hersen to an' fro', swaying her body back'ards and for'ards, an 'oo'd a bundle o' summat in her arms lying across her breast, an' 'oo strained it to her and made her moan. Her face were pale as death, an' her cheek bones seemed high an' sharp, an' th' skin drawn tight as a drum across 'em. An' her eyes were sunk in her yed, but black an' wild an' staring. An' her lips were thin and bloodless, an' there was a line of blood upon 'em as tho' she bled, an' her arms and hands were thin and skinny. Aw didn't know her, but aw stopped to see what ailed her. She wouldn't, talk for a bit; she'd do nowt but moan. An' then 'oo told me she'd been down to Huddersfielt to see th' Relieving Officer. Her husband wer' a cropper. He'd been thrown out o' work. His master'd put in two frames, an' he had to leave. He's down wi' th' rheumatic fever. They'd nowt to eat, an' nowt to sup. 'Oo'd been sucklin' th' babby, an' as time went on she'd no milk in her breasts for th' little one. 'Oo'd fed it for days by soaking a rag i' warm milk an' water an' lettin' it suck at that. But th' little thing had pined and pined, crying an' wailin' and, o' a night, pressin' its little mouth to her dry breasts an' drawin' nowt but wind. An' then it had th' convulsions, an' she had to leave her man ravin' i' th' fever an' hug th' brat to Huddersfield, an' there they'd nowt for her, an' 'oo must back agen wi' nother bite nor sup between her lips an' nowt the better for her tramp. She oppened her shawl, an' as I'm a livin' man, there wer' th' little 'un wi' a head no bigger nor mi fist, stark dead at its mother's breast; and its eyes starin' an' starin' an' its face all drawn wi' pain. It made my heart stand still, an' aw felt as if a strong man were clutchin' at my throat."

"Aw stood before her mute. Aw couldn't speak. An' just then I heard th' sound o' a horse's trot, an' I turned round an' there wer' Horsfall o' Ottiwell's coming up th' road. He wer' wipin' his mouth wi' th' back o' his hand, and' aw judged he'd stopped for a glass at th' Warrener. Aw don't know what possessed me, but aw nipped up th' child fra' its' mother's arms an' stepped right i' th' front o' his horse it swerved, an' he swayed in his saddle."

'Damn you, mind where yo're walking,' he said. 'Stand aside and leave the road free, yo' drunken tramp.'

"But aw stood stock still i' th' front o' his mare, an' aw held up th' child aboon th' horse's head an' I thrust it right to his face."

'Look at thi work, William Horsfall; look at thi work, an' be glad,' I cried. "Th' horse reared a bit, an' he leaned over its shoulder an' peered, for it wer' gettin' dark. Aw thrust th' poor mite close to his jowl, an' aw heard him catch his breath an' saw a great start in his e'en. An' then he drew his mare on to its haunches, an' lifted his stock high in th' air, an' before aw wer' aware on him, down he brought it wi' all his might an' main reight across mi face. Tha' may see th' weal. But aw didn't seem to feel it much."

"'Out o' mi way, you villain,' he cried, an' he dug his spur into th' mare an' she sprang on wi' a bound, an' he wer off up th' road, turning in his saddle an' shouting:

'Aw marked yo' George Mellor; aw marked yo', an' know yo' for what yo' are. Yo'n none heard th' last o' this.'"

"But aw cared nought for what he said. I gave th' wee body back to its mother an' all th' brass I had on me. And 'oo went her way and I came mine. But, as the Lord's above me, that blow shall cost William Horsfall dear."

I hated more than ever to do my errand now, but it had to be done. My neat little argument about machines went clean out of my head. I got George quieted down after a bit. It had done him good to let him tell his tale and storm on a bit. And then, when I thought he could talk sensibly, I said:

"Yo' won't like my errand, George, but I've settled to tell you, an' I thought I must come straight to yo' an' tell yo' what's in my mind."

"Well, what is it, lad, I'm easier now I've said my say."

"Yo' know what's fixed for next Saturday?"

"I do, that, Ben, an' all goes rare an' well. Aw've had word that a big force fra Leeds will join us near Rawfolds, an' some 'll be there fra Bradford an' Dewsbury. Th' movement's spreading, lad, it's spreading an' it's growing, an' th' time's at hand when General Lud will have an army that will sweep all before it."

"I shall be there, George."

"Why, of course tha' will, Ben. You an' 'Siah must lead the hammer men. Those doors o' Cartwright's will stand some braying, but yo' an' 'Siah can splinter his panels an' burst his locks, aw'm thinking."

"I shall be there, George, for my word's passed. But after that night—yo' must do without me."

"Do without thee, Ben? Tha'rt none bahn to duff? Tha'll noan turn tail, Ben? Why victory's at hand, man. One blow and the game's our own. Tha'rt joking, Ben."

"Aw never were more i' earnest, George. And it hurts me to tell thee. Yo' know what store I set on yo', George. We've been more like brothers nor cousins, an' tha knows, tho' aw'm not clever like thee an' high mettled, aw'm neither coward nor traitor. Aw've tried to think as yo' think, George, an' to see as yo' see. Aw know it's all true tha says about th' sufferings o' th' poor; an' what's to become o' th' working folk when more an' more machines come up, aw cannot tell. But we're on a wrong tack, George. Enoch's none going to stop machinery. Th' mesters are stubborn, an' they're English, too. We may break a thousand frames, an' clear every machine out of every mill an' shop in England, but better ones will take their place. We cannot go on for ever wi' midnight raids an' secret meetings. The law's too strong for us, George, an' we're kicking against the pricks."

"Then what would yo' have us do, Ben? Are th' working classes to sit down wi' their hands i' their pockets an' watch their families die by inches? If yo' don't like my methods tell me better. Do yo' think I like stealing about at night like a thief, or that I find any pleasure in smashing machines? If that were the be–all and end–all of our campaign, I'd have nowt to do wi' it. But it's only th' beginning, Ben, only th' beginning."

"And the end?" I asked.

"We'll strike higher an' further. Before many weeks are over I'll throw off all disguise. I'll call on every man that has a heart in his breast to join me in a march to London. We'll strike into the great North–road. We'll ransack every farm house by the way for arms and provisions. We'll take toll of every man in every town who has got rich by grinding down the poor. We'll make our presence and our power known at every hail and castle in the Shires. We'll strike terror into the hearts of every aristocrat who abuses his hereditary privileges to press down and rob the poor. We'll march with swelling ranks and a purpose firmer by every step we take, till we stand, an army, at the very gates of Westminster, and there we will thunder forth our claims and wring from an abject Parliament the rights, without which we are driven slaves."

"And have you counted the cost, George?"

"Aye, that I have. If we succeed, who can tell what we may not accomplish? These cruel lagging wars that keep corn beyond our reach, and are useful only to find riches and glory for the ruling families of the land, shall finish. The toiling masses of England shall clasp in friendship the hand of the uprisen people of France. We will drive from office and power those lords and landowners who for centuries have battened on the poor and used the great resources of this country, wrung from the helpless taxpayer, as their own privy purse. We will establish a Parliament in which the poor man's voice will be heard. We will sound the death knell of privilege and inequality; we will herald the glorious reign of equality and righteousness. And if we fail, why then, Ben, we shall have died in a glorious cause, and George Mellor for one would rather shed his blood in such a cause than sit mute and consenting, a crushed and heartless unit of a people hugging its own chains. Dost like the picture, Ben?"

"I'm with yo' George, in an open fight, tho' I seem to feel a rope round my neck as I say it. But, for heaven's sake, George, get into th' open as soon as tha' can. For aw've forgotten how to hold up mi head an' look th' market in th' face even sin' aw first put on a mask an' dodged behind a hedge at the sound of a trooper's horse. Tha's cozened mi again, George. Aw came to get out o' a conspiracy an' tha's nobbut pledged me to rebellion. I'm out o' th' frying pan into th' fire, wi' a vengeance. But at least I'st have mi own self respect, an' that's summot gained."

"Spoken like thi own self, Ben, an' now lets talk o' Saturday neet, an' no more looking back, an' yo' love me, lad."

CHAPTER VIII.

IT WAS nigh ten o'clock of the Saturday night when I slipped on my clothes, went on tiptoe across the bedroom floor into the little room where 'Siah slept—how the rafters creaked!—and roused him from his deep sleep. 'Siah sat up with a yawn that would have awakened any but those who slept the heavy slumbers born of honest toil and pure air, rubbed his eyes with his knuckles, yawned again, thrust, a stockinged leg from under the blankets, muttered something that did not sound like a blessing, donned his trousers and his smock, and followed me, with a clumsy attempt at care, down the stairs. In the kitchen we shod our feet, 'Siah in clogs, over which he drew a pair of socks, myself with thick hob–nailed boots. The dog rose from the hearth, stretched himself with a yawn, arched his back, and then lay down again with his jaw upon his fore–paw and eyes watchful from under shaggy brows. My mother had not kept her threat to lock me in o' nights, in fact I am not sure she could have done, had her will been ever so good. 'Siah opened the door, motioned the dog back to its place, and we turned out into the yard, doubled the house side, and strode off down the hill. We met not a soul nor spoke a word till we came to Kitchen Fold, and here, by the Black Bull, we came upon Soldier Jack. He gave us a quiet greeting, almost in a whisper. He handed an axe to 'Siah, and a huge sledge–hammer to myself. He showed us a pistol that he himself was to handle, and a small canvass bag of powder and ball. He fondled the weapon lovingly, and as we walked briskly along towards Huddersfield, kept on cocking it at the startled birds that sprung twittering from the hedges. Of Watch and Ward we saw no sign. There was half a moon in the sky, which was o'ercast by scudding clouds behind which she sailed, diving down as into troughs of ink, then showing a horn and riding triumphantly to the clear again, like a ship of fire in the billows of the sea. There was no rain, but the wind moaned, and save for its moan and the fall of our feet and the bark of a cur as we passed the scattered houses, and now and then a word from Jack, all was very still. We did not dally in the town, for the order was that each man should make his own way to the Dumb Steeple, a sign well known to all of us, hard by the Three Nuns, on the road side, near the old Convent of Kirklees. As we neared the spot we saw other figures moving furtively and quickly in the same direction. Some were dressed in smocks, and all had their faces part concealed, either by a mask or by a 'kerchief drawn across the lower face. One gaunt being strode on before us dressed in woman's skirts; but a pair of men's trousers, that showed at every step, and a manly stride were in ill keeping with the skirt. When we got near the Steeple I put on my mask and 'Siah and Jack theirs. From all sides, across fields, down bye–ways, from Roberttown, from High-town, men, singly and in small groups, were gathering. Some were even coming out of the Three Nuns, where lights were showing through the lower windows. But all were curiously still. So still I gave a start when a slim form moved by my side, sprung from I know not where, and John Booth's voice whispered:

"I knew you by your height, Ben, and the swing of your gait, and Soldier Jack is noan hard to tell by his limp. But here we are by th' Steeple, and here should be our leader."

We had not long to wait for George. He singled me out easily enough by my height, for I was a good three inches above any man there.

"Well in time, George. That's right, and 'Siah too. Give Martha a buzz fra me, 'Si, when tha' gets back to Holme. What! Soldier Jack! Ah! now we shall make a brave show, an' those Leeds lads will know what it means to have a soldier to smarten us up." And he was here and there and in and among and seemed to have just the right word for every one, and Soldier Jack began at once to busy himself in seeing how each one was armed. 'Siah slunk off towards the Three Nuns, muttering that if he had to die that night he should like to die with t' taste o' honest ale in his mouth.

"Come aside with me, Ben," said John, when none was bye to note him. "We've a good half–hour to wait here before we start. There are not above a hundred of us here all told; and we counted on five times that number. The Leeds men will meet us, or should meet us, nigher Rawfolds. But Bradford and Dewsbury have sent a mere handful of those that should have come. George is putting a brave face on, but he's sore vexed all the same."

"We've enough for th' job," I said. "If a hundred men cannot force Rawfolds a thousand cannot. We'd do well to start and know our luck."

"We must not start before I say my say, Ben. We shall see the ranks forming from here, and I may have no other chance."

"Well, John lad, what is it. Tha' looks as if tha'd seen a boggard." The pale light from the moon had fallen full on his face as we stood against the wall of Kirklees Park, a two or three hundred yards away from where the moving mass bulked large about the Steeple.

"Don't jest to–night, Ben. I cannot bear it. My heart is heavy with forebodings. I cannot, cannot shake them off, try as I will. This is my last venture, Ben."

"Aye and mine by moonlight, John Daylight or nowt, say I."

"It is my last, Ben. There will be sharp work at Rawfolds. The mill is well garrisoned, Cartwright is a bold, a resolute man. He will defend his machines at any hazard and at any cost. Still you need not despair. If you can but win your way in, you may overpower him and the men he has with him. But, Ben, have you thought of it? There will be bloodshed. There must be bloodshed. Cartwright will not ask quarter, nor will he give it. My father knows him well. If you break down gate and door, you will find him there, pistol in hand, and he will not scruple to shoot his assailant down."

"Tha'rt none feart, are ta, John. Tha can slip off, if tha likes. Aw'll ma'e some mak' o' a story to quieten George. Tha looks poorly enough for owt."

"Quit yo'r talking, Ben. I would not turn back if I could. But, Ben, this night's work will be my last. Something tells me my days are numbered I do not know I need greet for that. It's a weary world, and I'st be well out on it."

"Yo're just talking daft," I said, but I felt somehow that he was telling truth. I could not make light of what he said, though I tried.

"If I don't go back to Huddersfield with you, Ben, you'll find a paper at Mrs. Wight's, telling yo' what to do with my bits o' things. There's Hume's History of England. Yo've always said yo'd like to read it. Mi Bible's for Faith, and this ring for Mary, wi my love, an' give George th' silver buckles off my Sunday shoon. It'll be for you to tell my father and Faith. No one else must do it. Promise me that."

"Do ho'd thi talkin, John, an' dall thee, dunnot look so solemn. I'st be angered wi' thee in a bit." I wanted to feel angry, to work myself into wrath, for I knew if this talk went on, I should soon be fit for nowt myself.

"Nay, Ben, bear with me. Faith will be a lone lass, when I am gone. She loves me, Ben, with more than a sister's love. You see my mother died when I were born. I wish she were well wed, George. I should not fear leaving her if I knew she were plighted to a good man."

"There's yo'r father," I said; "but what child's talk we're talking. Tha'll noan fall, John; aw dunn't believe in forebodings an' such woman's fancies. It's thi liver, John. Let's go back; George 'll be missing us. Stick as close to me as tha can get, when we come to th' mill, an' aw'll see nobody touches thee, if I can help it."

"My father's an old man," pursued Booth, not heeding what I said. "An old man, wrapped in his books, and more helpless than Faith herself. Do you like Faith, Ben? I've fancied of late she turns to thee I know she trusts you and seems to lean on your strength. Women like power in a man, Ben, not wreck lings like me."

"Yo're noan a wreckling, lad. It's th' head folk measure men by, not legs an' arms."

"Ivy will cling to the oak, Ben, for all that, an' Faith's is a clinging nature. Yo'll stand by her, if th' worst comes to th' worst. Promise me, Ben. On thi word as a man, Ben, pledge me thi promise, an' I'll go to this night's work wi' a lighter heart."

A whistle sounded shrill and clear from by the Steeple. It was the signal to fall in. We turned to join our comrades. John held me by the hand, and his pale, thin face, with those large, soft, woman's eyes of his, was turned up to me, all entreaty.

"It needs no promise, John; but if it 'll lighten thee owt an' help thee to play the man this night, there's mi hand on it. An' now put this nonsense, out o' thi head. Stick close to me, all through. An' when it's ovver (end choose how it may) make straight for me or Soldier Jack, and we'll win home together. Come, the men wait, an' our work's before us."

George and Thorpe and Soldier Jack were forming the party into companies. There might be some two hundred of us, but I never counted them. Jack arranged us in the order deemed best. We were drawn up in a long line close by the Steeple. The men of the first company had pistols or muskets, firearms, of any sort. They were to march first. If soldiers were about I suppose Jack thought the men with firearms could drive them off if any of us could. But Lord bless you! Most of them couldn't have hit a hay stack at twenty yards. A few of them that had done a bit of poaching might give a better account of themselves. But, anyhow, they might fley the red–coats, and that would serve our ends just as well as shooting them. Behind the shooters were drawn tip, two abreast, the hatchet men, and behind them were to march my own lads, about a score of us, big men all, either in height or breadth, and each of us slung a hammer over his shoulder. I was captain of the hammer–men, and on my shoulder I bore a mighty weapon that few could sling. Behind my company was more or less of a rabble; men unarmed or with bludgeons only. What good they were, or expected to be, it would puzzle me to say. They were only in the way; but they were Luds, and that was enough.

Soldier Jack went down the line. Ben Walker moved by his side, carrying a lanthorn. I had not seen him till then. He looked sick and wretched. His hand trembled as he held aloft the light. Jack called the roll by its rays as he moved down the line.

"No. 1."

"Here."

"No. 2."

"Aw'm here."

"No. 3."

No answer.

"No. 4."

"That'll be me."

And so on down the line, while those who had made answer pulled their caps over their faces or fixed their masks more securely.

"And now, lads," cried George. "We'll waste no time in talking. We've three good miles to Rawfolds, and the night shortens. Before day break our work must be done. Show yourselves men but this night, and yo' bring the masters to their knees. Yo' fight; for home and hearth and the right to live. If there is one among you whose heart fails him, let him step out and leave us. William Hall, do you bring up the rear. If any turn tail, mark him. If yo' suspect treachery, shoot him. Sam Hartley, yo' know the way over Hartshead, walk by my side, and we will lead the way."

"And now, men, ready!"

"One, two, one, two, steady!" cried Soldier Jack, and we beat time as he had taught us in our drill, "one, two, left, right, left, right."

"Forward!" cried George, and he placed himself at the head of the column, and we moved steadily on in the dark, glad of the motion, for our blood was chilled with standing, and I, for one, thought less when I was moving, and the less I thought the better I was suited. 'Siah was in my company, and he, too, had a hammer, and well he knew how to use it. I took care he should not be far off me at all times. John Booth was in the rear, for he could use neither axe nor hammer, and pistols he would have nought to do with. As we marched along over the Moor, tramp, tramp, tramp, our feet falling pretty regular, and Soldier Jack sort of beating time for us by shouting "Left, right, left, right." There was a bit of breeze by this, and it was none too warm, but my spirits were rising spite of John's gloomy words and little as I liked the job. Every now and then George ran past me on his way down the ranks, and I could see his eye kindled and lit up with fire, for he had lost or thrown away his mask. Near the White Hart Inn, we halted; for here, if anywhere, we should be joined by the Leeds men; but there was neither sight nor sound of them.

"Shall aw go meet 'em an' hurry 'em up, General?" asked Ben Walker.

"Noa, tha winnot, tha'll stay here," said Soldier Jack, before George could reply.

I saw George was a bit huffed at Jack's putting his oar in so sharp, and he turned on him to say something Jack mightn't have liked, but thought better of it and checked himself.

"We cannot very well spare thee, Ben, we mun send some'dy whose legs are more use nor his arms."

"Send John Booth," I whispered.

"Why John Booth?"

"Nivver mind, George, I'll tell thee at after; send him."

"'Well, if it'll pleasure thee."

But John Booth wouldn't go. When George ordered him he flatly refused, and would only say that he had come out to fight, and not to run errands. John was a favourite with the men, who liked his pluck, and wondered often to each other such a fiery spirit was to be found in so frail a body. So they bore him out in his refusal, and a young lad from Huddersfield, who had been, better at home with his mother, as indeed we should all have been, was packed off over the Moor, to hurry up the laggards. I heard afterwards he met them a mile away; but when they heard the sound of musketry and our hoarse cries as we dashed at the barriers that kept us from our prey, they fair turned tail and slunk off to bed again. Anyway we saw nought of them.

"Do yo' know where th' soldiers are billeted?" I asked George.

"Ay, mostly at Haigh House in Hightown, yonder way," he replied, pointing into the darkness.

"Hadn't we better send a party to engage them and cut them off?" asked Jack.

"There's more at Millbridge yonder," said Thorpe. "They're all around us. If yo' try to stop one lot coming up, why not another?"

"There's summot i' that," said Soldier Jack; "anyway we mustn't stop shivering here. Yo' mun keep 'em movin, General. There's nowt men hate worse nor waiting i' th' dark. They get fleyed at their own shadders, an' start at their own thowts. Push us forward, George, an' let us get to close quarters, for every minute wasted now means a deserter."

"Right yo' are, Soldier. Aw've noticed more nor one slinking off; but aw thowt it best to say nowt," said Thorpe.

"Then forward, men! Th' Leeds lot will be here in time for th' shouting. All the more glory will be ours. Now forward and no more lagging."

We moved on again, turning sharply down a lane that led from the Moor towards the mill. We could see the buildings now, the mill itself, four stories high, with smaller buildings, the dyehouse, drying stove and such like, clustering near it. A brook ran rippling over rounded pebbles to the dam and from the goit to the great water–wheel. We could hear the water of the beck babbling when we started, but its murmur was lost in the thud of our feet as we closed on the mill. Not a light was to be seen. The moon shone at moments on the windows, but no ray came from within. But smoke came in a thin stream from the long chimney, and showed that the boiler fire was banked up ready for Monday's work. Now we neared with quickened steps to the mill–yard, and out into the night came from within the fierce baying of the watch–dog. It hadn't bayed two minutes when a single light shone out from the counting house, and we could see it move from window to window, and other lights glowed now from other portions of the mill. The watchers within had heard the faithful hound, and were doubtless speeding to their post's and standing, to their arms.

"Rush for the gate, hatchets to the front!" shouted George.

A band of men with hatchets sprang forward, and began to ply their weapons at the gates.

"Musket men line up," came the sharp command. "Give them a volley at the windows. Now, lads, spread yourselves. Cover the windows. Bullets and stones, mi lads, let 'em have it."

I caught sight of Booth. I seized the arm as he was hurrying past me. "Stand by me, John; stand by me and 'Siah. Dunnot leave our side, as yo' love yo'r sister."

"My place is elsewhere, Ben."

"Stand by me, aw tell yo. 'Siah, be with me. See! the outer door gives. They're in, they're in! Now 'Siah! follow me. Come, John."

I sprang forward, 'Siah gave a shout like the bellowing of a mad bull. I rushed into the mill yard. The glass was falling from the frames with crash upon crash, sticks and stones were flying above our heads as we streamed forward. The volleys of musketry made their din, and now from loop holes and from windows came answering shots. We could see the streak of fire from the barrels and hear the sharp ping of the bullets as they whizzed about our heads. Our men roared and roared again and yelled with frenzied cries. There were men there who could do nought but roar and yell and curse. They had only sticks and hatchets, and till the doors were down sticks and hatchets were of no avail.

"Way for Enoch!" I cried. "'Siah it's thee and me now."

"Way for Enoch!" came a ringing cry from the roaring crowd, and the men fell aside as 'Siah and I bounded to the front. The door stood staunch and true. I rushed at it with a curse and a cry and smote as I never smote before. You could hear the din of my every stroke rolling away into the emptiness of the mill within, and from the great bolt heads that studded the panels the sparks flew fast and thick as I thundered at the door.

"Bang up, Ben!" cried the voices I knew so well. "Damn the door, will it never yield?"

'Siah was by my side. There was room only for us two, and above the roar of the mob, above the yells and curses and cries, above the thud of stones and the crash of falling lime and glass, above the clanging of the mill bell, above the din of gun and pistol, rang out the mighty sound of Enoch's echoing thunder. With every blow that fell quivering shocks ran up my arm as the hammer dithered in my grasp, and still I pounded at the door, and still the stout timbers yielded not a jot. I wielded my maul fast and furious, but now with feebler blows, for my wind began to fail me; but 'Siah pounded on calm and stolid as if he stood in the village smithy.

"It's no use, Ben," I heard his hoarse voice in my ear. "It's no use, aw'm feart, but we'll keep braying. Howd thi strength, tha'll want it."

"Let's try at th' back," shouted George. "To the back, Ben. There's a way in at th' back, they say."

"To the back be it," I heard a voice within; "We'll be there to greet you."

And that was near the last sound I heard. I fell back from the door that had stood so well our fury and looked up at the window front. I think I raised my hand to my head to wipe away the sweat that was blinding my eyes. Then I was aware of a sharp burning boring pain in the muscle of my upper arm, and Enoch fell with a clatter into the cobbles of the yard, and I turned sick and dizzy and faint. The crowd were rushing away from the mill front round to the back, and I tried to follow them. But my eyes had a film before them, and I reeled and swayed like a drunken man, and when I tried to lift my arm a hundred daggers seemed to dig deep into my shoulder, and my arm fell useless by my side.

"He's hit! They'n hit th' mester," cried 'Siah. "Here, Soldier, tha're wanted here. Bear up, Ben, tha' mustn't fall. Brace thi' legs, man. By God he's wounded." And everything swam around me and I knew no more.

When I came to my senses, I was, for a time, conscious only of my agony. I was stretched on a pile of straw in a lofty room with bare walls of undressed stone and great bowks and rafters crossing the arched roof. A mere slit, high up in one wall, let in a stream of light, but the corner in which I lay was almost wholly dark. Someone was kneeling by my side and when I moaned in my pain an arm was passed under my head and a mug was pressed to my lips.

"That's reight, Ben, tha'rt better now. Tak' a swig at this; it'll do thee good."

It was 'Siah's voice, and the brandy and water that he poured down my throat set me coughing and choking, and every cough gave me awful stabs of shooting pain.

"Where are we, 'Si?" I murmured as I sank back again all faint and sick.

"Hanged if aw know, lad. But we're safe for a bit. It's som'dy Soldier Jack knows. We're noan far fra' Fixby, that's all aw can tell thee, an' here we'st ha' to tarry till we can move thee."

"An' th' mill? Ha' we ta'en th' mill? Where are all the boys? What am I doing lying here? Oh! I mind me now. I was hit i' my arm. Where's George an' Thorpe, and—oh! tell me all, 'Si."

"Tak another sup o' this an' lig quiet. Tha'd best noan talk so mich. There's a caa or two i' th' mistal theer, an' if tha'll be still I'll see it I cannot squeeze a drop aat on 'em. There's been a lass milking noan so long sin'; aw expect 'oo's noan left 'em dry if 'oo's like th' rest on 'em. Naa thee be still, an dunnot go swounding off agen, if tha' can help it, Ben. Tha' fleys me. Aw thowt tha were done for. Lig thee still, aw'll be wi' thee in a jiffy." And 'Siah lumbered off in the gloom, and I heard him straining a thin, and coy stream of milk into a can, whilst a cow's hoof stamped as if in protest at this renewed demand upon her stores.

The warm rich milk revived me, but when I strove to rise to my feet my strength failed me and I fell back again.

"There's nowt for it, Ben, but patience. Th' farm man here's known to Soldier Jack, an' as good luck will have it, his mester's away. So we're right for th' day, an' as soon as neet comes we're off."

"Tell me what has happened—I shalln't settle till tha' does."

"There's nowt much to tell. After tha' were hit aw caught thee i' my arms just as tha were falling like a felled bullock. Gow! what a weight tha are, to be sure, Ben. Then aw dragged thee to one side. Tha' were bleeding like a pig, but Soldier Jack were wi' thee i' no time. See yo' where he cut away thi' vest an' shirt. Then he put his finger i' th' hole where th' bullet is, an' didn't ta' groan. But he could feel nowt, so he bun thi up wi' th' tail o' thi shirt an' a handkerchief. But theer tha' lay like a log, and what to do wi' thee wer' th' puzzle. Aw' looked under a shed i' th' mill yard to see if ther' wer' owt we could hug thee on; but there wer' nowt. T'others were runnin' off i' all directions. Some were crying out to 'em to run, some wer' orderin' 'em to stop. George wer' like one off his yed. Aw see'd him jump on to th' sill o' th' lower window an' grasp a frame wi jagged glass all around an' shake it an' gnash his teeth at those in th' mill. But someone dragged him dahn. An' all th' while that damned bell wer' clanging like all that. Then som'dy cried out at th' sojers wer' comin', an' aw thowt missen aw heerd th' gallopin' o' horses' hoofs; but aw winnot be sure. Aw grabbed hold o' Mellor an' telled him tha wer' hit."

'Cannot yo' see to him?' he said.

'Siah an' me'll see to Ben,' said Soldier Jack, who wer' knelt down bi thi side.

'Thee see to thissen, George.' So George just gave a look at thi an' gay' a groan an' threw up his hands, an' shook his fist as th' guns kept popping fra' th' mill in a way 'at made me duck mi head every half second, an' off he skeltered after t' others."

"And what of John Booth. I hope no harm's come to th' lad."

"Oh! nivver thee mind about Booth. He's noan o' kin to thee at aw know on."

"But did he get safe away, 'Si? Did he go with George?"

"Aw'm noan his keeper, am I? Hannot aw enuff to do wi' thee o' mi hands wi'out John Booth? Go to sleep wi' thee, th'rt talking too much."

"Yo're hiding summot, 'Si. Na tell me, an' then aw'll be quiet."

"Well, there's nowt much to tell. Booth wer' hit, that's all aw know. Aw seed him liggin' on th' ground, an' he' wer' bleeding i' th' leg. But Soldier 'll see to him."

"Soldier?"

"Aye, he said' tha wouldn't be easy if tha thowt John wer' left, so after we'd tugged an' tewed an' hustled thee here, an' sich a huggin' an' a tewin' an' a hustlin' aw nivver had i' mi life afore, what wi' thee keep on swounding every fifty yards o' so, Jack first o' all went back an' gate some brandy. Aw dunnot know wheer he sammed it up, but Jack knows his way about, an' no mistake. We should ha' been fair done but for Jack. Then he said he'd hark back an' see what could be done for Booth; but he shouldn't come back here till neet, an' then we'd see what could be done about movin' thee. An' we wer to ca'er here till he come back. Naa, that's all aw know, except aw wish aw wer' a caa."

I was feeling very drowsy now and just remember murmuring:

"A caa; what for, 'Si?"

"So's aw could chew th' cud o' mi last meat, for aw'm awmost famished, an' aw cannot mak' a meal o' milk like a caulf."

And then I must have dozed off, for I heard no more for a long time.

The weary day dragged its lingering length. I slept by fits and starts. 'Siah, worn out, slumbered heavily. A swallow darted through the slit high up in the wall, skimmed round the rafters, intent upon nest building in the thatch—a rat ran across my feet. I could hear the crowing of a cock and the clucking of hens in the yard outside, and the song of a lark soaring in the heavens made me long for light and freedom. After what seemed an eternity of time the kine were driven in from the pastures for milking. I heard a voice coaxing them in:

"Coop—coop—coop." Then there were two voices, a man's and a woman's, and some talk I strained my ears to catch. "Luds," "sojers," "dead," and "poor lad"—this from the woman; but I could not piece the fragments to make sense. Then I judged the man was foddering his beasts, and I knew the hour of my deliverance was at hand. The gloom deepened, and all was still save for 'Siah's heavy breathing. Then I heard the sound of wheels, the door was opened cautiously, and a limp fell upon the flags.

"Are ta theer, 'Siah?"

And 'Siah creeped upon his knees to the limit of the hay bowk.

"Ger up an' ma' as little noise as tha can."

"Can ta walk, Ben?"

'Siah held me by the left shoulder, and leaning heavily on him I gained the door. Outside was our good old Bess. I could have wept to see her: such a flood of sweet home memories swept over me. The bottom of the cart was covered with hay and in one corner of it was our new roan calf. Soldier Jack and 'Siah between them lifted me into the cart,—and I sank exhausted by the effort and the pain, down by the dumb wondering brute that slobbered upon my face and gave a slimy lick at my lips.

"Tha mun drive, 'Siah. Go slow, by Deanhead. Aw'll walk on i' front, and if aw start whistlin' tha'll know som'dy's comin'. The sojers are scourin' th' country. Th' Luds are hidin' for their lives. There's small hell to play ovver this neet's work. Tha munnot hurry, an' keep out o' th' ruts an' jolt him as little as tha can."

"What's th' cauf doin' here?" muttered 'Siah.

"Tha dunderhead. We' mun cover Ben up wi' t' straw. Leave him his nose aat an' nowt else; then if we meet a search party they'll happen think tha'rt fetchin' a cauf wom. Tha' mun act as gaumless as tha' can, an' na' drive on an' ma' as if aw'd nowt to do wi' thee."

"Come up, Bess, woa, steady!" and we lumbered off past the top of Lindley, keeping well on the crest of the hill, whence we could see the light of Longwood and Golcar in the valley, and so, bearing towards the left, made for Lower Holme. We passed a party of mounted soldiers about half–way on our journey and, for-tunately, at the very moment of our encounter the calf staggered straddling to its feet, putting its hoof upon my right hand and sending shooting torments up my arm. It rocked and swayed in the cart and moo'd feebly at the soldiers as they drew rein.

"Have you seen any suspicious characters on the road, my good man, higher up the hill?" asked their leader.

"Nay, nowt out o' th' common," said 'Siah, "a tramp or two, an' a chap 'at looked as if he'd been feightin'."

"Ah! where was that?"

"T'other side o' Lindley; he wor makin' fra Grimscar."

"Forward, men!"

"Good luck," said 'Siah. "Ger on, Bess." And my heart began to beat again.

How my mother met us at the door, how my father stood aloof and would not speak one word, how 'Siah undressed me and put me into my own bed, what need to tell; nor yet set forth in detail how it came about that as I sank down into the cool, clean sheets, and laid my head upon the grateful feather pillow, stuffed with feathers plucked by Mary's own fingers, I heard the kitchen door open and a quick step ascend the stairs.

"Now Mrs. Bamforth, well Mary, where is he? let's have a look at him. Off with you now, all but 'Siah. 'Siah, you cut–throat rebel, shut the door and hold the candle for me."

It was Dr. Dean from Slaithwaite, hearty, hale and cheery, who had ushered me into the world and given me powders and pills in the little ailments of childhood. He took command of the whole house as by divine right. Even my mother recognised his prerogative and resigned her supremacy, and Mary was his willing and adoring slave. Before you could say "Jack Robinson" he had slit my sleeve with his scissors, lifted the rude bandages, now sodden and stiff with blood, and was handling my arm deftly and tenderly as a woman.

"H'm, bullet in biceps, hoemorrhage of the artery, acute inflammation, temperature equatorial, fever, ravings, pandemonium generally!" All the while probing for the bullet as if he were picking a periwinkle.

"Mrs. Bamforth," presently he said, "how do you feel?"

"Aw'm well enough i' body, doctor, but nowt to boast of i' mind."

"I don't think you are very well, Mrs. Bamforth. I detect in you symptoms, my dear lady, that give me grave alarm."

"Why, good gracious, doctor, whatever do yo' mean? Why my appetite's good . . . ."

"That aggravates the complaint."

"Aw sleep well, leastwise aw did till a neet or two sin, when aw started dreamin' o' washing clothes, an' aw knew it were a sign o' a burial i' th' family. 'William Bamforth,' aw said to th' mester, 'William Bamforth, as sure as yo're a living man there'll be a death i' th' family afore yo'r a month older, but little did aw think o' yar Ben bein' laid low. Aw put it down to my sister Matty. He did nowt but laugh, but he'll happen believe me now. It's a judgment on him for scoffing.'"

"Mrs. Bamforth, you must take to your bed at once; and you must not stir out of it till I give you leave. You must send Martha to the surgery at once and I'll make up a bottle, and three times a day you must take it."

"But I ail nowt, doctor."

"You may pour it down the sink."

Was the doctor off his head? But no, he went on:

"You must impress it on Martha, I'll tell her myself, that you are dangerously ill and every day I'll drive up myself to see you. You must tell Martha to mind she says nothing about it in the village, and then I suppose it'll be all over the Country in no time. And if anybody asks where Ben is, he's gone on his rounds. Now do you understand?"

I did anyway, and I pressed his hand gratefully.

"It may be a fortnight before Ben's fit to be moved, and then, mark you, he must be moved, and for my credit's sake, if for no other reason, not a soul out of this house must know Ben's within a hundred miles of this."

"God bless you, doctor. Aw've been wondering and wondering ever sin' 'Si' brought him home, whatever we should say to th' neighbours. An' yo've found a way all in a minnit. See what it is to be eddicated. Aw'll be i' bed afore yo're out o' th' house. An' mind yo' insense it into our William, for he's that stupid he'll spoil it all. An', for sure, aw don't feel very well; it's my heart, doctor."

And I think my mother came as near winking as ever she did since she made lovers' signals across the pews, when my father was courting her.

Dr Dean.

CHAPTER IX.

MY Father and Siah left home that very day with the waggon. It was given out in the little village that I was gone too, and it was soon town's talk that Mrs. Bamforth was sick and that Dr. Dean was visiting her twice a day. 'Siah came up to see me in bed before he started.

"Th' mester's awful put out," he told me. "Aw heard thi mother askin' him if he weren't bahn to come up an' say good–bye to thee, Ben. But he said nowt. Tha's put his back up gradely this time, lad, an' I expect aw'st have a roughish time on it missen. But hard words an' foul looks break no bones, an' aw'd rather be i' Macclesfield wi' Awd Harry hissen,' just nah, nor at wom among th' Luds. No more sojerin' for me, Ben. My yed's fair stunned wi' th' din. An' ne'er thee mind about thi father. He'll come rahnd, an' then he'll ma' it up to thee as if he'd been i' fault hissen. By gow, tha has getten a arm, to be sure. It looks like three pund o' lites, and they'd best keep th' cat out o' th' room when th'ar asleep, or 'oo'l be at thee, sure as God made little apples."

And soon afterwards I heard the cart lumbering out of the yard to the usual accompaniment of the dog's excited barking and 'Siah's apostrophes to Old Bess.

Then my mother and Mary took possession of me, and I am persuaded that never did my mother enjoy herself so thoroughly as during the three weeks or more that I kept my bed. Her own room adjourned the one in which I lay, and as she was supposed to be herself bedridden she had all the advantage of being at close quarters. She would come to my bedside a hundred times a day in her linsey petticoat and a red flannel jacket with big bone buttone that gave her quite a martial air, and at every knock at the house door she would skip back to her own room, tumble into bed, draw the clothes over her, and set to groaning as tho' in mortal agony. Then, when retreating footsteps assured her the coast was clear, she would steal back with a shame–faced look and busy herself about the room. How many times a day she dusted the furniture of my room and arranged and rearranged the odds and ends on the little dressing table, I cannot hazard a guess at. She spent hours each day listening at the top of the staircase to what was going on below, for she was tortured by the conviction that things were going to rack and ruin in her absence and that Martha and Mary were in a conspiracy to do all things they ought not to do and leave undone the things they ought to do. Nothing would persuade her that any cleaning was being done in the parlour, and she knew that when she was able to get about again she would be able to write her name in dust on the looking–glass and the chiffonier, that is if she should haply be able to get into the room at all, of which she was somewhat sceptical. When Mary brought my chicken broth and rice pudding, my prescribed diet, on which by the bye I soon began to lose flesh at an alarming rate, my mother would meet her at the stair head and herself bring it to the bedside, very jealous, as was easy enough to see, that he could not cook it herself. Such tasting of broth and puddings sure never was before nor since, nor such fault–finding. Some days the rice hadn't been soaked long enough, other days too long. Some days the broth was too strong, others too weak, or the salt was in excess, or the pepper, or a pinch of this or that would have improved the flavour. Poor Mary, did it ever set you thinking, I wonder, what an ideal mother–in–law your aunt would make?

Then, when the ball had been extracted from my arm and my shoulder began to look less like a lump of liver, it became clear to my mother that I was in need of spiritual comfort. The big Family Bible was brought from the parlour and placed on a little table by my bedside. I was perfectly capable of reading it for myself, but that would not have suited my nurse. She read with difficulty and had many a stubborn tussle with the hard words. At first I helped her with them but soon perceived she took a delight in the struggle and so left her to grapple with them. As she opined my illness would be a long one and she did not mean to be gravelled for lack of matter, she began at the first chapter of the Book of Genesis and advanced by slow stages to the tenth, when she floundered in a genealogical bog from which she brought forth, I fear, only one piece of abiding information, to wit, that the eldest son of Eber bore the same name as the crippled son of the village postmaster—Peg–leg.

Dr. Dean was her great comfort during this enforced confinement. Twice daily did that cheery visitor drive up to Holme, and from the long stay that his champing, stamping mare made by our door, the neighbours drew gloomy auguries as to my mother's desperate state. If they could have seen him sat in an easy chair, profaning the chaste sanctity of the bedroom with tobacco smoke, and relishing our best Hollands while he detailed the village gossip to my mother's delighted ears, they would have had less concern for the good soul's health. My mother declared the doctor's visits were worth a guinea apiece.

"Mrs. Garside's been enquiring after yo' Mrs. Bamforth." Now this was that Hannah Garside who had pulled up my mother's half–cousin, Sam o' Sall's, because of the eggs.

"She met save her breath to cool her porridge," was my mother's ungrateful comment.

"She says she freely forgives yo', ma'm."

"The imperence on her. Ah! wait till I get better, an' I'll gi'e her forgive me!"

"She promises to pray for you, Mrs. Bamforth."

"To pray for me! Hannah Garside, pray for me! Oh! this must be stopped, doctor. It's too bad 'at she's none content wi' makin' th' village unbearable an' nah mun' be bringing me into bad odour wi' th' saints above."

"She sends her compliments, ma'am, and says if I prescribe custards she won't venture to send any batter as it's well known your family knows a way o' never being short o' eggs."

"Oh! trust her for taking a mean advantage o' me, an' me laid o' mi back an' not able to stick up for missen. Take her a cruet o' water, doctor, an' say I'd be glad if she'd look into it an' turn it to vinegar. But yo'r taking nothing, doctor. Fill your glass, now do, and have another pipe. Never mind th' smoke. It's good for moths." And thus did Doctor Dean pass the time in those professional visits the portentous length of which gave so much anxiety to our friends.

It was Soldier Jack who told me the news of poor John Booth's sad end. Soldier had been chary of coming at first for fear of arousing the suspicions of our neighbours, but he was very useful in spreading the news of my mother's illness. He had her one day on the brink of death, another day rallying. One day it was current through the village that my mother had sent for Lawyer Blackburn, and the undertaker went about with a visibly expectant face. When Mr. Webster called, all hope was abandoned. When he went away without being admitted to the sick chamber, tho' my mother had to bite her tongue to prevent herself calling out to him from the stairhead, our kinsfolk of all degrees began to look up their mourning, and the stone–cutter at Powle Moor got ready a selection of appropriate head–lines.

At length Jack could keep away no longer and came one afternoon into my room, walking softly in on tip–toe of one foot and a limp of the other, as tho' I were dead or sleeping. Poor Jack, he looked sadly worn and harassed of these days and had lost all his swagger and even his cheerfulness.

"Yes, it's too true, Ben. Poor John Booth's dead as a nit. Shot through th' leg, an' no stamina to bear it. He died th' same neet.

"Tell me about it Soldier? Poor lad, poor lad."

"He died at Tommy Sheard's at th' Star i' Roberdta'n. He wer' a good plucked 'un, an' his father a parson too. His mother mun ha' been a none such, aw reckon."

"Who was with him Jack? Was he in much pain? Did he say owt? Tell me all about it."

"Well, as far as aw can gather, after we carried yo' off t'others didn't stay long behind. Th' game wor up."

"How did we come to leave Booth? We ought not to have left Booth. I promised I'd see to him, and a pretty way I've kept my word."

"Dunnot yo' fash yersen, Ben. Yo'd your work set wi' Enoch. John brought it on hissen. He wer' all ovver th' shop', egging th' men on. Aw told him to keep i' covver, but he seemed fair to run agen th' bullets as if he wanted killing. Well he gate what he wanted. Still if we hadn't had our hands full wi yo', we might ha' carried him off. But he's dead, so we should nobbud ha' had our wark for nowt, an' a mort o' trouble to account for th' corpse. Yo' mebbe hannot thowt o' that. What should we ha' done wi' a dead body wi' a leg smashed to mush, on our hands?"

Aye, what, I thought.

"Well, theer John lay among broken glass, an' stones, an' sticks, an' plaster, in front o' th' mill, an' Sam Hartley shot through th' lung an' vomiting quarts o' blood, not far off him. After a bit owd Hammond Roberson, th' feightin' parson, come gallopin' up wi' a lot o' soldiers, an' Cartwright oppens th' mill door, an' him an' his men comes out, an' they do say Cartwright took on rarely when he see'd th' mess we'd made o' th' mill front. Poor John were beggin' some o' th' folk 'at had run up to fetch him a drop o' water. Aw know what it's like when yo'r wounded. Yo' feel as if yo'd got a little hell o' yo'r own inside yo'. But Cartwright wer' noan for lettin' him have a drop, not even to wet his lips, till he'd gi'en th' names o' those 'at wer' th' leaders. But John tak' no notice nor Hartley nawther, but nobbut begged for water. Old Roberson, dam him, wor as bad as Cartwright. It wer' confession first, an' water after. But a chap called Billy Clough ran an' put a stone under John's yed, an' then fot him a drink. If awther th' parson or Cartwright had stopped him, aw'm told th' folk round 'ud ha' mobbed 'em. Aw can forgi'e Cartwright, for it's none calc'lated to put a chap into th' best o' tempers to ha' his mill made such a mullock on; but, curse Roberson, an' all such like, say I, an' him a parson, too!"

"But what of John, Soldier?"

"Well at last when he'd say nowt, water or no water, they put him on a gate an' carried him an' Hartley to th' Star. A doctor wer' noan long i' turnin' up, for them chaps smell blood like vultures. He said ther' wer' nowt for it but to hampotate th' leg, an' that wer' just more nor John could stand, an' he cheat both th' parson an' th' gallows, an' deed like a man an' a Briton at he wor.

"How cheat th' parson, Jack?"

"Well owd Roberson wouldn't let him die i' peace, but wer all th' time naggin' him to confess. Then when Booth knew his end were near, he called old Roberson to stand ovver him, an' th' owd sinner's face lit up wi' glee, an' he stepped up to John as brisk as a bee."

"You see, gentlemen, the power of the Church! And now, my good man."

"Can yo' keep a secret, sir?" said John, in a whisper; but all were so still yo' could have heard a pin drop. Even Sammy Hartley, who wer' deein' fast, stopped moanin', they say; tho' that mun be either accident or fancy."

"Can yo' keep a secret, sir?" whispered John.

"I can, I can," said th' parson.

"An' so can I," said John, wi' a smile, an he put his head back an' never spak' no more; an', oh! Ben, when aw talk on it aw'm fit to blubber like a child. He wer' a rare un, wer' John."

Mary was there and my mother, and Mary's face was buried in the counterpane and I heard her sob, and a tear trickled down my mother's cheek, and I turned my face to the wall and mourned for my friend.

"We got his body," went on Jack after a long pause. "Mr. Wright, th' saddler, saw to that. It wer' brought to his house, an' th' funeral wer' fra' theer. He wer' buried i' Huddersfield Churchyard, an' all th' town wer' theer. George Mellor and Thorpe walked after th' hearse, an' all th' folk, hundreds on 'em, 'at could lay the'r hands on a bit, wore white crape around their arm. It wer' a gran' funeral."

"And Faith?" said Mary.

"'Oo leaned o' Mrs. Wright, 'at wer' like a mother to her. Th' owd father weren't theer. But Faith looked just all brokken to pieces, poor wench."

"I'll go to her, straight away," cried Mary.

"Aye, do, Mary," said my mother, "and bring her up to Holme wi' yo'. She wants some kitchen physic as well as other folk."

"Yo' forget yo'r ill i' bed, aunt," said Mary, "and Ben's away to Macclesfield."

"Well, if aw amn't, aw soon shall be, if this mak' o' wark goes on. Oh! George, tha's a deal to answer for, an' it's much if tha doesn't break thi mother's heart afore tha's done, an' then there 'll be an end o' poor Matty, too."

I fret a deal over John Booth's awful death and felt in a manner that it lay at my door. Faith's sad face haunted my fevered dreams, and I reproached myself not a little that I had not taken more care of the lad. And yet, looking back, I do not see that I could have done other than I did. I spoke with Mary on the matter.

"It's a bad job for Faith losing her brother like this, Mary. I doubt she'll take it sore to heart. Her whole life seemed centred and wrapped up in John. They might have been twins. I blame misen shocking that aw left him to shift for hissen."

"I don't see how yo'r to blame, Ben. From all I can make out, yo'd enough to do to look out for yersen; and it's only natural that 'Siah an' Soldier, anyway 'Siah, our own man, should look to yo' first an' foremost, choose how others fared."

"But I promised Faith that I'd have an eye to him."

"Well you did your best, and th' best can do no more. It's no use thee working thissen into a fever, an' tossin' about as if tha wer' on a hot backstone, an' kickin' th' clo'es off thee as fast as aw can put them on, over summat at's done an' can't be undone."

"Yo'r only a Job's comforter, Mary. Aw should have thought tha'd more feeling in thee."

"Feeling! aw've feeling enough. But it's time to talk a bit o' sense. There's been mischief enough an' to spare o' late about feeling. It's feeling baht sense 'at brought yo' into this mess, an' yo'r noan aht o' th' wood yet. Happen tha'll live to envy John Booth, an' wish tha'd been left for dead at Rawfolds i'stead o' 'scaping to find a worse fate. I declare aw never hear a step come to th' door but my heart goes into mi mouth an mi knees shake so aw can hardly stand. There's feeling for yo', if yo' like. Mr. Chew says it's a hanging job for them 'at's caught."

I flushed at this you may be sure, tho' Mary only put into words the thought that had tortured my waking hours and made my dreams hideous. That was a subject not to be dwelt on. So I made haste to revert to Faith.

"Aw hannot told yo' yet, Mary, that I made a promise to John, too."

"Yo seem to ha' been precious free wi thi promises."

"Nay, Mary, what's come ovver thee? Its noan like thee to turn agen them 'at's i' trouble. It wer' at Kirklees, just before we started for Rawfolds."

And I told Mary of what had passed between John Booth and me.

"Well, what is it all leading to?" she asked.

"A've been turning things ovver i' mi mind, Mary, as aw've laid o' mi back. Yo' see, Faith's nobbut a poor weak thing, an' fra all aw can hear her father's awmost as bad. Don't yo' think we ought to do summat to help her?"

"With all my heart—as how?"

"Nay, that's wheer aw'm fast. Cannot yo' suggest summat?"

"Yo' might happen ask her if she wants a home—Martha 'll mebbe be so accommodatin' as to mak' room for her i' th' house. Martha could get another job fast enough, an' then yo'll have Faith under yo'r own e'en, an' it'll be little trouble to look after her then."

"The thing's preposterous, Mary. The idea of Faith scouring and, milking and such like."

"Yo' might perhaps offer her work at the spinning."

"Why, Faith's been brought' up a lady," I cried.

"It's no more nor yo'r mother an' me does every day of our lives. But to be sure I'm not a lady. But, perhaps, yo'd like to make Faith a present or allow her a pension. I'm glad to see things are mending wi' yo', Ben. Aw allus thowt yo' had nought but what yo' addled, an' that's like to be little enough for many a month to come. But, perhaps, tha's come in for a fortin', an' been keepin' it secret for fear o' killin' us wi' joy. Tell us on it, Ben. Aw'll try to bear it, if it isn't too dazzling."

"Do quit thi teasing, Mary, an' talk some sense. It's no jesting matter for poor Faith."

"And that's true enough, cousin, and I'm a wicked girl to run on so. But yo' aggravate me so wi' thi wild schemes an' foolish talk."

"How foolish!"

"Why, how can ta help Faith? It were reight enough for poor John to speak to yo'. I expect his heart wer' full, an' it eased him to speak to thee. But now what can yo' do? Tha has nowt, an' half nought's nought all th' world over."

"I could be a brother to her, Mary."

"Oh! a brother! I should ha' thowt yo'd had enough o' brotherhoods to sicken thi for life. Aw've no patience wi' thee. There's Faith living at Low Moor wi' her father, an' needed there, aw've little doubt, an' wi' her hands full enough, an' now yo' mun strike up a brotherhood wi' her. Aw suppose we'st ha' yo', as soon as yo'r up, settin' off every week end to Low Moor to play the brother. Yo'll ha' to take yo'r sister out for long walks aw suppose, an' to buy her rings an' keepsakes an' all that. Yo'll find it cheaper to buy her a plain 'un to begin wi'."

"Well, and why not?" I said, getting nettled, for Mary had told me some home truths that had been none too pleasant in the hearing and digestion.

"And why not?" I repeated. "Faith's a sweet lass, and a good one an' true. She's over pale an' thin mebbe, for everyone's fancy."

"Oh! beauty's in the eye of the beholder," put in Mary, tossing her head.

"But she'd cure o' that, wi' plenty o' good milk an' fresh air such as we han at Holme. An' aw think she leans a bit to me. Don't yo' think so yoursen, Mary.

"Dunnot ask me. My head doesn't run on such trash. What's ta talking to me for? Aw'm noan Faith. Yo'd soon have an answer, an' one 'at 'ud tak' th' conceit out on thee if owt could. Ask hersen."

"Well! I happen will," I said. "Aw've a good mind."

"It's a pity to spoil a good mind then. I'd waste no time about it, chance some'dy snaps her up. An' while th' art abaht it, yo might ask her to come an' nurse thee, so's 'oo'll know what's afore her."

And Mary bounced out of the room in a tantrum.

The frame of mind in which she left me was certainly not one that Dr. Dean could have desired for a feverish patient. It. was clear to me that my own position was anything but an enviable one. Large rewards had been offered, I knew, for such information as would lead to the conviction of those concerned in the attack on Rawfolds, and machine breaking had been made a capital offence. My own participation in that affair was known to scores, and suspected by hundreds more. An incident that befel shortly afterwards aggravated my alarm. My father was still away. A letter had come from him, written in an obviously bad temper, complaining of the awful state of trade and driving my mother to distraction by telling of the trial and punishment of the Nottingham Luddites. However, I had so far proceeded to convalescence as to leave my bed, and I was looking forwards to being out and about in a few days, and I was turning over in my mind the feasibility of leaving home for a few months till things blew over a bit. I did not feel safe at home and that's the fact, and I was on tenterhooks to put a hundred miles and more between me and Justice Radcliffe, who was scouring the district for Luds.

I was meditating on these matters and wondering why George Mellor never came near me even to ask after my recovery, when I heard the dog give tongue in the yard and the sound of horses' hoofs. I managed to support myself to the stair-head. I heard a clatter at the door, which was opened by Martha.

"Does William Bamforth live here?" asked a voice, and there was the pawing of a horse's hoof, the jingling of a bit–chain, the sound of one swinging himself heavily to the ground, and the clinking of spurs.

"Does ta' mean Bill o' Ben's?" queried Martha.

"I mean William Bamforth."

"Well yo'see, there's a seet o' Bamforths i' Holme, an' four on 'em's Bills. It'll be Bill o' Luke's yo'r wantin', or happen Bill o' Nan's Back Side."

"I mean William Bamforth, who has a son called Ben."

"Well, he's noan at wom. He's i' Macclesfield. But aw munnot stop talkin' here. Aw'm churnin', an' th' butter's just on th' turn. Aw'll tell him a felly come to see him."

"Not so fast, my good woman."

"I'll trouble yo' to keep a civil tongue in yo'r head. My name's Martha. Don't 'Good woman' me, if yo' please."

"Where's yo'r mistress?"

"'Oo's i' bed. 'Oo's ill. 'Oo's getten th' small pox, an' tha'd better be off afore th' smell on it comes dahn stairs an' smittles thee."

"I'm sorry to seem rude, my sweet Martha. But duty's duty. I must search yo'r house."

"If tha comes in aw'll set th' dog at thee. Here Vixen, Vixen." And Martha called to an imaginary bitch.

There was a slight scuffle, and someone strode into the house.

"No one here anyhow. Now for upstairs." My mother had fled to her bed and drawn the clothes about her. For me, I lay back in my chair incapable of thought or movement. The stairs creaked under a heavy tread. Mary stood by my side, my hand stole into hers, and she faced the door, battle in her eyes. A big, burly trooper pushed it open, ducking his head as he advanced over the threshold. It was Long Tom with whom I had fought at Marsden.

"What want you here?" cried Mary. "How dare you force your way into decent folks' house in broad day?"

"The gamesome wench that slapped my face!" cried Long Tom.

"Aye, and will slap it again if yo'r not off."

"Gently, Mary, gently," I said. "The sergeant has doubtless business here. Your errand, sir?" I said. "You see you intrude."

"Why this beats Banagher, where the cows run barefoot!" exclaimed the soldier. "If this isn't the youngster spoiled my beauty for me. Nay, sit still," he went on, as I tried to rise.

"What! bandaged, too, and in the forearm. A queer treatment for small pox."

"Sir, if you have business here, I pray you do it."

"Is your name Ben Bamforth?"

"It is."

"The son of William Bamforth?"

"His son."

"And what the devil are yo' doing here, you thundering young idiot? Why in the name of common sense aren't you a thousand miles away if horse or mail could carry you?"

"And what the devil are yo' doing here, you thundering young idiot? Why in the name of common sense aren't you a thousand miles away if horse or mail could carry you?"

"I am not accountable to you for my actions that I know of. Again, your business?"

My mother had issued from her room in petticoat and scarlet jacket.

"Keep your distance, good woman, if its yo' have the small pox. If I must be riddled let it be with pellets not pustules," cried the soldier, starting back in horror.

"Oh! good Mr. Soldier. What do yo' want with our Ben? A quiet, harmless lad, as ever lived, that never harmed a flee. I'm sure he's done nothing wrong, and him bedfast these six months past."

Now heaven forgive you, mother!

"He played a mighty heavy fist for a sick man not three months gone, anyhow, good dame. Nay, keep your distance. Good God! if the old lady isn't going to kneel to me."

For my mother made as if she would throw herself at the soldier's feet.

"Mother, calm yourself," I said. "Pray, sir, you see I am in no case to bear much talking. What is your will with me."

"I'm sorry, I'm very sorry. A man like you that ought to be fighting Mounseer, and a proper Life Guardsman yo'd make, for sure. Well, well, of all the tomfoolery! However, I see no help for it."

And Long Tom strode about the room in evident perplexity, muttering to himself: "A brave lad," "a sad case," "too good for the gallows," and "I owe the wench one, too."

I seemed to watch the working of his mind, and hope stole trembling back into my heart.

Another too was scanning his face as anxiously as manner marks the witness of the skies.

"And so, madam," he said, "you are his mother, and I suppose this tale of small pox is all flam. And you, Miss, what is this long–limbed game cock to you?"

"Oh! Sergeant," cried Mary, "I am sure you have a good heart, and are a brave and generous man. You must not think ill of Ben for besting you when yo' fought. It was all for me."

"I don't' think any the worse of him, pretty. I think all the better of him. It served me right, and if I hadn't taken a drop too much, I shouldn't have tried to steal a kiss. Tho' you will admit the provocation." And here the gallant sergeant doffed his shako and made a low bow to Mary, who blushed and curtsied and cast down her eyes.

"But I owe you some return, miss, for my ill manners, and as for the trouncing, a soldier bears no malice. But you haven't told me, yet, what is this Ben here to you? Your brother?"

"No, good sir, my cousin!"

"H'm. Aught else?"

Then did Mary catch her breath and hold me tighter by the hand; and for a moment I could hear my own heart beat.

"He is my sweetheart, sir, an't please you. And we're to be wed when he's well. And oh! sir, it will kill me if yo' take him from me."

"And a lucky dog he is to have so fair a bride. Well, well, I'll risk it. But hark you, Ben Bamforth, you've had a narrow shave. I won't enquire how you came by that bandaged arm. Perhaps I know more than yo think. A change of air will do you good. I say no more than this: 'Next time yo' go out of nights, take missy with you. Veils are dangerous, especially with such eyes behind them'" — another bow to Mary — "but masks are worse. You take me."

Indeed I did take him.

"And now I'm off. You need fear nothing from my report. But be careful of the company you keep. A wink's as good as a nod, they say, and there's a man in your confounded league who has no love for Ben Bamforth."

"Good day, ma'am, and I wish you better of the small pox."

Long Tom clinked his heels together, drew himself up to the salute, nearly knocking his head against the rafters as he did it, and turned to go. He had reached the head of the stairs.

"Stay, sir," cried Mary, her face as red as a peony.

He looked back.

"I thought yo' wanted a kiss t'other night."

"Aye, but yo' refused me smartly."

"Well," and here Mary drooped her head and played with the corner of her apron. "Well — I've, I've changed my mind."

And Tom laughed a great laugh and stooped over my cousin and she raised her crimson face to his.

"Gad! Bamforth, my lad, I'd change places with you this minute and risk Jack Ketch. Good luck and good day."

And Long Tom strode down the stairs. There were three other mounted soldiers in the yard.

"A false scent again," we heard him say. "Only an old woman in a fever. The bird's flown."

"It isn't often you stay upstairs so long with an old woman, sergeant!" laughed a trooper; and they shook their reins and clattered out of the yard, the hens scurrying with beating wings, and the ducks waddling, quacking loudly, out of their way.

I made to thank Mary, but she fled from my room and I saw her no more all that day, and when, the next morning, she brought me, instead of the bowl of porridge on which I break my fast when hearty, a dish of tea and a buttered egg, and I would have drawn her to my heart, as surely lover may draw his mistress, Mary held aloof.

"Why, Mary, lass, surely tha'll give me a kiss now?"

"And why now?" she said, as cold as ice.

"Why, after what yo' said yesterday to Long Tom, 'at yo' an' me wer' engaged to be wed."

"Oh! that wer' nowt. I just said it because I thowt it might help thee."

"And then, don't yo' mind, Mary, that neet after I'd fought Long Tom at Marsden—how yo' come behind th' chair an' kissed me."

"Well, what o' that?"

"Dost ta mean to say, after that, tha cares nowt about me more nor common?"

"It it comes to that, Ben, didn't yo' see me do much th' same wi Long Tom yesterday?"

"In truth, I did, Mary. And I think it was unnecessary, not to say unmaidenly."

"Thank yo', Ben. I'll mind my manners better i' future. But at least yo' mun see that yo' munnot argy from what aw did when yo'r eye wer' blacked i' Marsden; for bi the same token Long Tom might leap to conclusions. And heigh–ho! Long Tom's a proper sort o' man, and I'm awmost stalled o' Sloughit. Sup thi tea, Ben, afore it gets cold, an' if tha'rt in such a hurry to get wed, remember yo'r more nor hauf promised to Faith Booth."

Long Tom was true to his word. Justice Radcliffe was hot on the trail of the Luddites. The patrols were more active than ever, and first one and then another was summoned to Milnsbridge House and questioned keenly as to his doings, but for a time nothing came of all this questioning, except that there grew up among the Luds an uneasy feeling that there was a tell–tale in their midst. I lived in daily dread of a visit from Justice Radcliffe, but I never came across him but once. It was about this time, when I was just beginning to get about a bit, my father and 'Siah being back from the markets, and I supposed to be returned with them, I was going through Milnsbridge when I was aware of Mr. Radcliffe on horseback riding towards me, a handsome hearty man as ever you saw in your life. "A fine old English gentleman," his friends all called him. He drew rein, and at his motion I stood by his saddle.

"Ben Bamforth of Holme, if I mistake not?" he questioned.

"At your service, sir," I said, with confidence in my voice and little in my heart.

"Good Mr. Bamforth, the clothier's son.

"The same, sir,—his only son."

"And following his trade, I hear."

"What there is of it, sir."

"A worthy man is your father, Master Bamforth, and a loyal subject of His Majesty. You have been sick of late they say."

Who said? I wondered but dared not ask, so muttered:

"Nowt to speak on, I'm all right now."

"Still yo' must be careful. Who's your doctor?"

"Dr. Dean."

"What, my good friend Dean? The sly dog! Still a patient's a patient" — this rather to himself than to me. "And has Dr. Dean said nothing to you about avoiding the night air for a time?"

"I don't know that he has, your worship."

"Well tell him you've seen me, and that my advice is that yo' keep in doors these spring nights, fine or dark, and ask him if he doesn't agree with me."

"It is unnecessary, sir, I am entirely of that opinion myself."

"Come that's good hearing. Mind you stick to it. And, hark ye, thank God as long as you live that you'd a good father before yo' and that Justice Radcliffe doesn't give heed to every idle tale that's brought to him."

And he touched his hat as I uncovered and bent my head to him, for I knew all our precautions had been in vain, and that Justice Radcliffe had in his keeping a secret that could send me to the gallows.

But who had betrayed me?

Sir Joseph Radcliffe.

CHAPTER X.

I HAVE told how I met Justice Radcliffe and what he said to me. That was after I was better and about. But many things had happened before that, of which I have yet to tell, and I scarce know how to frame the telling. Events so crowded one on the heels of the other that it is difficult to write of them connectedly and in order.

It was Tuesday, April 28th, something more than a fortnight after the affair at Rawfolds, and I still kept my room but not my bed. I had seen nothing all this time of my cousin George, and took it hard that he should not have come near me, but found excuses for him in the thought that perhaps he feared to bring notice on our house by being seen to visit it. Martha that night had gone into the village to meet the carrier's cart by which my mother expected sundry things that she had ordered from Huddersfield. It drew late, and my mother began to fidget and to worrit about the difficulty of getting a servant that would not tarry to gossip whenever sent an errand and the readiness with which young women lent themselves to gallivanting, so different from what it was when she was a girl, when, she gave Mary and me to understand, a self–respecting maid entrenched herself in a barricade of frigid reserve that only the most intrepid, the most persistent and the most respectful approaches could surmount. About nine o'clock, however, Martha came home, and my mother called to her to come upstairs to give an account of herself, and presently we heard her panting up the steps. She dropped into the first chair she came to—

"Oh! my poor side," she gasped. "That broo 'll be the death on me yet. Such a pain as awn got an' sich a gettin' up th' hill as never wor, an' th' pack hauf as heavy agen as ever it had used to be, an' me awmost running, all th' way for fear sum'dy sud be afore me an' no one to oppen th' door to 'em. Aw do believe aw'st faint." And indeed Martha was in a very bad way.

"If yo' didn't stop talkin' wi' every young felly tha' met at's nowt better to do nor be tittle–tattlin' wi' ony idle wench he meets, tha could tak' thi time an' not come home an hour late an' lookin' as if tha'd been rolled i' th' hedge bottom, a sight not fit to be seen in a decent house," said my mother severely.

"Oh! Mrs. Bamforth, God forgive yo' those words. Yo'll live to repent 'em, an' yo'll never die easy till yo'n said so, an' me that keeps misen respectable tho' sore tempted."

Now if ever kindly Nature laboured to shield a helpless virgin from the craft and allurements of man, it had so laboured on behalf of honest Martha.

"But p'r'aps yo' dunnot want to be hearing th' news, an' aw'm sure aw can do wi' all th' wind awn got i'stead o' was–tin' it wheer its noan wanted. So aw'll just put th' shop stuff away an' yo'll happen count yo'r change an' I'st go to bed, for it's little supper aw'st want to neet or for mony a neet to come, if we live to see another neet. But yo' needn't be so sure o' that. It's more nor likely we'st all be murdered i' our beds, an' th' mester and 'Siah away when they're most wanted."

"What is it's upset yo', Martha?" asked Mary, giving Martha a little cold tea which had been left in the pot.

"It's about Edmund Eastwood."

"What o' Slough'it? What on him?" asked my mother. "I'll lay he's had a stroke. Aw told their Lucy only th' last time aw seed her he wor puttin' on flesh a deal too fast for a man o' his years."

"Well it's noan a stroke, so tha'rt off thi horse this time, missus, choose how, an' so's Eastwood too, come to that."

"Don't be so aggravating, Martha," said I. "If you've ought to tell, let's hear it."

"Well, there's all maks o' tales dahn i' th' village, an' aw stopped to get th' reights on it, if aw could, for aw thowt it wer' no use bringing hauf a tale, an' it's little thanks aw get for my trouble. But there's justice i' Heaven, that's one comfort, for there's little on earth, certain sure. But as aw wer' sayin', Eastwood wer' comin' fra' th' market, an' they do say he rode hard, for he wer' trying to catch up wi' Horsfall o' Ottiwells."

"Aye, they oft rode home together," I put in.

"Weel, they'll nivver ride home together again if all they sen be true," continued Martha. "Eastwood had just getten sight o' Horsfall opposite Radcliffe's Plantation, when bang coom a shot out o' th' wood, an' he seed, they say, a felly jump on top o' th' wall an' wave his arms. An' Horsfall fell off his horse just as Eastwood wer riding up."

"Dead?" I gasped.

"Who said he wor dead? Noa, but as good as dead by all accounts. Eastwood's horse swerved at him as he ligged across th' road, an' Edmund wer thrown off into th' road. But he sammed hissen up an' bent ovver Horsfall, an' a lad caught th' mare up th' road as it wer' makin' for home as if Owd Harry wer' behind it, as he might be for owt aw can tell. But Eastwood nivver stayed for th' mare. He set off for Huddersfield as fast as he could split to fot a doctor."

"And Mr. Horsfall?"

"They carried him to th' Warrener, an' in a bit Eastwood comes back in th' gig wi' Dr. Houghton fra Huddersfield, they say i' a hand gallop an' covered wi 'sweat. Th' doctor jumps out o' th' trap an' runs into th' inn an' Eastwood wer' following him. But th' doctor comes running out again. He'd left some on his tools behind him."

"Aye, aye, most haste least speed," from my mother.

"And th' lad come up wi' Eastwood's horse, an' he up into th' saddle an' galloped off to th' town helter–skelter, an' reight at th' corner o' th' churchyard, just as if th' sensible crittur knew that were where th' rider wer' bun for, it threw him agean. They sen he's twisted his innards, an' they do say it's a toss up which 'll go first, him or Horsfall."

"What! is Mr. Horsfall so badly hit?"

"Aye, he's at th' Warrener. They cannot move him wom, and Mr. Scott o' Woodsome's theer to tak' his dying speech an' confession."

"Deposition," I corrected.

"Well, it's th' same thing, an' aw'm no scholar to crack on. An' little use learnin' is, it seems to me, if folk cannot keep theirsen out o' such mullocks as this. It's a mercy 'Siah's away, say I, for if they can they'll put it on to th' poor folk, an' let their betters go scot free, tho' its them as puts 'em up to it."

I did not sleep a wink that night. Horsfall shot dead! A man done to death in broad daylight by a shot from an assassin lurking behind a wall! It comes home to you when you know the man, when you know well the very spot on which he fell, when you can see in your mind's eye the murderers crouching behind the stones of a wall on which you have rested in many a homeward walk. How much more does it touch you when, as you ponder this picture of these crouched and waiting men, a face starts forth, with murder in its eyes, and the face is that of one you have loved and leaned on! I could not be certain, but I felt the hand of George Mellor was in this awful deed, and every instinct of manliness, of fair play, of humanity, rose up within, me and cried shame on the bloody deed. I remembered what George had said the night Horsfall had struck him with his riding–whip. I knew how his proud spirit must have chafed at our repulse at Rawfolds. But murder! oh it is an ugly thing. To stand up in fair fight, to pit strength against strength, craft against craft, to stake limb for limb, life for life, why, that, who shall cry fie upon. But to steal upon your foe in the dark, to stab in the back, to smite him unawares, to speed him unsummoned and unfit to judgment—there is no cause so righteous as to redeem an act so dastard. And that George, so frank, so full of sunshine and gay candour, should do this cowardly deed, passed comprehension. And yet who of all the others would dare? And if the thing had to be done, was George one to leave to others what he shrank from doing himself?

It was a night of torture. I looked back on the night I had passed in the barn after the fight at Rawfolds, and it seemed by comparison a night of restful bliss. Once, about midnight, I thought I heard the rattle of a pebble against the window pane. I stole softly out of bed and raised the window. But all was still around, and not far away in the little village a widow mourned a murdered husband and anguished hearts cried to heaven for just revenge.

After breakfast my mother set off to the village in quest of news. Work was out of the question. Mary busied herself about the house, and I tried to fix my mind upon straightening the books, which, after a fashion, it was my duty to keep. Alas! the invoices to be made out were few and slight, and an hour or so a week was enough for all the accountancy our business called for.

To me, thus engaged, tho' with wandering thoughts, came Martha, care upon her brow and secrecy in her gait.

"There's som'b'dy in th' shippen wants thee, Ben. Oh! dunnot let Mary know. He doesn't want any but thee to know he's here."

"Who is it?" I said beneath my breath. "It's him," said Martha, and nodded to me significantly.

"George?"

"Aye, George."

Just then Mary came out of the parlour with a duster in her hand, and I made pretence to be wrapt up in my ledger. Martha turned to go.

"What are yo' two whispering about?" Mary said suspiciously.

"Oh, nought," said Martha.

"Summot an' nought," I said, for Mary kept looking from one to the other.

"I don't believe you, Ben. What's agate? oh! Ben, don't trifle wi' me this morn for aw feel as if th' world were coming to an end, and more mysteries and horrors will drive me mad."

I reflected. If George were indeed anything to Mary, who had so much right to see him now as she? Anyway the day had gone by for me to be mixed up with any more secrets.

"There's George in th' mistal, Mary, he wants to see me by misen."

"Tell George Mellor to come in here and show himself like, a man," cried Mary. "Go this minute, Martha, and bid him come to his aunt's house as a man should come. Tell him, I, Mary, say so." And Martha went.

I rose from the little desk at which I sat and stood upon the hearth. Mary stood by my side, her face pale, her eyes lustrous, her breath coming short. The door opened slowly, and George came in. My God! I see him yet! I had passed a sleepless night, but George looked as if he had known no sleep for weeks. His face was white and drawn. His eyes were deep sunk in his head, and even by this they had a hunted shifting look—and when they looked at you, which by rare times they did, they seemed as tho' they asked a question and feared the answer. His neckchief was all awry, his boots clay covered, his breeches soiled, his hands were stained with dirt and torn with thorns, and his whole body seemed bent and unstrung. He advanced but two uncertain paces into the house. I stood my stand upon the hearth. George half lifted his hand to meet mine. For the life of me I could not raise my own, and words died from my lips. And Mary moved closer to my side, and half her figure drew behind me.

"What ta, Ben?" and George moaned and flung up his arms and sank upon a chair by the little round table in the kitchen centre and bowed his head on his arms and great sobs shook his frame.

"Leave us, Mary," I said very soft.

"I winna, aw'st see it aat. Tha't too soft, Ben."

I shaped to lay my hand on George's shoulder, but even as I raised my arm the thought of the murdered man came like a shock at me again, and I stood stiff and still once more. The convulsion passed, and George lifted his face.

"Tha knows all, Ben?"

"All I fear, George."

"And tha flings me off?"

"I fling thee off."

The angry colour came to his face, some of the old fire to his eye. He sprang to his feet, something of a man once more.

"And is this thi trust and this thi loyalty; hast ta forgotten thi oath, Ben?"

"I have forgotten nought, George."

"And yo' desert the Luds? Our greatest enemy lies low. I have struck the blow that others feared to strike, and terror palsies the oppressors of the poor. And in the supreme hour of our triumph you draw back?"

"I draw back."

"You brave the consequences of your broken oath, you earn for yourself the hatred of the poor, the obloquy and the doom of the traitor?"

"I brave them."

"Then out upon you, Ben Bamforth, for a false and perjured knave. The hour of trial and of danger has come, and it finds thee false. Oh! bitter the day and cursed the hour I took yo' to my heart, and bitter the rue thou'st sup for this. And yo' Mary, I've a word to say to yo'. But cannot I speak to thee alone?"

I made as tho' to leave the house, but Mary stayed me by a touch.

"Say what yo' have to say before Ben. Yo' can have nought to say to me he cannot hear."

"Nay I care not if tha does'na. He may listen if tha likes. All th' world may know for me. It has to be said, as well now as another time, tho' it's a rum courting to be sure. Tha knows aw love thee, Mary; tha knows aw've sought thee and only thee this many a month back?"

"I know yo've said so, George."

"And yo' did not say me nay. Yo' bid me bide my time, said yo' did not know yor own mind, that yo' were ower young to think o' such things yet, and put me off. But tha did not send me away wi'out hope, Mary, and I thought that in the bottom of your heart there was a tiny seedling that in time would flower to love."

"And so it might have done, George, but when it was a tender plant, a cold frost came and nipped it."

"I cannot follow yo', Mary, I am distraught in mind. All this night I have wandered the fields and in the lanes. A hundred times I have set my face over the hills to leave this cursed country."

"And your work behind you!" I put in, but he heeded me not.

"But the thought of you, Mary, held me back. I must know your heart, your mind to me. If yo' will be mine, if yo' will give me your word to wed me in quieter days, I will quit this work. Things will quieten themselves. A month or two and the Luddites will be forgotten. Our secrets are well kept. The Government will be only too glad to let sleeping dogs lie, and in another country, under another sky under the flag of the free Republic that has spurned the fetters of its English mother, you and I will seek fortune, hand–in–hand."

"There is blood upon your hand, George Mellor. Mine it shall never clasp again."

"So be it I need not stoop to woo too humbly. My star is o'ercast now, but a day shall come when yo' will regret the hour yo' spurned George Mellor's love. And yo! Ben Bamforth, traitor to your friend's confided love," . . . . and he turned upon me fiercely with flashing eye and clenched fist, and all his wrath surged to his lips and he would have gladly poured it out on me.

"Nay, George, I have not said my say," Mary broke in. "Yo' have told me yo' loved me, and when first I knew you I think I could have been easy won to love. But you were here when Ben Walker told how Long Tom had outraged me. Yo' heard every word he said, and I grant yo' you talked big. But what did you do? The girl yo' woo'd for your bride told her tale, and yo' — yo' made a speech and went home to bed, leaving to another arm to wreak the punishment you only threatened. My love, such as it was, died that night, that was the icy breath that killed it, and from that night I have almost loathed myself that ever I wasted a tender thought on you. But go, leave this house, your mind should be on other things than love. I ask no questions. But if my fears are true, it is of making your peace with an offended Maker you should be thinking, and crying for mercy rather than suing for love."

"You have had your answer, George," I said, as Mary hastened from the room leaving us confronting each other.

"Aye, I have had my answer. Yo' have stolen my love from me, yo'r desertion will wreck our cause, and now, finish what tha has begun, go to Justice Radcliffe, tell him George Mellor did not sleep at his father's house last night, put the blood-hounds of the law upon my track, and when tha draws the price of blood make a merry wedding for thissen an' th' lass tha's stolen to lay her head upon thi false an' perjured heart!"

And he waxed me off as I strode towards him, and made with quick step across the yard, and for many months I saw George Mellor no more.

Horsfall's death had an effect just the opposite to that expected by the Luds. It did not bring the masters to their knees: on the contrary it hardened and united them. It did not embolden the Luddites; rather they became alarmed at their own extremes. A reward was offered for the discovery of those concerned in the attack on Rawfolds, and a large sum, three thousand pounds, if my memory serves me, was put together by the millowners and given to Mr. Cartwright to mend his windows and to reward his pluck. Another reward, of two thousand pounds, was offered by the Government to anyone, not the actual murderer, who should betray to justice those who had shot Mr. Horsfall. Justice Radcliffe never rested. The least rumour that reached his ear was sufficient to justify an arrest, and no one knew when it would be his turn to be summoned to Milnsbridge House and have an ugly half–hour in the sweating room where the magistrate examined the men, women and children he hauled before him. I do not know what warrant Justice Radcliffe had for such examinations—probably none. But, then, how were ignorant folk, half frightened out of their wits, to know this; or if they knew it, how was their knowledge to serve them? To refuse to answer would be construed as a sure sign of guilty knowledge, if not of actual partnership: so people made themselves as gaumless as they could, and when driven into a corner lied like blacks.

The manufacturers who felt themselves or their goods in danger took heart. All eyes at this time were fixed on Marsden. Enoch and James Taylor, who made the new cropping frames, were looked upon as marked men, and Woodbottom mill was fortified as if for a siege; soldiers sleeping in the mill at night.

"Arthur Hirst's a main clever chap," said 'Siah, with unwilling admiration.

Arthur Hirst was the engineer at Woodbottom.

"How so, 'Siah?" I asked.

"Why mon he's laid a trap for th' Luds 'at 'll give 'em what for, if they pay a visit to th' Bottom. It's like th' owd nominy, 'walk into my garden said th' arrunder to th' flea.'"

"What's the' trap, 'Si?"

"Why he leaves a door open that leads ovver th' wheel race; an' there's a false flure ovver th' race, an' if anybody wer' to walk ovver it, it 'ud give way an' souse into th' race he'd go. Then up wi' t' shuttle, in with th' watter, an' in a jiffy th' wheel 'ud be turnin' an' hauf–a–dozen Luds turnin' wi' it, if so be as they be so obligin' as to walk into th' trap."

But no one did. Woodbottom was not attacked. The midnight raids became rare, and then ceased, and people went about saying the power of the Luds was broken and that we should hear no more of them. For my part I asked for nothing better.

Mary was true to her promise. She went to Low Moor and returned with Faith, a paler, thinner, sadder Faith. And Mary was very kind to her, very gentle with her, which surprised me not a little, for more than once she had been somewhat waspish whenever I had spoken of John's sister. But all that was past and over, and Mary and Faith seemed as thick as thieves. They slept in the same bed, and would go about the place with arms about each other's waists—a pretty picture: Mary in her blue print, with rosy cheeks and plump figure, and dancing eye and saucy speech; Faith in a plain close fitting dress of some black stuff, pale and pensive, with many a sigh and at times a tear of chastened sorrow when her mind fled back to the brother she had lost.

Of George Mellor we never spoke, though he was not long absent from the minds of any one of us. Mary put me on my guard.

"Yo' thought, Ben, 'at Faith wer' sweet on yo'!"

I made haste to disclaim the impeachment.

"Now it's no use lying, Ben, yo' six feet o' vanity that ye' are. An' what's more yo' were wi'in an ace o' bein' i' love wi' her."

I vowed by all my gods that this was false.

"Oh, yo' may swear as hard as yo' like; but aw know ye', Ben. Yo'd gotten into yo'r head 'at it wer' yo'r mission i' life to look after folk i' general an' they'd nowt to do but look ailin' an' pinin' as if they couldn't stick up for theirsen, an' yo' wer' ready to tak' them an' their trouble on them big shoulders o' yo'rn. That wer' th' way thi vanity showed itsen."

"I was sorry for Faith, Mary. But bein' sorry an bein' i' love 's two different things."

"Pity's o' kin to love," quoted Mary. "An' aw tell ye', wi' precious little encouragement an' th' chapter o' accidents helpin', yo'd ha' been sprawling at Faith's little feet, an 'ud ha' gone to yo'r grave believin' yo'd loved her sin' first yo' set eyes on her."

"And who was it taught me the difference atween love and pity, Mary?" I asked.

"How should I know and why should I care quoth Mary.

"No voice has ever told me, Mary, but the voice of my own heart; no words that maid e'er spoke, but a pair of arms around my neck and a maid's kiss upon my brow."

"Then if that's all yo'r warrant, I'd 'vise yo' not to be over certain on it. There's many a slip 'twixt the cup 'an the lip, an' a woman doesn't like a felly to be too sure."

"Nay, if yo'd have me plead on," I began and asked nothing better than to say my say; but Mary had ever a way of slipping from my grasp.

"Do yo' think I've nowt better to do nor listenin' to this nonsense? We wer' talkin' about Faith, an' how we wandered off aw' cannot tell."

"Well what of Faith?"

"Aw tell yo', Ben, Faith thought more of George Mellor's little finger nor of all yo'r big body. Aye an' still thinks. He's her hero. Her brother stuffed her head wi' such a pack o' nonsense that she thinks George the finest man that ever lived, and yo' not much better nor a coward for deserting him. She frets because he doesn't come here, and there's no tellin' what mak' o' folly her silly fancy mayn't lead her to."

"But George cares nowt for her," I said.

"What's that to do wi' it? Let a felly go sighing an' pinin' after a wench—an' it's long odds she'll laugh i' his long face. Let him seem beyond her reach an' it's just as likely she'll break her heart longing for him."

"Does she know about Horsfall?"

"Of course she does."

"What, all?"

"Aye, all. I took care she should."

"Well?"

"Well, she doesn't believe a word of it."

CHAPTER XI.

MAY came, sweet, fair and smiling. The crops bade fair to be good, and we looked forward to hay–making time with every assurance of a rich harvest. Everything was quiet as quiet could be. Of George I saw nothing at all. True I did not seek him, rather I shrank from meeting him. Our household settled down into its accustomed ways, and, such is the elasticity of the human mind, I began to look back upon the winter months as a troubled dream, only an occasional twinge in my right arm giving me a sharp reminder of the days I slung a hammer and pounded at the massive door of Rawfolds. I was wondrous happy. Health returned to my frame like the sap to the branch, and my heart was filled with all the sweet delight of love given and returned. There was no troth plighted as yet between Mary and me, but there grew up between us an unspoken acknowledgment of our love that bettered words. Faith was still with us, and as the weeks grew to months her melancholy melted away and a pensive content took its place. You did not find her singing like a lark, carolling the live–long day, as you did Mary, but there was about her an air of serene restfulness and calm that won all our hearts. With Mr. Webster she was an especial favourite, and she began, to his great delight, to teach a class in the Sunday school at Powle Moor. Faith was a rare scholar, tho' not, of course, learned in foreign tongues like John had been. She could write a beautiful hand and draw beautiful designs of birds and flowers and faces, which she wove in a marvellous way into the flourishes in her copy–books. And her figures and summing were like print. She taught the girls at the Powle to read and write, and she taught them so well that the boys rose in revolt and demanded that they too should join Miss Booth's class. It was a sight to see her leaving chapel of a Sunday afternoon. The scholars, boys and girls both, would wait till service was done that they might walk homewards with Miss Faith, and it was as sweet a sight as ever gladdened the eye of man to see her crossing the fields by the narrow lanes through the waving, nodding, rustling grass, that now began to sigh its own dirge, for hay–time drew near, a crowd of children in her train, a toddling urchin on either side clutching with chubby hand the folds of her skirt, and an advanced guard of sturdy lads marching on in front prepared to face imaginary lions and tigers in defence of their beloved teacher. Little Joe Gledhill and Jim Sugden fought a battle royal on Wimberlee because Faith had kissed Joe, whereas she had only given a lollipop to Jim, and on the strength of the kiss Joe went about bragging that when he was a man he should wed Faith and live happy ever after, the envy of all the boys in Slaithwaite, Lingards and Outlane.

Wonders never cease. At this time Soldier Jack turned religious, and began to be very constant in his attendance at Powle Moor, and there was much rejoicing in the camp of the godly over this brand plucked from the burning. Of a surety there is more rejoicing over one sinner that is saved than over ninety and nine righteous men. And Jack announced his resolve to forswear sack and live cleanly. He took a little cottage in the village, which he minded himself, and it was a picture of cleanliness, tho' it was not over stocked with furniture. You should have seen Jack polishing his fender, pipe–claying he called it.

There was a stormy scene, folk said, between him and Widow Walker, the buxom landlady of the Black Bull, the day Jack paid his last shot and announced his resolve to frequent that hostelry no more. The lady wept and stormed and even threatened Jack with the terrors of the law; but Jack was adamant.

"Dost think awn goin' to tak' up wi' that owd swill–tub's leavin's?" Jack asked when I questioned him as to his rupture with the hostess of the Black Bull.

"Yo' used to crack on her famous," I replied. "Ah! that wer' i' mi salat days, Ben, an' aw'll thank yo' not to throw them days of darkness i' mi face."

"But what's converted yo', Soldier?" I asked.

"Parson Webster."

"H…m"

"Aye, tha may h…m, that's ever the way wi' scoffer's an' unbelievers. Aw tell yo' th' little man's getten th' reight end o' th' stick an' owd Chew at th' church isn't fit to fasten th' latchet o' his shoes, as th' Book says: an' if tha thinks contrariwise I'll feight thee for it big as tha art."

"That's what they call muscular Christianity," I said.

"An' a very good sort, too," quoth Jack.

Anyhow a great change had undoubtedly come over the man, and none of us was surprised when he broached to my father and mother his schemes for establishing himself in life.

"It's about time, Mrs. Bamforth, aw settled dahn. Aw've had mi fling an' sown mi wild oats, an' nah it's time aw turned mi hand to a reg'lar job."

"Yo' should get wed," said my mother, very promptly.

"Would yo' reilly advise me so, maam?" asked Jack.

"Indeed aw should an' th' sooner the better."

"Aw dunnot see as how I can afford."

"Oh, fiddlesticks, what 'll keep one 'll keep two, an' God never sends mouths but he sends meat."

"That's cheering anyhow. But don't yo' think awm too old, Mrs. Bamforth?"

"An' what age may yo' be, if aw may make so bold?"

"Well yo' see awm noan rightly sure. But put it at forty–two or three, an' a gamey leg to boot."

"Limps dunnot run i' fam'lies," replied my mother with conviction. "There was that lad o' Crowthers 'at fell off a scaffold twenty foot high an' had to be taken to th' 'Firmary at Leeds, an' came back wi'out his arm an' went about wi' th' left sleeve o' his jacket pinned across his chest an' wed Kerenhappuch Hoyle, which aw shall allers say were no name to give a Christian woman, tho' Mr. Webster did say it meant 'the horn of beauty': an' yet when th' first child came, an' Kerenhappuch that anxious as never was an' not knowing for certain whether to mak th' long clo'es wi' one sleeve or two, it had two as fine arms as ever yo'd wish to see on a babe. So it's clear arms isn't like squints, which it's well known run i' families same as bald heads, an' it stan's to reason if arms dunnot legs winnot, not to name a bit of a limp."

"That seems to settle it," admitted Jack.

"An' han yo' fixed yo'r mind on anyone particler, Jack? Awm sure yo'n ta'en time enough, an' reason enough too you should. Marry i' haste an' repent at leisure's God's truth, an' aw've no patience wi' young folk weddin' 'at could awmost go to th' hedge an' see their nippins."

"Nay, ma'am," said the foxy warrior, "In so weighty a matter aw thowt it best to seek advice, and who can counsel me better nor yo'rsen."

"Aw thank yo' for the compliment, Soldier, Aw will say that it's th' army for puttin' a polish on a man if he do get but little moss. All i' good time for th' moss. An yo'll be lookin' maybe for a tidy body wi' summot o' her own put bye. A decent, quiet, God–fearing, steady woman, that could manage a house an' make yo' comfortable. There's Betty Lumb, now, o' th' Town End. She's pretty warm, I'll be bun, for she spends nowt."

"'Why she's forty, ma'am, if she's a month, an' wi' a tongue like a flail."

"An' what age might yo' be thinkin' on, Soldier?" asked my mother with asperity, suspicion in her voice.

"Well, aw haven't fixed to a year or two, but she mun be younger nor that. Else what about discipline, ma'am, what about discipline? 'Discipline must be maintained,' the Duke always said, and, zounds, I agree with him."

And Jack made his escape leaving my mother the agreeable task of turning over in her mind all the single women of middle age for miles around, weighing their merits and by no means unmindful of their failings.

With my father Jack's converse was on sterner matters. It seemed the Soldier was not without a little money laid by, and he was anxious to engage his modest capital in some enterprise in which his want of experience, would not be fatal. Farming he rejected with little consideration as being too tame a pursuit, tho' Mr. Webster, who was also taken into council, pointed out the excellency of beating the sword into a plowshare and the spear into a pruning hook.

Jack's doubts were, as often happens to man, rather solved for him than by him. Say what folk will, Rawfolds was not attacked nor Horsfall shot in vain. Those two events pleaded harder with our masters in Parliament than Mr. Brougham. They were arguments that could not be resisted. In June of that year, on the 18th to be exact, the Orders in Council were repealed, and our Valley and all the West Riding was soon busy with the stir of a revived industry. It was as tho' we breathed free after the weight and pressure of a long nightmare. The markets briskened at once, as tho' under a fairy's touch. Men went about shaking each other by the hand and with glad smiles upon their faces and in their eyes. The idle looms began to click, the roads were again busy as of yore with the traffic of great waggons departing laden and returning empty of their load. The canal began to be used freely for the carriage of piles of pieces. We could not make goods fast enough. The ports were once more open, and it seemed as if, all the world over, the nations were crying for our goods. It was as if the waters of commerce, frozen and banked up, had been thawed by a sudden heat and hounded forth in tumultuous volume. The church bells all over the Riding rang out the glad news. The manufacturers of our parts had a great dinner at the Cherry Tree and many another hostelry besides, and for the first time in my life and the last, I saw my father overcome by strong waters. He held down his head many a day at after before the awful face of my mother.

We shared in this great outburst of glorious sunshine. Our house was filled with pieces that my mother had vowed could have no other end than to be eaten by moths and rats. They found now a ready market, and the cry was still for more. We were all as busy as Thropp's wife from morning till night. I could not be spared from my own loom and from the warping and seeing to the bunting and country work. And so it came about that Jack went with my father on one of his rounds and proved himself so apt at cozening customers and became so great a favourite with the farmers' wives that came to buy suit lengths, that he was in time deemed fit to be trusted with a load on his own account. He bought a horse and waggon, established a round of his own, where he wouldn't clash with us, purchased his goods for the most part of us, and in a smallish way began to build a business, and laid the foundations of a thriving trade for his son and his son's son.

But with it all Soldier ever delighted to spend his nights at Holme and his Sundays at Powle Moor. I soon found he wanted none of my company. He had eyes only for Faith. He would talk to Faith by the hour of the singular virtues and the unparalleled learning of poor John, and that was a theme Faith never wearied of. What a saint, what a hero, what a philosopher they made of him between them! I only hope Jack believed half of what he said: else, there was a heavy account scoring against him somewhere.

We were all very happy during those months of summer and early autumn, lulled in a false security. We might have known that sooner or later the authorities were bound to get the information for which they never ceased to seek. In the middle of October it was rumoured in the market that George Mellor and Ben Walker had been arrested by Justice Radcliffe, but after a few hours detention had been released for lack of evidence. I breathed freely after this, and itched to go to George and hear all he had to tell. But I had to bite my thumb and wait, for, apart altogether from the coolness between George and me, it would never have done to be seen in his company just then. Still it was something to know that the police could make out no case against him and Walker, and we all felt that was more than a little in our favour. Then, like a bolt from the blue, came a piece of news in the "Leeds Mercury." Mr. Webster was the first to tell us of it, for we did not, at Holme, see the daily paper till after Mr. Mellor the schoolmaster had done with it, he and my father joining at the cost of it. I have the paper still before me as I write, tho' it is now yellow with age and hangs together very loosely and it is worn through at the creases. I may as well copy out what Mr. Webster read to us, and you may judge for yourself what a flustration it threw us into:

"A man has been taken up and examined by that indefatigable magistrate, Joseph Radcliffe, Esq., and has given the most complete and satisfactory evidence of the murder of Mr. Horsfall. The villains accused have been frequently examined before." —I never heard of but once—"but have always been discharged for want of sufficient evidence. The man charged behaved with the greatest effrontery till he saw the informer, when he changed colour and gasped for breath. When he came out of the room after hearing, the informer's evidence, he exclaimed 'Damn that fellow, he has done me.' It appears that this man and another have been the chief in all the disgraceful transactions that have occurred in this part of the country, especially at Rawfolds. This will lead to many more apprehensions."

When he had read this aloud Mr. Webster handed the paper to me, and I read the bit he pointed out to me again and again, for I was too stunned to take the sense of it in at first. The paragraph referred to the murderers of Mr. Horsfall. Well, I was clear of that at all events. You see my first thoughts were of myself and my own neck. It is no use pretending to be different from what I am, and I may as well confess that my first feeling was one of relief that the murderers of Mr. Horsfall only were indicated by the paragraph. But the feeling was short–lived. If Walker, for of course it must be Walker, it never entered my mind to question that, if Walker had told about the murder of Horsfall, would he hold his tongue about other matters. And if he told about the doings at Rawfolds, how many weeks purchase was my life worth. "This will lead to many more apprehensions." These words stood out and stared me in the face, and I broke out into a cold sweat and my hand trembled as I gave the paper back to Mr. Webster.

What was to be done? My father was all for flight, but Mr. Webster thought that would be of little use, for, said he, six feet two are not so easy hid as three feet one. He should like to see Ben Walker's father, who was or had been one of his deacons, and learn from him the exact truth of the matter. But he was fearful lest he should bungle the business, being as he said little used to the subtleties of the law and having a fatal habit of being prodigal in the matter of the truth.

"There's Soldier," said my father, who had unbounded confidence in our new foreman's resources, and who also probably felt that whatever qualms Jack might feel about parsimony in the matter in which the parson was prodigal he would be able to overcome.

"But Jack's in it knee deep," I objected.

"He'll wade out," said my father. And Jack was fetched from the scourhole, and came in with his arms bare and sweating from the steam, and smelling abominably of lant.

The paragraph was read to him.

"Phew! so George is nabbed. Well he'll noan split aw hope."

"'It appears that the man and another have been the chief in all the disgraceful transactions that have occurred in this part of the country, especially at Rawfolds' read Mr. Webster again. 'The man and another . . . . especially at Rawfolds?' You see the betrayal has not been confined to the murder of that unfortunate but head-strong man—'The man and another.' Who can the other be?"

I looked at Soldier and Soldier looked at me.

"That'll be me," said Jack.

"Nay, me," I said.

And the silence of dismay fell upon us all.

"Nay," said the good parson at length, and never did dying absolution from priestly lips bring more comfort to a penitent—"Nay, that can hardly be. This pa-per was published in Leeds yesterday morning. The information must have been in the possession of Mr. Radcliffe for some days. If either of you had been impli-cated you would have been under arrest ere this."

I breathed again.

"Well, Jack, what do yo' say?" asked my father.

"Say? Well aw say I'm noan goin' to be kept on th' tenterhooks. Awm goin' to know all at is to be known. I'm goin' to reconnoitre. They can't hang me for a spy, any road, an' that's what they nearly did in Spain. Just yo' cower quiet, Ben. I'm off to th' Brig. There'll be more known there. Just you leave it to me; an' I'll be back wi' my budget bi th' afternoon drinkin'."

And Jack set off without parley, and left us to our anxieties.

He was back by four o'clock. Mr. Webster had been in and out half a dozen times, having passed the afternoon in reading the Scriptures with a distraught air at the houses of those of his flock who lived at Upper and Lower Holme.

Jack's face was very sober when he came into the house and found us waiting, Mary and Faith with us, for I had not thought it necessary to hide from them the serious aspect of our affairs, and we had all gone about all day, my mother de-clared, as if we had th' bailiffs in, which to her mind was far worse than a death.

"It's Walker's split, sure enough," said Jack coming to the point at once. "Him an' Bill Hall. George Mellor and Thorpe and Smith have been taken and sent off to York under guard. That's for Horsfall's job they say. John Walker, Ben's own brother, 's pinched for Rawfolds. So's Jon'than Dean an' Tom Brook an' two or three others, but I couldn't reightly find out who an' how many more. But there's no gainsayin' them. An' more nor likely there's more to folly. When aw got to th' Brigg there wer' a crowd round Buck Walker's house, booin' an' callin' out 'black sheep, black sheep.' But that'll do no gooid. There wer' some o' those new consta-bles at Mr. Radcliffe's brought up i' th' front o' th' house, an' bar a stone or two thrown at th' windows no harm wer done. Aw made mi way in, an' gate a word wi' Mrs. Walker, Ben's mother."

"But George—where was he taken? Cannot yo' tell us more of him?"

Jack glanced covertly at Faith. She sat with fingers tight interlaced upon her knee. Her eyes were fixed on Soldier, wide dilated. Her lips were parted, and she scarce breathed.

"Oh, tell us of George," she sighed rather than spoke.

"He wer' ta'en at th' shop. He wer' workin' with th' shears, an' like as not thinkin' o' nowt so little as th' sodjers. They'd come up, about six on 'em, very quiet, an' owd Radcliffe hissen wer' with 'em wi't officer wi' th' warrant. Radcliffe come reight up to th' door as bold as brass afore anyone i'side wer' aware on him, an' Ben Walker wer' wi' him. Ben sidles into th' shop, an' George turns to speak to him but his eye fell o' Mr. Radcliffe stood i' th' door way."

'Hows a wi' yo, George?' says Ben, an' holds out his hand.

"But George took it all in in a jiffy, an' he maks a spring at Ben, an' they say he'd ha' run his shears into him if he'd got at him. But th' chap wi' th' warrant rushes for'ard an' th' soldiers run in at a word fra Mr. Radcliffe. 'Judas,' hissed George, and fixed his eyes on Ben an' nivver took them off him while they put th' darbies on him an' Thorpe 'at wer' taken at th' same time. 'Judas, yo' cursed Judas!' and Walker cowered behind th' stout owd magistrate like th' cur at he is. But, quick, look to Faith."

Mary and my mother sprang to Faith's side, and Mary caught her in her arms as she was falling unconscious to the ground. The poor lass had swooned away. Jack supported her to the parlour, and laid her on the horsehair sofa and my mother and Mary busied themselves in bringing her round.

"Drat me for a tactless fool," said Jack, when he returned to the kitchen. "Aw cannot ha' th' wit aw wer' born wi' to be ramblin' on like that an' her there. Well, well, it's a pity her heart's so set yonder, for awm feart her thowt's 'll be where her eyes 'll nivver rest again." And for a long time Jack could not be moved to continue his story. It was only when Mary returned to say that Faith was quite recovered, and that the mother would stay with her in the parlour that he went on:

"George wer' game to th' last, an' Thorpe, they say, wer' just as unconcerned as if he wer' used to bein' charged wi' murder every day o' his life. When they thrust 'em into th' coach they had i' waitin', George raised his hand as well as he could for th' irons, an' called out, 'Three cheers for General Lud.' But th' crowd wer' fleyed to death. A lad or two in th' throng cried out i' answer, an' a woman waved her shawl, but everyone feart to be seen takin' his part, an' folk 'at had known him fra a lad held back fra him same as if he'd getten th' small–pox."

"Oh! the cowards, the heartless, ungrateful wretches!" cried Mary with flashing eyes. "I wish I'd been there. I'd have, stood by him if his own mother had disowned him!" And I have no doubt Mary would have been as good as her words.

"Well and then?" said my father to prod on Soldier, who seemed to have only half his heart in the story, for he kept his eyes fixed on the door of the parlour, and seemed to be listening with all his ears for what might be passing within.

"Well, they hustled him off wi' a clatter, th' soldiers mounted their horses, three o' each side o' th' coach, an' off i' a gallop to Leeds on their way to York. Ther' wer' more dragoons waiting for them by th' Brigg for they feared a rescue, but, Lord bless yo', when they'd getten George they'd gotten all th' heart an' all th' pluck to be fun' wi' in a mile o' th' Brigg. A rescue say yo'? A swarm o' rats not worth feightin' for. That's my judgment on 'em all."

"But you saw Mrs. Walker yo' said?" queried my father. "Had yo' no speech wi' Ben?"

"Nay, they took good care o' that. Owd Radcliffe has him safe enough, an' he'll noan let him slip aat o' his clutches till he's kept his bargain an' put th' noose round George's neck. He's to be ta'en, they say, to Chester, an' kept theer till th' York 'sizes. They'll noan gi' th' Luds a chance o' stoppin' his mouth wi' an ounce o' lead, worse luck. For awm noan so sure aw wouldn't ha' a try at him misen."

"And what had his mother to say?"

"Oh! lots. A cunning, contrary bitch, that aw sud say so! There's no wonder Ben Walker wer' what he wer' wi' a dam like yon, whinin' an' quotin' th' Scriptures, enough to mak a man turn atheist."

"But what did she say?"

"Oh! I cannot burden mi mind wi' all 'oo said, about it bein' th' Lord's will, an' submission to th' ways of th' A'mighty, reg'lar blasphemy aw call it, callin' in religion to cover up a piece o' as damned rascality as ever wer' done by man. But there's something aw munnot forget. It concerns thee, Mary."

"Me! what can she have to say to me."

"That's what aw wanted to get at. But 'oo'd noan send any word bi me. She particler wanted to know if ther' wer' owt 'atween yo' an' Ben here."

Mary flushed and tossed her head.

"The impudence o' some folk," she said.

"Aw axed her what business that wer' o hers' an' towd her aw thowt 'oo'd best turn her thowts to prayin' for that scamp o' a son o' hers. But 'oo stuck to her guns. 'Oo wants to see thee, Mary."

"'Oo may want," said Mary.

"Well it's for yo' to judge. She made out it mut be waur for Ben here if tha didn't go."

"Mary 'll noan go near such like wi' my consent," I cried.

"Whativver can th' woman want?" mused Mary. "Aw've a good mind.... Ben Walker's away to Chester yo' say? For good an' all?"

"Aye, they'll keep him fast enough yo' may rest content."

"I've a good mind...," continued Mary. "Waur for our Ben, did she say? I'll go."

"Yo'll do nowt o' th' sort!" I said.

"An' since when wer' yo' mi mester, cousin Ben?" she asked. "I'st go and aunt 'll mebbe go wi' me."

"Not an inch," snapped my mother, who had left Faith in a great measure composed "Aw'd be poisoned if aw' breathed th' same air."

"Then aw'st go by misen. Yo' can see me to th' Brigg, Ben, if tha likes. But I'll hear what 'oo has to say. She cannot harm me, an I'st happen get to know something that may help us."

"Mary's right," said Soldier. "My word, Ben, thee's getten thi mester," he whispered to me on the sly.

But it has been a sweet thraldom. When Mary had made up her mind she was not one to let the grass grow under her feet, and the very next evening she told me to get me dressed if I meant to go with her to th' Brigg. So off we set together by Kitchen Fold, over Crossland Moor, past the plantation where Mr. Horsfall had been shot, and so dropped down into th' Brigg. I pointed out to Mary the marks of the bullets on the wall on the road side opposite the little wood; but Mary shivered and drew her shawl tighter about her and hurried on, casting frightened glances at the clump of trees and bush as if she feared to see a ghost. She would not let me go with her to Walker's, bidding me meet her in an hour's time on the Brigg and be ready to company her back. So I thought I might as well comfort myself with a glass at th' Nag's Head. It was not so long since that the landlord would have fussed about me as I drank my ale and offered me a treat. But now, as I sat aloof from the little company and took my drink, he talked pointedly to the other customers about the honest way he had always kept his house, saying he would have neither Luds nor their brass at th' Nag's Head and their room was better nor their company. But I would not be hurried for the likes of him, and called for another gill and made it last out my hour just to spite him.

Mary did not keep me waiting long on th' Brigg, and fain I was to be off, for little knots of people were clustered in the street and many a look was cast at me, not over friendly; and faces that I knew well enough looked stonily at me, and one or two that knew me well enough, and to whom I gave the day, made as tho' they did not know me from Adam. It was plain as a pike–staff that the folk at th' Brigg were fleyed out of their wits of being suspected of having ought to do with the Luds. They altered their tune later on, when th' first panic had passed, but for a week or two after George and Thorpe were taken every man was on his best behaviour, and a good many lived in hourly fear and trembling.

Be sure, then, we did not loiter in Longroyd Bridge. There was nothing there to tempt us to stay, and Mary was in a greater hurry to be gone than even I. She was very pale. She had had no spirits to talk of since we had heard George was taken, but now she was more down nor ever. Not a word spoke she right up th' moor till we got to th' top and turned round to look on th' town lying at our feet. She was panting for breath, and I drew her to the roadside and made her sit upon the wall. There was nobody about, and the early night of late autumn had closed in. I tried to steal my arm about her waist, tho' Mary was ever coy of suffering any such show of my love. But she put away my arm very gently—"Yo mustn't do that again, Ben. It's all ovver now. We'n had our dream, an' it's been a sweet 'un. But I've had a rude wakening, an' it's all ovver, it's all ovver." And Mary hid her face in her hands and bent over as she sat, and tears trickled from under her hands down upon her lap.

I let her be, and she wept silently. Then she sprang to her feet and dried her eyes and tried to smile and would have had me take the road again; but I would not budge, and she had to sit by my side. The road was quiet enough, and what mattered it if all the world saw us? We'd as much right there as anyone.

"Now, Mary, tell me, like a sensible lass, what it all means."

Mary did not speak to me. I saw she was considering so I did not hurry her. I was getting used to the ways of women. There's nought like loving and courting for teaching a man th' way to handle 'em, tho' they're kittle cattle to shoe at the' best o' times.

"There's summat aw hannot told thee, Ben. Happen aw should ha' done."

"Aw think aw can guess it."

"Tha nivver can."

"Is it about Ben Walker?"

Mary nodded.

"Martha towd me."

"Oh!"

There was a look passed over Mary's face which I took to mean that Martha would have a piece of Mary's mind first chance that offered.

"Well?" I said.

"Well, of course, I'd ha' nowt to do wi' him."

"Aw should think not," I said, moving a little closer to her.

"And at first he thowt aw'd promised George."

"That comes fra not knowin' thi own mind." Mary drew further off.

"I told him so misen," I said.

Mary sprang up as if she'd been shot.

"Yo' did?"

"Aw did."

"Then yo've a deal to answer for, Ben Bamforth. His mother says that's what made him peach on George."

"The devil!" I said, and there was silence, and we sat thinking our own thoughts.

"It wer' happen my fault," said Mary at last, sitting down again. "Anyway it's no use quarrelling about it."

"Nor crying over spilt milk," I said.

"But that's not th' worst on it by a long chalk," said Mary.

"Well, let's hear it?"

"She's a horrid woman, that Mrs. Walker. Just like an owd witch, an' such wicked, wicked eyes, a peerin' at yo' an' a peerin' at yo', an' wantin' to stroke yo'r hair like as if yo' wer' a cat. But aw'll begin at th' beginnin'."

"That's th' best way," I said, and my arm now was where it should be, and Mary reckoned not to know. I'd looked up th' road an' down th' road an' nobody was coming.

"When aw got in, 'oo dusted a chair wi her apron, an' not afore it wanted it. Th' house wer' like a pig–stye. But I sat down, an' 'oo stood afore me an' looked me up an' down same as if 'oo wer' vallyin' me. 'Aw hope yo'll know me again next time yo' see me, an' that won't be soon if I've my way' aw thowt, but said nowt.

'An' so yo'r Mary o' Mally's?' 'oo said at last.

'At yo'r service,' aw said.

'Yo're not much to look at,' 'oo said.

'Thank yo' kindly,' aw answered as polite as never were.

'But yar Ben's a reight to ha' his own way now he's a gentleman.'

'A what?' aw cried.

'A gentleman. A real gentleman at can ha' th' pick o' th' country side. He's nowt to do but howd up his finger naa. It'll be whistle an' aw'll come to yo', mi lad.'

'He's altered strangely,' aw said.

'Aye, two thousand p'un' does mak' a differ,' says th' owd hag.

"And then aw remembered about th' notice in th' paper.

'It'll do him no good,' aw says. 'It's blood money. There'll be a curse on it.'

'It's good gold, lass!' 'oo says. 'Good gold, leastways it will be when th' 'sizes is ovver. An then yar Ben's off to 'Meriky, an' nowt 'll suit him but yo' mun go wi' him.'

'Then he'll noan be suited,' aw says.

'Hoity–toity, mi fine wench,' 'oo cries. 'Don't thee be too sure o' that. Yo'r happen thinkin' o' ta'in up wi' Ben Bamforth. Leastways that's what yar Ben heerd just afore he wer' off to Chester. That's what aw've sent for yo' for.'

'What's it to him, who aw wed?' I asked, but aw wer' all of a tremble.

'It's this. It'll be yar Ben or nobody sin he's set on it. 'See her yoursen, mother,' he said, an' these were awmost his last words afore he set off wi' Justice Radcliffe, two gentlemen together. 'See her yo'rsen, an' tell her that th' same tongue 'at's teed a rope round George Mellor's neck can tee' one round Ben Bamforth's, an' will too, unless she speaks the word that'll stop my mouth.' Now, what's ta say, mi fine lass?'

"And what could I say, Ben," sobbed Mary, hiding her face on my shoulder. "Aw saw she meant it. She gay' me a month to think on it, an' if aw don't say yes 'oo swears Ben Walker 'll give thee up to th' law, an' it's a hangin' job, sure an' certain."

"What did yo' say, Mary?"

"At first I towd her aw wouldn't wed their Ben if there weren't another man i' all England. Aw'd rayther wed a toad, aw said, an' aw meant it. But oh, Ben, tha'rt i' their power, an' aw'm noan worth hangin' for. And what would yo' have me do, Ben? Aw mun tell her in a month."

"There's one thing tha shalln't do," I cried. "Aw'd rayther hang a million times ovver nor tha should ha' a thing like him. Let her do her worst. Not if it would save me from ten thousand times ten thousand base deaths shall Ben Walker call thee wife. That aw'm fixed on. What say'st ta, Mary?"

"Eh, awm fair moithered, Ben. Aw know this, if wed him I must aw'll mak' a hole i' th' cut th' same neet," and Mary sobbed again.

And I declare that I was happier whilst I soothed her and whispered words of bye and pressed kisses on her cheek and lips than ever before. For never till then had I realized to the full all the sweet privileges of our love.

CHAPTER XII.

I HAD got my affairs into, a pretty tangle, and for the life of me I could not see my way out of the mess. I lived in daily terror of arrest. I was not even supported by what appeals so strongly to a young man's vanity—popular good–will. When a man gets older he comes to esteem the applause of the world at its proper worth, largely indifferent to it and content if happily he can be assured of the good–will of his own conscience. But even the poor solace of the public voice was just now denied the poor Luds. The murder of Mr. Horsfall had revolted the general mind. So I found myself quaking at every step that approached the door when I kept the house, and met with looks averted or openly hostile when I took my walks abroad, which was not oftener than needs must be. Then there was that diabolic threat of Ben o' Buck's, which I had no reason to hope he would not make good. I could not essay to save my own skin by counselling Mary to have Ben Walker. Even had I not loved her myself I could scarce have brought her to that. Add to this the reflection that, innocently and honestly enough, I had probably been the means of drawing upon George Mellor's head the spiteful hatred of the traitor by giving him to believe that it was a made up thing between Mary and George. I tell you I could neither eat nor sleep these days for thinking of all these matters. And Mary looked worn and ill. The rose's began to fade from her cheeks, she had scarce a word to throw at a dog, and as the days grew to weeks her gloom deepened and misery showed more plain upon her face.

I took counsel of 'Siah. I was in such straits that I could have found it in my heart to seek wisdom from the town fool. 'Siah had a short cut out of the whole perplexity.

"Yo' mun get untwisted, Ben," said 'Si.

"What's untwisted?" I asked.

"I cannot tell wher' yo'r wits are these days," said 'Siah impatiently. "Theer tha sits by th' fireside, counting th' co'wks' an' glowerin' into th' ass–hoil, as if that 'ud do thi ony good. Tha shud stir about, mon, an' hear whats a foot. There's more i'spiration, as th' parson calls it, to be fun' at th' Black Bull i' hauf an hour nor i' a week o' sulkin' at whom bi thissen."

"Aw've no faith i' th' counsel 'at's to be found at th' bottom o' an' ale–pot, 'Si."

"Who want's thee to ha? Th'art as bad as Martha for preachin' these days. Ther'll be no livin' for sermons soon. There's summat beside drinkin' goin' off in a public."

"Well, lets hear it?" I said passively, for I had not much faith in what 'Siah might have picked up in his haunts.

"Aw tell thee tha should get untwisted."

"Well?"

"Well and well an' well. Can ta say nowt but well? Doesn't ta know what aw mean, or mun I tell thee straight out?"

"Aw've no' more notion nor th' babe unborn," I said.

"Yo' know Mr. Scott o' Woodsome?"

"Of course aw do. Didn't aw sit next to him at th' audit, last year?"

"Well yo' know he's a magistrate, an' main good to th' poor folk, everyone says he is. He's everyone's good word, an' that's summat out o' th' common for a justice."

"And how can Mr. Scott help us in our troubles? I fear they're a bit aboon his power."

"Why, he can untwist thee, mon."

"Untwist?"

"Aye! untwist! There's Doad o' Jamie's an' Lijah o' Mo's an' a seet more on 'em 's gate untwisted, an' it costs nowt, an's just as easy as sinnin', an' a heap more comfortin' by what they say."

"And what in the name o' wonder is it?" I asked, thinking 'Siah might have penetrated deeper into the mysteries of the law than I, and having much respect for him, as one who had more than once slipped through the constable's hands and left him clinkin'.

"Yo' know th' oath we took at th' Buck," replied 'Siah, lowering his voice and looking cautiously round.

I nodded.

"Well, Mr. Scott's untwisting th' oath off th' Luds for miles around. Yo'n nowt to do but go to Woodsome an' say yo'r soary an' let on to tell all yo' know, an' that needn't be more nor yo' can see wi' both e'en shut, an' he untwists yo'. It's same as th' Catholics, tha knows."

"Why that's king's evidence," I cried.

"Yo' may call it what yo' like, but it's cheap an' easy, an' 'll do nobody any harm."

"What give evidence again mi own cousin? I'd be as bad as Ben Walker."

"Nowt o' th' sort. They'n getten witnesses enew baht thee, an' Mr. Scott 's a friend o' thi father's, an' 'll let thee dahn soft for auld acquaintance sake. It isn't as if tha wer' th' first to split, nor as if owt tha can other say or do 'ud pull George out o' th' boil or thrust him further in."

"I'll ha none of it, 'Si," I cried. "And what's more yo' an' me quarrel if yo' do owt o' th' sort thissen. Why man, aw sud nivver sleep another wink nor howd up mi head agen if aw lowered misen to that, an' whativver tha does, 'Si, keep thissen cleaner nor Ben Walker. Aw'd never speak to thee agen, no more would any on us'. Has ta' spoke to Martha on it?"

"Well awm not free to say but what aw han."

"And what does Martha say?"

"Well if aw mun speak th' truth she says th' same as thee. All fools in a lump, say I, but gang thi own gate, an' dunnot fear aw'st cross thi will. But its hard liggin' for all that."

So I got no comfort from 'Siah.

Then, as if we hadn't troubles enough of our own, my Aunt Wood, George's mother, came from the Brigg to see my father about George's case. It must not be thought we had not worried about him. We had, and more than a little. Whenever I pictured to myself my cousin and more than friend, eating his heart out in a prison cell, I was near beside myself with grief. As for the end of it all, I dared not think of it. I had parted from George in anger; but I made no account of that. I was safe in Mary's love, and those who win can afford to be generous. And if these Luddite troubles had blown over, George might have come round, and tho' our relations might never have been what they had been, still we could have patched up a work–a–day friendship that would have served. But now George was in prison, charged with the most awful of all crimes, and tho' my gorge rose at the deed, I sorrowed for the man.

It was sad to see the change in my Aunt Wood. She was never a strong woman, least–wise in my knowledge of her; but now she was piteous to look at. She was crushed by the burthen of sorrow and shame. Sorrow's bad enough: but add shame to it, and it's more than human soul can bear. My mother fair wept over her.

"Eh, lass," she said, when she had taken my aunt's shawl and poke bonnet and got her seated by the fire, whilst Mary busied about boiling the kettle and making some tea. "Eh! lass, that ever we should live to see this day."

My aunt drooped her head. She did not greet nor moan. I think the fountain of her tears was dry.

"My heart's sore for yo', Matty, and glad I am yo've come to me i' yo'r trouble."

"I had to come, Charlotte, for if yo'r William cannot help me, I dunnot know wheer to turn."

"Aw'll do owt aw can. Yo' know that, Matty. Aw set a deal o' store on George. We all did. Aw cannot think what possessed him. More aw think on it, more awm capped, for George wer' noan o' th' sort to . . . . It's fair beyond me. What does Wood say?"

"It's that's brought me here, William. It's a cruel thing to say; but in his heart o' hearts aw think mi husband's fair glad they'n fetched our George. He never took to th' lad, nor George to him. But yo'd ha' thowt at naa, when aw want all th' comfort aw can get, mi own husband 'ud be th' first to help."

And Aunt Wood's lips trembled and she pressed her thin hand to her throat to keep down the sobs that choked her.

"Dunnot tak' on, Matty," said my father. "We'st stand to yo', wet or fine."

"Aw shud think so i'deed," cried my mother; "my own sister. If yo' can't look to yo'r own in th' time o' need, what's relations for aw shud like to know. Onybody 'll stan' yo'r friend when yo'r i' no need o' frien's. It's trouble tries folk. Nah, thee drink this cup o' tea, Matty, an' nivver heed drawin' to th' table. Sit wher' tha art an' keep thi feet on th' fender. An', see yo', there's a drop o' rum i' thi tea, tho' aw dunnot hold wi' it as a reg'lar thing, for wilful waste ma'es woful want, but it'll warm thee an' hearten thi up. Tha' looks as if tha hadn't a drop o' blood i' thi body, poor thing."

"Hast ta any notion o' what tha'd like doin' for George?" asked my father.

"Nay, it'll be a law job, that's all aw know. But see, awm noan come a beggin'. Aw dunnot know what William 'ud say, if he knew; but yo'll noan tell."

And my aunt lifted her dress and from under the skirt drew a linen bag, which she placed upon the table.

"Count that." she said.

My father turned over the greasy, dirty notes, pound notes of the Huddersfield Commercial Bank, Ingham's, wetting his forefinger and counting aloud, very grave, as he always was whenever he counted money. He used to say it gave him a turn, when he went to the Bank, to see the flippant way the young men handled the money across the counter—"But they don't know its valley, or they'd noan finger it so free," he would say.

"A hundred pounds, neither more nor less," he said, after the third counting and blowing of each note to see two hadn't stuck together. "Wherever did ta get it, Matty?"

"Aw saved it out o' th' housekeepin' brass 'at Wood gives me. Aw'd meant it for George' on th' day he should be wed—but nah!"

"It'll come in useful ony road," said my father. "Am aw to keep it for thee?"

"Aye, it's for th' law."

"Has ta any fancy?"

"Nay, tha knows best."

"What does ta say to 'Torney Blackburn? He's allus done my bit."

"Aw dunnot know. Aw reckon there's not much to choose among 'em he mun be th' best brass can buy."

"Well there's young Allison; aw don't know but what he'd be more cut out for a job like this. But they say he's for th' Crown. Him an' Justice Radcliffe ha' been here, there an' everywheer huntin' up evidence agen th' 'sizes."

"Aye, trust th' quality for havin' th' best o' everything," spoke my mother.

"Well, if tha thinks 'Torney Blackburn can be trusted, tha can set him on. But awm feart them lawyers is all in a string. Yo' never know who yo' can trust these days."

"Well yo' see," said my father, "we'n got to trust 'em an' pray for th' best. Aw supposes there's summot i' th' nature o' th' law 'at makes it difficult for th' best on 'em to be ony better nor he sud be; an' happen if they warn't a bit crooked theirsen, they'd noan be fit to straighten other folk's twists. But 'speak of a man as yo' find him,' say I, an' aw've allus fun 'Torney Blackburn as straight as they make 'em. But aw wish we could ha' had Mr. Allison all th' same."

"Why?" asked my aunt.

"Well, somehow he'st th' name o' bein' thicker wi' Owd Harry; an' that goes a long way i' law."

And so it was settled that the defence of George should be entrusted to Mr. Blackburn, of the New Street.

I went with my father the very next day to see Mr. Blackburn. I did not like being seen about, but there seemed nothing for it but to brazen it out and take my luck. I had never been to a lawyer's office before, and felt as if I were going to have a tooth pulled; but my father opened the door of the outer office as bold as brass. There was a little old wizened man with a face like yellow crinkled sheepskin, and a suit that had once been black, maybe, but now was rusty brown and white at the seams.

"Is he in?" said my father.

"Sit down, Mr. Bamforth, sit down. Come to the fire. Your son, sir? Pleased to know you, sir. A chip of the old block, Mr. Bamforth, a chip of the old block."

And my father actually looked pleased, tho' if I were a chip of the old block there was a deal more chip than block.

Mr. Blackburn was in, and presently we were ushered into an inner room. It would have turned my mother sick to see the dust that lay about, and the frosted windows that gave on to the New Street looked as if they hadn't been washed for a century.

Mr. Blackburn shook us both by the hand in a jerky way, and offered my father a pinch of snuff from a big silver box. My father took a pinch with the result that he never ceased sneezing till we were out into the street and he had hurried to the Boot and Shoe and drunk a pint of ale to wash the tickling out of his throat.

"And now, Mr. Bamforth, what can I do for you?" asked Mr. Blackburn, pushing his spectacles on to his brow and laying a large brown silk handkerchief, snuff coloured, over his knee.

"It's about George Mellor, yo know," said my father.

Mr. Blackburn did not look as if he did know.

"Him 'at's ta'en for Horsfall's job, yo' know," explained my father.

"Well, what of him?"

"He's my nevvy, yo' know."

"Yo'r nevvy? Phew! this is an ugly business, an ugly business."

"Awm feart so."

"Well?"

"Aw want yo' to defend him at th' 'sizes."

"Why my good man, what defence is possible? Allison tells me the case is as clear as crystal. Not a loop hole in it."

My father's face fell. Then he pulled out the bag of notes.

"There's a hundred pound here, Mr. Blackburn. George shalln't stand up i' Court wi'out one soul to take his side. Guilty or not guilty, whatever th' law can do for him shall be done. It'll happen soothe him at the last, if th' worst comes to th' worst, to know at some hearts felt for him, an' that what brass could do to get him off, wer' done."

"It's a noble sentiment, Mr. Bamforth, and does you credit I'm sure. Well, well, no man's guilty in this country, thank God, till he's proved guilty. But I can't make bricks without straw, you know. What's the defence?"

"Nay, that's for you to find out," said my father, more cheerfully. "That's' what th' hundred pound is for."

"But we don't make evidence, my dear sir. There can be only one defence— an alibi. The man was shot, that's plain. It wasn't an accident, that's clear. Who ever did it, did it of malice prepense. There can only be an alibi. This young man now"—turning to me—"the prisoner was your cousin?"

"Yes, sir."

"And doubtless you were on good terms?"

"The best."

"And equally without doubt you saw a deal of each other?"

"We did."

"He visited you and you him?"

"That's so."

"And you remember the night of the—what day was it?"

"Tuesday the 28th of April last."

"And you remember that day?"

"Only too well."

"Now perhaps—I only say, perhaps, mark you—your cousin George spent the evening of that day in your company? A respectable young man like you— your word would go a long way."

But I shook my head. No, I could not swear I was with George that fateful day.

"Well, well, perhaps someone else can. I must see the prisoner, and when I've heard what he has to say, I shall be better able to judge what is best to be done. Another pinch, Mr. Bamforth? No? a bad habit, a bad habit, don't you begin it, young sir, but clears the brain. Good day—Jones, give Mr. Bamforth a receipt for £100. "Rex versus Mellor." Good day—we'll do our best, and a case is never lost till it's won."

"Did' yo' notice th' books, Ben?" asked my father, as we crossed the street to the Boot and Shoe. "Wonderful isn't it? Aw dunnot wonder a man wants some snuff or summat to life th' weight o' all them books off his brain. Aw wonder how he crams it all in, for his yed's noan so much bigger nor other folk. Wonderful."

When we got home that night we had to tell in detail all that we had said to Mr. Blackburn and all that Mr. Blackburn had said to us. Soldier Jack and Mr. Webster were of our council.

"It's a tickle business is an alibi," Jack commented. "Them lawyers turn a chap inside out. Aw once tried to get a felly out o' a bit o' a mess afore th' justices at Bristol. He wer' one o' th' line an' had used his belt in a street broil. I went to swear him off."

"I hope, Soldier, not to perjure yourself," said Mr. Webster earnestly.

"Well not to say perjure," said Jack. "They say if yo' kiss yo'r thumb i'sted of th' Book, it's noan perjury. But aw did better nor that, aw'd a ready reckoner i' th' palm o' my hand, an' aw kissed that. So aw reckon aw wer' clear ony road."

Mr. Webster sighed and shook his head.

"But it wer' o' no use. Ther' wer' a little chap at wer' persecutin', an' he looked that innercent yo'd ha' thowt ony sort o' a tale 'ud go dahn wi' him. But aw nivver wer' so mista'en i' a chap i' my life. He began to cross–question me mild as milk. He wanted to know what aw'd had for mi breakfast an' wheer aw took my ale an' a hundred thousand things, an' raked out th' whole history o' mi life awmost fra mi pap bottle up'ards, an' he twisted mi answers so, an' th' magistrates began to look at me as if aw wer' th' worst specimen o' a criminal they'd ivver seen; an' he back'ards an' for'ards, lopin' like a flea fra this spot to that spot o' mi tale, till aw didn't know whether aw wer' stood o' mi head or mi heels. An' he looked at mi wi' an eye like a gimlet, an' for th' life o' me aw couldn't tak' mi e'en fra his, tho' aw'd ha' given owt to do it. An' then aw saw aw'd contradicted misen, not exactly a lie, but a bit o' a slip, an' aw saw he'd twigged it, an' aw saw he saw aw saw he'd twigged it; an' ther' come a quiet smile o' his lips, an' he looked at me as much as to say 'what a clever fool yo' are,' an' he played wi' me like a cat lakin' wi' a mouse, an' aw broke out into a sweat an' aw'd ha' swapped places wi' th' prisoner an' given summat to boot. Phew! it mak's me warm yet to think on it! It's risky wark is a haliby, aw tell yo', an chance it."

"I suppose the Crown will rely mainly on the evidence of Ben Walker?" asked Mr. Webster.

My father nodded assent.

"But I think I have read that a man cannot be hanged on the unsupported tes-timony of an informer. If they have only Walker's evidence to go on, or indeed that of any other participator in the deed, the case may break down."

"It's no go," said Jack. "There's others beside Ben o' Buck's ha' leaked. As soon as it wer' known he'd split there wer' a reg'lar scramble to turn informer. Everyone wer' anxious to be i' th' swim. There's Joe Sowden."

"O' th' Yews?" I asked.

Jack nodded. "Th' same felly."

"Why what could he say?"

"Th' story is that th' day after th' job wer' done, George went into th' croppin' shop, an' him an' Thorpe towd Sowden all about it."

"What, that they had shot Mr. Horsfall?" exclaimed my father, in a voice of horror.

"Nowt else. An' they made Sowden tak' a oath to keep th' secret an' sweer all th' others to keep th' secret. Everyone i' th' shop wer' sworn. There weren't a soul i' all John Wood's that weren't sworn. And folk say George held a pistol at Sowden's head while he read th' oath off a bit o' papper an' made 'em all kiss th' book."

We stared at each other blankly.

"But is this known to the Crown?" asked Mr. Webster at length.

"Sowden's takin' his tea at this minnit i' Chester Castle, livin' o' th' fat o' th' land, a guest o' th' king, feastin' like a fightin' cock, an' yo'll nivver set eyes on him agen till yo see him i' th' witness–box at York 'sizes," said Jack. "An' there's more to tell. They say George borrowed a Russian pistol fra William Hall."

"Well, I'll vouch for Hall, ony road, for all awm worth," I burst out. "He'll noan turn traitor. He wer' allus th' keenest o' th' lot on us."

"Tha'd lose thi brass," said Jack quietly. "Hall's sat just nah opposite Sowden, like as not drinkin' success to honesty. He lent his pistol to George the very day Horsfall wer' shot, an' seed him load it with ball an' slugs."

"Why Hall lodged at Wood's an' slept wi' George, i' th' same room if not i' th' same bed," I murmured.

"Skin for shin, yea all that a man hath will he give for his fife,' so says the Book." Thus Mr. Webster.

"And after Horsfall wer' shot, choose who shot him," Jack went on. "George Mellor an' Thorpe went to Joe Mellor's at Dungeon Wood an' hid two pistols, an' one on 'em, they do say, is th' self–same pistol 'at Hall lent to George afore th' job wer' done."

I do not know whether any of us till then, clung to a hope that George might be cleared of any share in the murder. For my own part I had known from the first minute I set eyes on George when he came to me at Holme the day after the deed, known without a word spoken, that he was guilty. All the same the law's the law, and it was none of my business to tell what I thought. Thinking's not evidence, and if there was a loop–hole for him anywhere I'd widen it for him rather than stop it.

"All the evidence points one way," said Mr. Webster despondently.

"Oh, no! it doesn't, beggin' yo'r pardon for contradictin' yo'," said Jack. "There's plenty think George 'll scrape through."

"As how?" I asked.

"Why on th' halibey. Mr. Blackburn 'll have summat to go on. Yo' know John Womersley, th' watch maker' i' Cloth Hall Street?"

"Aye, aye."

"Well he says he wer' talkin' wi' George just after six bi th' clock opposite th' Cloth Hall, an' had a glass wi' him at th' White Hart."

"Well?"

"Why it wer' just on six when Mr. Horsfall wer' shot on Crosland Moor, an' if George were i' th' White Hart at hauf past six, it stan's to reason he couldn't be shootin' folk on th' moor at six."

"Womersley's a decent man, and his word will have weight," said my father with relief in his tone. "Perhaps we've been misjudgin' the lad after all."

"Let's hope so," said Soldier. "An' like enough others 'll turn up 'at can give similar evidence. But it's a tickle job is a halibey, best o' times."

And so our council ended, Jack engaging to search high and low for any scrap of testimony that might help the prisoners.

The month within which Mary must give her answer to Walker's mother stole on. I scarce could trust myself to look on Mary so sad and wan was she. But one morning towards the middle of December after she had sided the breakfast things she donned her Sunday clothes, a thing rarely done on week–days in our house, except for visits of more than common ceremony, or for weddings and parties.

"I'm going to Huddersfe'lt and mebbe a step beyond," she told my mother.

"To see thi Aunt Matty?"

"I'st happen see her."

My heart quaked.

"Yo'r never goin' to Walker's?" I asked when I could speak to her alone.

"Trust me for that," she said. "I'd rather walk a good few miles another way."

"Then where'st ta goin'?" I persisted, "an' winnot yo' tak' Faith? Th' walk 'll happen do her good if she wraps well up."

"Faith mun see to th' mixin' o' th' Kersmas cake. Awn towd her how to mix th' dough, an' aw'll hope 'oo'll mak' a better job on it nor 'oo did o' th' parkin o' Bunfire Day; but it's never too late to larn, an' awm thinkin' it won't be long afore she'll need to know summat more nor to play on th' spinnet an' to sing hymns an' love ditties. They'll boil no man's kettle."

But of her errand to Huddersfield I could get no inkling, and off she set in the forenoon through the snow with warm hood over her head and thick Paisley shawl and mittens, and pattens to her feet, as sweet a picture as ever went down that hill before or since.

It was night, eight o'clock, when she came home, and many a time I'd gone into the lane and strained my eyes across the valley to watch the road from Kitchen Fold. The snow was falling thick, and when Mary entered her shawl was covered with the flakes and little feathery sprays were on the curls that twined and twisted from beneath the hood. Her cheeks that had grown so pale were a rosy flush with the keen frosty air, her eyes were bright and glad and there was the first smile upon her lips had played there for many a doleful day. She shook her shawl at the house door, whilst Vixen yapped and gambolled about her and Faith made haste to remove her pattens and knock the clogged snow from the irons while Mary smoothed her hair before the little glass by the window.

"An' how's thi Aunt Matty?" asked my mother; "an dun yo' want owt to eit? Yo'll be ready for yo'r porridge aw sud judge. Is 'oo bearin' up pretty well, an' did ta see John Wood, an' is he lookin' as ill favored as ivver?"

"Let th' lass get her breath," pleaded my father.

"Has ta met a fairy?" went on my mother. "For a month an' more tha's been mopin' an' turnin' thi nose up at good victuals an' comin' dalin o' a mornin' lookin' as if thi bed wer' made o' nettles i'stead o' honest feathers, as well aw know 'at plucked 'em, an' nivver a word nor a look for anyb'dy, an' wouldn't see th' doctor nor tak' th' herb–tea aw brewed thee, an' me thinkin' all th' time it wer' a tiff atween thee an' Ben, an' him lookin' waur nor a whipped cur, which it's to be hoped yo'll both learn more sense when yo'r well wed, for it'll be as th' man said 'Bear an' forbear' then or yo'll ha' a sorry time on it; an' now yo' set off wi'out a wi' yo'r leave or by yo'r leave an' come back fra goodness knows where lookin' as if yo'd been proved next o' kin to a fortin', which it's enough to make anyone think it wor all make believe, tho' me that anxious as aw sud be fit to shake yo' if so aw thowt."

My mother paused to get breath.

"I've summat to make me look cheerful," said Mary. "Yo' little know wheer I'n been this afternoon, an' who I've talked to and had a cup o' tea into th' bargain. Aw don't feel it's real yet. Nip me, Faith, to let me know if I'm dreamin'!"

"It's a dream we should like to share in," said Faith in her quiet way, taking my mother's hard, thin hand, much worn by work, and soothing it caressingly, a way she had that always ended by bringing a reposeful look upon that eager ner-vous face and made my mother declare Faith was as good as hops in your pillow for restfulness.

"Well aw suppose I'st ha' to begin at th' beginnin'," said Mary, settling herself for a long talk and smiling into the fire. My father filled another pipe, and my mother let her ball of wool roll upon the floor so as to have a long reach of work before her.

"Yo' maybe hannot guessed at Ben Walker wanted me to wed him."

"What Ben o' Buck's o' th' Brigg? Him as turned informer?" asked my father, letting his pipe out in his amaze.

Mary nodded.

"That comes o' thi flighty ways," commented my mother with severity. "If a lass dunnot keep hersen to hersen, but will ha' a nod for this an' a smile for that an' a joke for t' other, she may know what to expec'. There wor a differ between decent gells an' hussies when aw wer' young, but if there's ony now it's all i' favour o' th' hussies."

Mary flushed angrily.

"Nay, nay, Charlotte, yo' dunnot mean that for yar Mary, aw know," said my father. "Go on wi' thi tale, lass. Thi aunt's put out a bit, these days."

"Well he did," continued Mary, "and of course aw'd his answer ready for him."

"Aw shud think so indeed. It was well for him aw didn't catch 'im at it. What did ta say, Mary?"

"Nay, aunt, yo' wouldn't ha' me cumber mi mind wi' such trash. Any road aw sent 'im packin'. Then, about a three week sin', his owd mother sent for me."

"Did 'oo send a broom for thee to ride on, th' owd witch," put in the tireless tongue, more by way of expressing an opinion of Ben Walker's mother than a question.

"And aw went," said Mary.

"More fool yo'."

"And 'oo said 'oo'd heard aw'd ta'en up wi' Ben here an' axed me if it wer' true."

"An' of course tha'd thi answer to that too," said my mother triumphantly.

"Well, yes," admitted Mary.

"So that put a spoke i' that wheel," said my father, knocking his pipe head on the fire–grate bar.

"Not a bit on it," quoth Mary. "On th' contrary she seemed rayther glad to hear it. But 'oo said he'd noan ha' to ha' me."

"Who, ya'r Ben?"

"Aye, yo'r Ben."

"Who's to stop him?"

"Mrs. Walker o' th' Brigg, by yo'r good leave, aunt. She said 'oo'd gie me a month to think on it, an' if aw didn't gi'e mi word to ha' their Ben, she'd just speak a word to th' Government ovver that Rawfolds job as 'ud send Ben here to keep George Mellor company."

The knitting fell from my mother's hand, the pipe from my father's They stared at Mary and at me.

"So that's what's ailed yo' this three week back. Herb–tea might well be wasted on yo',", at length my mother managed to gasp.

"That wer' just th' complaint we were suffering fra, wern't it, Ben?"

"An' beyond any physic aw ever heard on," I said. "But tha seems to ha' fun a cure."

"But you won't have him," said Faith eagerly. "Oh! the wretched plotter. Say you refused, Mary?"

"A varmint not fit to be touched wi' a pair o' tongs," remarked my mother.

"But to save Ben here?" asked Mary, maliciously.

And my parents looked at each other. It was a dilemma's horns.

"Don't look worried, ma'am," said Faith. "Mary's only plaguing us. She has found a way out, it's plain to see. She wouldn't look as she does if she hadn't."

"Then till beseems her to be fleyin' her elders out o' their wits an' mi heart goin' pit–a–pat that fast at aw may be took any minnit," said my mother.

"Awm sorry, aunt," said Mary, quickly crossing the hearth and putting her arms round my mother's neck and kissing her brow. "Aw shouldn't ha' done it if aw'd thowt; but awm so happy awm hardly misen. Theer, aw'll tell mi tale."

"Well, then, yo' may be sure after aw heerd owd Mother Walker's threat aw wer' bothered aboon a bit. Aw wer' noan for weddin' her lad, even if he hadn't turned informer, but what use 'ud Ben here be to me hangin' i' irons off York gibbet. Aw could na see a road aat, look choose which way aw would. Well yesterday aw heerd uncle here say my lord an' lady Dartmouth wer' at Woodsome."

My father gave a corroboratory nod.

"So aw thowt it ovver all neet, an' to make a long story short awn been to Woodsome this very day."

"An' seen my lord?" cried my father.

"Aye, an' mi lady, too. When aw gate to th' big door lookin' on to th' lawn— an' yo' should ha' seen th' deer down th' big avenue made o' trees like th' pillars o' a cathedral aisle—when aw gate to th' door aw gav' a knock at th' big knocker, an' it made such a clatter aw could ha' fun it i' my heart to run, but aw thowt aw'd come so far aw'd see it through. A felly oppened th' door. A reg'lar nobob. 'It's mi lord hissen,' aw thowt. He'd a powdered wig, an' epaulettes, an' a brown plush coat wi' big buttons wi' figurin' on, an' a scarlet weskit, an' plush shorts an' silk stockin's an' oh! such an air o' haughty pride. He pulled hissen up when he seed me. 'Yo' sud ha' gone to th' tradesmen's entrance,' he says. 'Aw want to see his lordship,' aw says as loud as aw could, but aw could scarce hear my own voice, an' aw dropped a courtesy, 'an' a reckon yo' mun be him, tho' aw didn't reckon to see so big a man, for Mr. Scott told me ye' wer' nowt much to look at.' And then aw heerd a loud laugh, an' i' th' gloom o' th' big hall aw spied a littlish man very plain dressed. 'Admit: the lady,' he said. And aw wer' shown into a room on th' reight hand, an' th' little man came in an' made me sit dahn, but not afore he'd helped me off wi' mi shawl, which wer' wet wi' snow, an' made that stuck up jackanapes tak' it to be dried. 'An ask her leddyship to spare me a minnit,' sez he. Then there came in a young leddy, just such another as thee, Faith, an' so pleasant i' th' face. An 'oo smiled at me, an' wouldn't hear a word till aw'd warmed misen by th' fire, an' 'oo made me drink a glass o' wine."

"Did yo' tell her who's lass tha wer'?" asked my father. "But he'd noan know me. Th' owd lord 'ud ha' known me. But this 'un's nobbud been th' earl a year or two, an awn nobbud seen him once or twice."

"Well, anyway he didn't say he didn't," said Mary diplomatically. "And then," continued Mary, "aw up an' tell'd them all about it, about Ben o' Buck's pesterin' me an' about Long Tom an' about Ben's arm an' about thee, aunt, bein' confined to thi bed an' havin' th' doctor to thee an' all time ailin' nowt...."

"Aye, an' what did they say to that?"

"Well, th' little lord laughed like a good 'un, an' said th' doctor 'ud ha' to be sent to th' 'sizes for bein' a summat after the fact, not a necessary, what wor it? — oh! an accessory. But aw seed he wer' jokin! Then aw began to tell about Ben Walker's mother, an' her ladyship told th' little Earl he'd better go out o' th' room, an' when he'd gone aw just down o' mi knees i' front on her, an' 'oo drew mi face to her an' aw had a good cry, an' 'oo drew mi face everything just as yo know it."

"Well, an' then?"

"Why she looked very grave and said it wer' a serious business an' a very delicate matter for his lordship to meddle in. She told me summat aw didn't quite mak' out about their party not bein' in just now."

"Of course not," said my father. "Aw could ha' told yo' that."

"But any way,' says she, 'my uncle's in the ministry and good friends with th' Secretary of State. So cheer up, Mary; th' men may manage th' State; but we know who manages th' men, an' my name's not Fanny Legge if yo'r lover shan't go free.'"

"Did she say Fanny?" said my mother.

"She did," replied Mary, "just plain Fan an' never a countess to it, and what's more she gave me this locket wi' her picture in it, an' told me to wear it o' mi weddin' day, an' wear it aw shall an' will, an' mebbe those 'at come after me." And Mary drew from her bosom the portrait you, my children, know so well of that young countess who so untimely died.

"Aw think that settles it," said my father, smiting his thigh.

"Of course it does," said my mother. "An' aw hope, William Bamforth, 'at after this yo'll vote blue an' side wi' th' quality. T'other lot's good enuff for shoutin', but gi' me th' owd fam'lies when it comes to th' stick an' lift."

And this profound political aphorism may close a chapter too long drawn out.

CHAPTER XIII.

I NEVER in my life passed so gloomy a Christmas as that of 1812. We killed a goose as usual, and there was the usual seasoned pudding and plum pudding, and Faith and Mary made a bit of a show with the holly and the mistletoe. But it was no use. We couldn't brighten up our hearts nor take our thoughts from the Special Commission which was to sit at York in the fore–end of January to try the Luds. Even our neighbours felt we could be in no mood for rejoicing, and neither the Church singers nor the Powle Moor lot came near us, and as for wishing each other a merry Christmas the farce would have been too ghastly.

It was arranged that my father, Mr. Webster and I should go to York for the trial, and at the last moment Faith pleaded for leave to accompany us. I wanted Mary to go too, but she was very decided in her refusal. She wasn't going to leave her aunt alone these long wintry nights, she said, tho' I don't think that was the real reason, for was there not Martha? I wonder if women ever give the real reasons for their actions. Why should Faith make a point of going, I asked myself, and Mary demand to be left at home. On the first point Mary herself enlightened me, being more ready to speak of Faith's actions than her own.

"It's plain enough why she wants to show George a kindness now," said Mary.

"Aye?"

"Can't ta see her heart's reproaching itself? She were more nor hauf i' love wi' George, an' no doubt thowt she could never fancy another."

"Well?"

"An' if there's one thing more nor another a woman sets store by, it's her own constancy."

"Indeed!"

"Yes, and indeed. And now Faith feels herself slipping, an' she's going to try to make it up to George for a treachery he'll never know of by sitting through the trial. It's noan so much to please him as to satisfy hersen."

Anyhow it was my father and Faith and Mr. Webster and myself that the Cornwallis took up at ten of the clock one morning in January at the sign of the Rose and Crown in Huddersfield. We might have joined it in Slaithwaite on its way through the village from Manchester, but we wanted to have as little talk and stir as possible. Mr. Blackburn's clerk had got us decent lodgings near the Castle with a widow woman who made a living by letting her rooms to witnesses attending the Assizes, and whose whole talk was of the counsellors she had heard plead.

She was pleased to express her satisfaction when she learned we had secured Mr. Brougham to defend George.

"Is he so clever a lawyer then?" asked Mr. Webster as we rested in the parlour after our long, cold, tedious journey, and warmed ourselves as well as we could before a fire on which it seemed to me the coals were put on with the sugar tongs.

"Well," said Mrs. Cooke, for that was the garrulous old lady's name, "Of course he is a clever lawyer, tho' they do say not so far learned nor so deep as some we've known in York in my time, but it isn't that will help you in a case like this."

"I do not take you, madam," observed Mr. Webster.

"You see Mr. Brougham has a great name in the city with the Whigs, and if yo' can get a sprinkling of them gentry on the jury it will go a great way in the poor young man's favour."

"All we ask is an upright and an intelligent jury," said Mr. Webster.

"That's all very well for you, sir, that's safe and sound by a good fire and a clean soft bed before you. But from what I've read, sir, that young friend of yours will do better with a jury that will lean a bit; and trust Mr. Brougham for making the most of his chances with the jury."

"Will he be allowed to speak to them?" I asked.

"Dear me, no," said the lady, proud to air her knowledge of the law. "And a mercy it is it is so, for if such a counsellor as Mr. Brougham could talk to the jury for a prisoner, half the rogues now hanged would be walking the county. But there's ways an' means sides talking, a shrug, a question to a witness, a meaning look at the gentlemen in the box, and above all a quarrel with my lord."

"What! quarrel with the judge?" exclaimed my father. "Surely that would be fatal."

"Not a bit of it," explained our landlady. "It's the safest card of all to play. You see the judge is sure to be against the prisoner."

"Nay, my good lady, surely nay," remonstrated Mr. Webster. "'Ye shall do not unrighteousness in judgment: thou shalt not respect the person of the poor, nor honour the person of the mighty: but in righteousness shalt thou judge thy neighbour.'"

"Ah! that's in the Bible, I take it," said Mrs. Cooke; "but the Bible's one thing and York Assizes is another, and so you'll find, unless I'm very much mistaken. The Government will take care to send judges that mean hanging, and that's so well known that it sets the back of the jury up a bit, particler if a touch of politics can be dragged into the case. That's Mr. Brougham's chance, and if he can make the jury think the judge is pressing things too hard against your man, I won't say but he may have a chance. But it isn't much to cling to after all, poor lad."

The night before the trial, which was fixed for Wednesday the sixth of January, Mr. Blackburn was to see George in the Castle cell. By much insistence he prevailed on the Governor to permit Mr. Webster to accompany him, a great favour, and one, we understood, little to the liking of the prison chaplain. When the little man returned to our mean lodgings, he was pale and downcast and sat for a long time silent, bending over the sullen fire.

"God preserve me from such a scene again," at length he said. "To think that one whose face I have seen upturned to mine in my own chapel should now be prisoned in yonder noisome cell. Oh! my friends, 'surely the ways of transgressor are hard.'"

"If it were not to distress yo' too much we should like to hear all from the beginning," said my father.

"Well, when we got to the gate of the gaol," said Mr. Webster, "Mr. Blackburn rang the bell. A jailor opened it after such unlocking and unbarring as you never heard."

'To see a prisoner,' said Mr. Blackburn.

'An attorney, sir? Your name?'

'Mr. Blackburn, of Huddersfield. For George Mellor and others to be tried to–morrow.'

'And your friend?'

'Mr. Webster, a good minister of the gospel.'

'He cannot enter, sir, unless by special order of the governor.'

'It is here.'

'Then enter and follow me. Write your name and address in this book.'

"He was a big, burly man, and treated Mr. Blackburn with great respect; but he looked hard at me from under his bushy eyebrows, till I bethought me to slip a crown piece into his hand, when he became more civil. He had a bunch of great keys by his side, and they jingled as he walked. We followed him across a court-yard, where there was more unlocking of gates and doors, and at length we were in a stone–flagged corridor with whitewashed walls, and on either side of these the cells. There was a little spy–hole in the door of every cell, through which, I judged, the warders might watch the wretches chained within. Before one door the warder stopped."

'This is your man, sir,' he said, and selecting a key turned the lock and threw open the door. 'I'll stand outside, sir.'

"Mr. Blackburn nodded and entered the cell, I at his heels, much daunted by the cold and the gloom. It was a little while ere my eyes got used to the darkness, but as we entered I heard the clank of irons, and was aware of some form in the gloom rising in the corner from under the grated window. It was George; but oh! how altered! he was gaunt and thin, and his eyes that I have known so bright and lit by the joy of life, were dull and fixed in sick despair. I forgot the crime of which he stands charged and saw only a brother, nay, a son, suffering in mortal agony, and all my heart bled for him."

"Poor George! Poor Matty," murmured my father, passing the back of his hand over his face, and Faith's eyes were fixed with pained intentness on the preacher's face, her lips pale and parted as she held her breath and waited on his every word.

"'Mr. Webster!' he cried, for he could see better than I, being used doubtless to the little light. 'Mr. Webster, oh! this is good of you!' and he seemed to take no heed of Mr. Blackburn, and as well as he could for the irons that cribbed his arms, he stretched out his hands to me, oh! so wildly and so lovingly, and I took both his hands in mine and must have done tho' I had seen the deed with my own eyes. And George bowed his head, and tears fell upon our clasped hands that were not wholly his nor wholly mine, and I drew down his head and kissed him on the brow."

"The good Lord bless yo'," sobbed Faith.

"And Mr. Blackburn stood a little way off fumbling with his papers and taking snuff very rapidly and in great quantities."

'Have yo' seen mi mother lately?' asked George; 'does she bear up? Is she here in York?' "His first thoughts were of her, poor lad."

"Yo' munnot forget to tell her that, Faith," said my father, and Faith nodded, and I know she did not forget, and it comforted my Aunt Matty in the after days.

"I told him only you and Ben were here," continued Mr. Webster. "'Not Mary?' he asked, and I told him no. 'Better not, happen better not,' he said at last; but he seemed disappointed that Mary should not be here, I know not why."

"Did he ask for me?" said Faith, very softly.

"Nay," said Mr. Webster. "He did not ask for thee; but I told him yo' wer' here and would not be denied."

"And what said he?"

'Faith! Faith Booth? Ah! poor John's sister. 'Oo'd over a tender heart, an' I loved her brother next to Ben.'

"Yes, he loved my brother," said Faith, "but not as John loved him." And after that she was very silent; only once I heard her murmur to herself, "Yes, he loved mi brother."

"Well then," said Mr. Webster, "for a while Lawyer Blackburn talked with George in a low voice so's the warder at the door might not hear what passed, and I tried to compose my thoughts, so that I might, if time and opportunity favoured, say some word that he might take to his heart to solace him withal. And when Mr. Blackburn began to tie up his papers and bid him bear himself like a man, on the morrow, and hope for the best, I asked George it he would pray with me. He did not refuse; but sat upon a little block that served for his seat, and I fell upon my knees and the lights streamed upon my face from between the bars. Mr. Blackburn turned his back and affected to busy himself with his bag, and the warder jingled his keys, impatient to be gone. And then I prayed the good God and Father to send peace and comfort to our dear brother, that. He might be pleased that this great sorrow should pass and this black cloud be lifted; but throwing all upon the mercy and compassion of the Heart that feels for all, for all, even for the outcast and the sinful. For the love of that Heart passeth the love of man and of woman, else woe and still woe, aye even for the chosen ones of Israel."

And Mr. Webster's voice broke into a sob, and he bowed his head upon his breast and would say no more, and more we did not seek to know.

In the evening I strolled into the city, walking round that great Cathedral of the North, and marvelled at the piety that had raised so splendid a temple to the glory of God. Then my steps turned towards the Castle, and I gazed from afar at the gloomy keep, and wondered behind which of the barred windows so high and narrow, lay my helpless cousin, tossing, I doubted not, upon a sleepless pallet, his mind wracked with thoughts of the morrow and his pillow, perchance, haunted by the image of him whose blood, I could not but think, was upon his rash and impious hand. I wandered by the narrow streets that approach the Castle, streets abandoned to squalor and to vice, my feet turned ever toward that monster dungeon, drawn by I know not what silent fascination. But as I walked as in a dream, I was brought to a stand by a gruff voice:

"Halt or I fire!"

And peering into the dark, scarce lightened by the oil–lamps that swayed in the streets, I saw that a company of soldiers was drawn across the street, and a sergeant in command held his musket at my breast.

"Have you business at the Castle and a pass?" he asked, and on my answering him nay he bid me begone. I turned sadly away, and when by chance I tried another street that led Castle–wards my fate was the same. So I turned my back upon the gloomy fortress and wended my way back to our lodgings. The city was filled with troops, and every avenue to the Castle strongly guarded; for a rescue was feared. Had they known the Luds as well as I they might have spared their pains.

The morning of the trial came, dark and threatening, with snow that wrapped the city as in a winding sheet, which befitted well a day so pregnant with all ill. We were at the Castle gates betimes, and yet the entrance to the Court was besieged with those like ourselves furnished with a permit to view the trial. My inches stood me in good stead, and by dint of good play with my elbows, I made way through the crowd for those that companied me. It seemed to me that all the ways that led to the Court were held by troops, and men stood to their arms on the very steps and to the great doors of the Hall of Justice. Faith hung trembling upon my arm, but craned her neck nevertheless to see the gallant show when the judges drew up, clad in crimson robes, with the sheriff and his chaplain by their sides, the heralds blaring their trumpets and the soldiers grounding their arms to make the pavement ring.

We made our way into the little Court and gazed upon the arms of England fixed high above the judgment seat, and when we saw the wigged gentlemen below the Bench rise to their feet we rose too, and when they bowed we bowed too, but the judges, tho' they bent their heads to the gentlemen of the long robe, took scant enough notice of our reverences, which methinks was neither in keeping with the civility that man owes to man nor yet in accord with our constitution: for if the judges draw their dignity from the Crown, whence, I ask, does the Crown derive its title and its lustre? But alas! the people of this country, even yet, are little conscious of their own strength and of what is due to the commons even from their princes and governors.

"Which is Mr. Brougham?" I asked my father, who I knew had heard him speak at a great meeting of the Whig voters.

"Him that Mr. Blackburn's speaking to," answered my father, and I followed his eyes to the attorney's well and saw a little man, sallow and clean shaven, with a long lean face, something like a monkey's with its skin turned, to parchment.

"What him?" I whispered in amaze.

"Aye, that's him sure enough."

"What! the great Brougham, our Brougham?"

"Yes, yes," said my father testily. "He's not much to look at; but yo' should hear him talk."

But soon there was a hush in Court. The prisoners were being brought into the dock, and the Cryer was calling his quaint "Oyez."

George Mellor, William Thorpe and William Smith stood there, heavily ironed and guarded by armed warders, confronting the judges and the jury, arraigned for that they did feloniously, wilfully, and of their malice aforethought kill and murder William Horsfall, against the peace of our lord the king, his crown and dignity. The jurors were sworn, the challenges allowed, the indictment read by the Clerk of Arraigns, and the prisoners given in charge to the jury, the clerk gabbling the words as I have heard a curate in a hurry read the lessons in Church. "How say you, George Mellor—guilty or not guilty," and George with a voice that did not falter and a look upon judges and the jury that did not flinch, cried "Not Guilty." I had eyes and ears only for him, neither then nor to the end. Thorpe and Smith might not have been there, for me. I kept my eyes fixed on him throughout, nor missed one single movement of his nervous fingers that clutched the rails of the dock, nor one glance of his eye. Nay, even now, right through the years, I can see the curl of his lips when Benjamin Walker with craven look and uncertain step, his eyes shifting, his voice whining, stumbled into the witness-box. All through, I had eyes, I say, only for George. When Mr. Park, the counsel for the Crown, addressed the jury, I scarce listened; I watched only George's face, and judged rather what was said by the play of his pale features than by ought I gathered from the long speech to the jury. And right through that weary trial, that lasted from nine o'clock of the morning till near the same hour of the night, never was there a moment that George bore himself save as those who loved him would have him. He almost looked at times as tho' he did not hear what passed around him, his eyes being fixed, not upon the judge but beyond him, with a far away gaze as tho' scenes were acting in a theatre none but he could see, and which concerned him more than what passed around. Once when his eyes ranged the faces that thronged the Court, and he saw our little group, a look of recognition passed upon his face, and he smiled faintly, with quivering lips; but presently turned away his head and glanced our way no more. Only when Ben Walker stood in the box did he rouse himself to the full, and he looked the slinking wretch straight in the face with curling lip: and Walker blanched and tottered and half raised his hand as tho' to ward off a blow. My God! rather would I raise my naked face to meet ten thousand blows from an iron hand than meet such a look as George cast upon that perjured miscreant. A low hiss went through the Court, a sibilation of hatred and contempt; and even the counsellor that examined the man did not conceal his loathing. We looked for Mr. Brougham to cross–examine Walker, but that was done by Mr. Hullock, whether that Mr. Hullock was the senior counsel and took this part as of right, or that, as some had it afterwards, Mr. Brougham knew from the first that the case was hopeless and did not care to be prominent, where defeat was certain. Tho' this surely must be of malice. But it mattered not: the end was certain even before Mr. Justice le Blanc summed up, and in a few words, not without their truth even we felt, brushed away the flimsy edifice of an alibi that had cost Soldier Jack so much scheming and ferreting out of witnesses. "Even supposing the witnesses to come under no improper bias or influence in what they are saying, they are speaking," commented the judge, "of a transaction which not only took place a long time ago, but was not imputed to the prisoners at the bar till a considerable time after it had taken place, and nothing happened immediately after the transaction to lead persons who have spoken as to the prisoners' movements at the time of the murder, particularly to watch, so as to be accurate in the hour or time on that particular evening, when they saw these persons at a particular place, and we know how apt persons are to be mistaken, even when care is taken, in point of time."

That was all we got from judge or counsel for our money, my Aunt Matty's hundred pounds, and many a good guinea to that which my father paid Mr. Blackburn, and I question whether it was worth the brass. But I would not have had George undefended for all that, even if it were all to do over again; for to have him spoken for was the only way now left us to show our care for him.

I never saw sentence of death passed but that once, and it will do me my life–time. "That you, the three prisoners at the bar, be taken from hence to the place from whence you came, and from thence, on Friday next, to the place of execution; that you be there severally hanged by the neck until you are dead; and your bodies afterwards delivered to the surgeons to be dissected and anatomized, according to the directions of the statute. And may God have mercy on your souls."

"Amen!" said many a hushed and awe struck voice, and I heard a moan and a hasty cry from Mr. Webster. A piercing shriek rent the stillness, and Faith fell fainting into my arms.

But one day intervened between the trial of Mellor, Thorpe and Smith and their execution. Mr. Webster was allowed to see the three condemned men the night before the Friday on which they were to make their piteous end. He shrank from that last interview in the cells with the sensitiveness of a woman; but he had a great soul in a little body and nerved himself to the painful ordeal. He told us something of what passed. Thorpe was stolid as ever, and simply asked to be let alone, and not pestered with questions. George declared that he would rather be in the situation he was then placed, dreadful as it was, than have, to answer for the crime of his accuser; and that he would not change situations with him, even for his liberty and two thousand pounds.

"Well said," cried my father, when Mr. Webster, with many a sigh, brought his tale to an end: "well said, there spoke our George. There spoke the lad we used to be proud on, and he's in the right on it, and so folk will say for all time to come."

"I urged him to forgive his enemies and to leave this sinful world in charity with all mankind."

"An' what said he to that?"

"He said he'd nought to forgive to anybody but Ben Walker."

"Well, and him?"

"I urged him to forgive even Walker. 'Vengeance is mine: I will repay, saith the Lord.'"

"Well, did he?"

"Nay, I found him obdurate on this point, though I pressed him hard. He reiterated that before he forgave Walker he'd like to give him something to forgive too. I could not but tell him he was entering the presence of his Maker in a most unchristian frame of mind."

"Are yo' clear, Mr. Webster," asked my father, "that religion calls on George to forgive Ben Walker?"

"There can be no question of it," was the answer. "Do we not pray 'Forgive us our trespasses as we forgive them that trespass against us?'"

My father shook his head pensively. "It may be Scripture, parson, but it isn't Yorkshire. Hast ta never heard that a Yorkshireman can carry a stone in his pocket for seven years, then turn it and after another seven years let throw and hit his mark?"

"It is an evil, an unforgiving, an unchristian frame of mind," quoth the parson.

"That's as may be," replied my father, doggedly. "But what's born in the bone will out in the flesh. For my part I'st uphowd George, an' if he'd said he forgave that spawn o' the devil I should ha' thowt he met be a saint, but he wer' a liar an' a hypocrite for all that. It's agen natur, Mr. Webster, it's agen natur."

Mr. Webster hastened to change the subject. "George sent a message for yo', Ben. He knows how it is between you and Mary and he wishes you all happiness, and asks you to forget and forgive the hasty words he spoke when last you parted. He said you would know what he meant."

"God bless him, sir, I had forgiven them long ago."

"And if it will not go too hard against the grain he wants you to be at the execution and to stand where his eye can fall upon you. He says he should like his last thoughts to be of Holme and the dear ones there. He seems strangely wrapped up in the old spot even to the exclusion of his own mother."

"Aye," said my father. "George never got over Matty marryin' again. If 'oo'd never wed that John Wood but made a home for her own flesh an' blood this met never ha' happened. But what is to be will be, an' that's good Scripture anyway."

"Foreseen and foreordained even from the beginning," assented Mr. Webster.

Now this request of George was to me of all things most painful. It was common enough in those days for people to witness public executions; and public executions were common enough in all conscience. But I had ever a horror of such ghastly exhibitions. Nay I liked not even the cock–fighting and bull–baiting that were as much our ordinary pastimes in my youth as cricket has come to be the sport of my grand–children. People called me Miss Nancy and mawkish and molly–coddle; but none the less, neither for such sports, if sports they must be called, nor for prize fighting, had I any stomach. But if it could give any help to George to know one was in that vast crowd whose heart bled for him and whose prayers went heavenwards with his soul, I could not but do his will.

And so it befell that Mr. Webster and myself were in the crowd of many thousands that stood before the scaffold. Two troops of cavalry were drawn up in front of the drop. We might be a hundred yards away, and when George, heavily ironed, was led to the verge of the platform to make his last dying speech and confession, there was a great silence on the multitude. Even a party of the gentry, as I suppose they called themselves, that had secured the upper window of a house looking on to the scaffold, and that were drinking and jesting and exchanging coarse ribaldry with the light o' loves in the mob, ceased their unseemly revelries and lent ear to what might be said. But George spoke little. His eye fell on me and on Mr. Webster, whom I lifted from his feet so that George might know that the little parson at Powle was faithful to the last, and hoping that even at the eleventh hour repentance might touch the stubborn and rebellious heart. And who knows but it did, for the last words on earth that George spoke were said with his eyes fixed on Mr. Webster's face, and they were spoken belike to him alone of that great and swaying crowd: "Some of my enemies may be here. If there be, I freely forgive them," and then, after a pause and with an emphasis which we alone perchance of all that concourse understood, "I forgive all the world and hope all the world will forgive me."

"The Lord above be praised!" exclaimed Mr. Webster, as these words fell on his ears, and as the cap was fixed and the noose adjusted, he raised his voice in the well–known hymn, and strange tho' it may seem, yet none the less is it true, thousands of voices took up the words:

> "Behold the Saviour of mankind
> Nailed to the shameful tree!
> How vast the love that Him inclined
> To bleed and die for me!
> Hark how He groans! while nature shakes,
> And earth's strong pillars bend:
> The temple's veil in sunder breaks;
> The solid marbles bend.
> 'Tis done! the precious ransom's paid—
> 'Receive my soul,' He cries;

See where He bows His sacred head!
He bows His head, and dies!
But soon He'll break death's envious chain,
And in full glory shine:
o Lamb of God! was ever pain,
Was ever love like Thine!"

There was a haze before my sight. I did not see the bolt withdrawn; only as through a mist see the quivering, swaying form. A long drawn sigh, that ended in a sob like one deep breath from a thousand hearts, proclaimed the end, and Mr. Webster and I made our way from that tragic scene.

CHAPTER XIV.

AFTER this, life for many months was very grey at Holme. We did not talk much about the grim days we had passed through. They were pleasant neither to talk of nor think on. My father's mind was chiefly exercised about the portentous length of Mr. Blackburn's bill of costs, and upon some of the items he delivered himself at large:

"'Attending you,'" he quoted, "'when you instructed me to see John Quarmby and James Eagland with a view to procuring their proofs for this defence, 6s. 8d.'"

"Think o' that now," he would say, "actually charging me for calling to tell him what to do, to put him up to his work, so to speak. My certy, lawyers may well ma' their brass quick! Aw've a good mind to ha' it taxed."

"What's that?" asked my mother.

"Why, there's a chap i' London 'at's put on by th' Lord Chancellor to go through 'torneys' bills an' see they ha' not charged too much."

"He'll be a lawyer hissen, 'aw reckon?" queried my mother.

"Aye, aye," said my father, 'set a thief to catch a thief,' tha knows."

"Tha'd best pay up, aw doubt na, awn heard folk tell o' fallin' out wi' the devil an' goin' below for justice, an' this taxin' 'll be after th' same fashion. Th' first loss is th' least loss, an' 'what can't be cured mun be endured.' If folk will ha' law they mun pay for their whistle, an' you've had yo'r run for yo'r money."

"Aw could ha' thoiled it better if they'd let Mr. Brougham speik to th' jury. Here's twenty guineas to him, to say nowt o' two guineas for his clerk, that did nowt 'at aw can hear tell but draw th' brass for his mester, an' him never allowed to oppen his mouth to th' jury!!"

"But he's had th' brass ha' not be?" asked the partner of my father's joys and sorrows.

"Aye, he's had it safe enough."

"Well, by all accounts," concluded my mother, "it's ill gettin' butter out o' a dog's throat." And the bill was paid: the only discount my father got being a pinch of snuff from Mr. Blackburn's silver box.

Faith was not with us now, nor did she return till hay–time. She had gone home to her father at the vicarage at Low Moor, but not without a promise to return in the summer. And about that time too, Soldier Jack became slack in his attendance at Powle Moor, tho' abating nothing in his respect for Mr. Webster.

He had been away for the week–end, having said nothing of his intentions, but it turned out he had been to Low Moor to see Faith and her father, and after this Jack began to go, in a rather shame–faced way at first, to Church. I asked him what was the reason of this right–about face.

"Well, yo' see, Ben," he explained, "th' service at th' Church is more reg'lar like an' more constitutional."

"As how?"

"'Well, yo' see, I'm a soldier, an' aw believe i' discipline."

"Yo' broke it often enough, bi all accounts," I ventured to remind him.

"Na, Ben, no back reckonin'! Yo' mun consider that aw wer' young then an' lawless. Aw'n sown mi wild oats nah, an' settled down an' aw begin to see that law an' order's a very guid thing, an' authority mun be respected."

"Well, cannot yo' respect it as much at th' Powle as at th' Church?"

"Now, aw cannot; an' yo' cannot, nother. Yo' see yo're dissenters at th' Powle, an' heresy an' schism an' rebellion against constituted authority are i' th' air, so to speak, on Powle Moor. Yo're all Republicans at' heart up yonder, an' aw'll tell yo', another thing, if there'd been no dissenters there they'd ha' been no Luds, an' George Mellor 'd noan ha' danced out th' world on nowt."

"But Faith Booth were Church an' yet she went to th' Powle while she wer' wi' us, an' had a class there into th' bargain."

"Faith's a woman," said Soldier, "an' women ha' no sense o' principle. She wer' your guest, an' wouldn't pain yo' by going elsewheer. That's what yo' call nat'ral politeness, an' we should be none the worse i' Sloughit for a little more on it. But what we're talkin' on now is a matter o' th' head not a matter o' th' heart, an' i' matters o' th' head a woman's nowt to go by. Yo' shud hear her father, th' owd vicar at Low Moor!"

"Oh! he's yo'r text, is he?"

"He put it i' this way. Th' Church o' Christ is an army—the Church militant, he called it. Th' king, God bless him, is th' head o' th' Church, jus' same as he's th' head o' th' army. Th' Archbishops is commanders–in–chief, th' Bishops is gener-als, the Rectors an' Vicars is colonels an' captains, an' Curates is th' lieutenants."

"And what of corporals and sergeants?" I asked.

"Th' vicar's warden, to be sure," said Jack promptly, "an' just yo' see if aw dunnot live to be vicar's warden afore aw dee o' old age: an' if yo' want to speer further into it, th' Collect an' th' Liturgy is th' Orders o' th' day an' the surplice an' hood's nobbud a uniform. So theer!"

And Jack looked at me triumphantly.

"An' wheer do th' Dissenters come in then?" I asked.

"Well aw reckon you're like these volunteers 'at come up when folk wer' fleyed o' Boney comin'. An' its th' same way i' religion. Folk turn Methodies when they're in a scare about their souls; but for reg'lar defence i' ordinary times, th' Church, as by law established, is enough to ward off th' enemy o' mankind."

"And what does Faith say to all this?" I asked.

"Faith's a very sensible lass, an' wi' a very proper notion o' discipline," replied Jack. "I tried her t'other day wi' th' text 'wives, submit yourselves unto your own husbands as unto the Lord. For the husband is the head of the wife, even as Christ is the head of the Church.'"

"Well?" I asked.

"An' Faith upholds every word of it, an' thinks 'at a woman 'at has a husband 'oo can respect an' look up to, 'll ma' no bones about obeyin' him in all things lawful."

"Well, well," I said, "I've no doubt some strapping young fellow will come along some day, and Faith will have a chance o' squaring preaching wi' precept."

"Aw don't know so much about a strapping young felly," said Jack, curtly. "Yo' young chaps think a wench has no eyes for owt but inches an' spirits. Faith's noan o' that breed. 'Oo thinks a husband owt to be older nor th' wife, so's 'oo can lean on him an' look to him for guidance."

"Aye," I said, "Faith's just turned twenty. Th' man owt to be five–an–twenty."

"Five–an–forty, if a minnit," cried Jack.

And I laughed in his face.

"What, Jack! caught at last! And what about the decent elderly widow 'wi' summat i' th' Bank 'at mi mother's lookin' for'?"

"Ben, quit thi jokin'; it's no jokin' matter, isn't this. Aw tell yo', Ben, if aw can win Faith Booth for mi wife, aw'st go dahn o' mi knees an' thank God wi' all mi heart for th' best gift even God can give—a pure an' good woman. Th' owd Book well says—'A crown unto her husband.' An' aw'm not wi'out my hope, Ben. But aw'm fleyed on her, man; aw'm fleyed on her."

"What! a soldier fleyed on a woman, Jack?"

"Aye, Ben, aw'm fleyed on her! Sometime's when 'oo's sat quiet by th' hearth, there's a look comes on to her face, that aw shouldn't be surprised any minnit if th' ceiling oppened up, an' 'oo just floated away to Heaven. An' yo' nivver see her in a temper, like other women, th' best on 'em; an' yo' nivver hear a cross word fra her, nor hear her gigglin' an' laughin' like other lasses—peas in a drum, th' cracklin' o' thorns under a pot, that's what they mind me on. She's just too good to live, is Faith, an' aw'm not worthy 'to touch the hem of her garment,' an' that's a fact."

And Jack made off with an agitated limp; but from such like talk and a hint or two that Mary let fall, my mother ceased her quest for the prudent elderly widow, tho' not without giving a very uncompromising opinion that there was no fool like an old fool.

"Tho'," she added, "if it wer' to be a young 'un, it couldn't ha' been a better nor Faith, an' that aw will say; but as for wives being obedient to their husbands"—for

I had taken, occasion to enlighten her as to Jack's views on the blessed estate — "it's well known St. Paul, good man, was a bachelor, an' bachelors' wives is same as owd maids' childer, like nowt in heaven above, nor the earth beneath — nor in the water under the earth," she added, to complete the text.

It was about this time that Mary had an unexpected visitor. It would be in July, as near as I can remember. I was piking in the barn, and there being a good yield that year, it needed all my height and a long pike to reach to the top of the hay bowk when it neared the roof. Mary and Faith were raking in the field, and Martha had been with the last bottle of home–brewed for the hay–makers.

We had always three or four Irishmen that came regularly year after year to earn their rent at the English harvesting. One of them, Micky, taught me to count up to twenty in Irish, so that I may claim to know a little of foreign languages, and if they are all like Irish, I pity the man that has to learn more of them. I had gone to the barn door, looking placidly across the field where Bob stood in the traces yoked to the hurdle on which we dragged the sweet new hay to the mistal; the sun was westering, and the grateful breezes fanned me with cool and gentle touch. The girls in the field had thrown off the large straw hats they wore in the noon heat, their tresses had escaped their coils, and they moved but slowly with the rakes, following the wake of the hurdle, for we had had a long and hard day, and all were fain our work was nigh done, and the hay, thank God, well won. My mother had gone into the house, for she had long ceased to take any part in the hay–making, and I made no question she was getting ready the baggin'. I saw her come to the house door, and heard her shout:

"Mary! Ben! come hither; aw want yo;" and she waved her arms to motion us in.

"Throw yo'r rakes dahn, an' come naa," came another cry, and there was that in my mother's voice which told us this was no ordinary summons to a meal.

Mary and I made for the house hot–foot. My mother met us at the door.

"There's Ben Walker i' th' parlour an' his mother," she said; "an they've come to talk to thee, Mary — aw thowt Ben had better come as weel."

"Aw winnot see 'em," said Mary.

"That's right," I said. "Tell 'em to tak' their hook, mother. They're none wanted here."

"Tell 'em thissen, Ben. It's more o' yo'r business nor mine, an' more or Mary's nor yo'rs. Both on yo' see 'em's my advice, an' if yo' think they'll eit yo', I'll stand by to see fair play."

"Aw'm none fit to be seen. Wait till aw tidy misen up a bit," said Mary, fastening her dress at the neck and prisoning some stray tresses of her hair.

"Yo're good enough for the likes o' them," said my mother, "an' aw'm none goin' to have 'em sittin' on th' best furniture i' th' house longer nor aw can help. They'll noan do it ony good. Let's in, an' ha' it ovver, an' dunnot pick yo'r words, either, wi' that lot: aw shannot, yo' may depend."

You never did see in your life such a beau as Ben Walker that day. His mother was fine dressed, with a big gold brooch and a gold chain round her neck and reaching like a rope down to her waist, and all the colours of the rainbow in the silks she wore. But Ben! you should have seen him! It was a sight for sore eyes. They called his father "Buck," but him I never saw in the days of his glory. But if he could out–buck Ben he was a Buck indeed. Why, his vest was a flower garden in miniature, and if he'd dipped his head in the treacle pot it couldn't have been stickier. Somebody must have crammed him that the tailor makes the man: but Lord! a tailor from heaven, if there are such there, couldn't have made a man of Ben Walker. Neither could ale nor strong waters. He had evidently been trying for a bit back to import courage from Holland, for his face was patchy and mezzled and his eye was filmy and his body jerky. We had heard that he was making the money fly down at th' Brigg, tho' it was not easy to get anyone to drink with him. However, here he was, and it was not difficult to guess his errand.

My mother eyed the pair of them with a look of fine disdain and offered them neither a hand nor a chair.

"Well, what's your business here," she said, "onybody 'at knew owt 'ud know this is none a time for visitin', th' hay out an' th' glass goin' down wi' a run, 'at awst be' capped if it doesn't knock th' bottom out, one o' these days."

"Aye, the weather's very tryin' indeed for th' poor farmers," said Mrs. Walker, "an' for them 'at has to depend for their livins on a few pounds worth o' hay. But yo' see gentlefolk needn't bother their yeds abaat sich things. Wet or fine doesn't matter so much to them. When it's too wet for walkin' they can ride."

"Aye," put in my mother, "we all know weel enough where a beggar rides to, if yo' put him on horse–back. But what's yo'r business, aw say?"

"Can't yo' speik, Ben?" said Mrs. Walker, "what's ta stand theer for, like a moonstruck cauf?"

"Aw wud like to speak wi' Mary here," said Ben.

"Well, it's a free country," said Mary, "an' there's no law agen speakin'."

"By thissen, aw mean."

"Well, tha cannot, that's all. If tha's owt to say to me, tha mun say it afore Ben Bamforth."

"Ben Bamforth, indeed!" said Mrs. Walker. "Mind yo'r manners, lass, or it'll be worse for yo', an' speik more respectful when yo' speik to yo'r betters. Does ta know tha'rt speikin' to two thousand pund?"

"Aw sud say t' same if aw wer' speikin' to th' king's mint, if Ben Walker wer' one o' th' stamps," retorted Mary hotly.

"Yo'll alter yo'r tune afore th' week's out, my lass," put in Mrs. Walker. "In a word, will ta ha' our Ben here? What he's so set on thee for 'mazes me. But he is set on thee, an' yo' sud be thankful he'll cast a look yo'r way when it's wi' th' quality he sud be speikin' at this very minnit, i'stead o' draggin' his mother up this rutty owd hill to a tumbledown ram–shackle owd sheep–pen not fit for a lady to put her foot inside on. Will ta ha' him, an' be a lady in silk an' satins, an' a servant o' yo'r own, an' a gig to drive abaat in, an' th' fat o' th' land to live' on?"

"Noa, aw winnot, aw winnot, aw winnot, so there's yo'r answer, an' if he comes near me or after me agen, there's one'll fetch as many colours on his back as th' weaver's put in his weskit."

"Then awst dahn to Milnsbrig this very neet," said Ben Walker, "an' tell owd Radcliffe all aw know abaat Rawfolds, an' that long–legged tally o' yo'rn shall go th' same gait as Mellor an' Thorpe."

And now I had a lucky inspiration—like a flash came into my head what Mr. Radcliffe had said to me: 'Thank your stars, Justice Radcliffe does not listen to every idle story that comes to his ears.' So I drew a bow at a venture:

"Go to Mr. Radcliffe and welcome," I said. "Tha's been before, an' told him all tha knows, an' more nor yo' could prove, an' yo' know nowt came on it. Dost think he'll tak more heed o' a second telling?"

Ben Walker and his mother exchanged glances and their faces fell, so I gathered courage and pushed my advantage.

"Go! aw tell yo'. Aw've known 'at yo' tell'd him long sin' all yo' knew about me, an' he put it aside. Aw've noan yo' to thank 'at aw'm here to tell yo' on it."

"Who telled yo'?" gasped Ben, off his guard. "Mr. Radcliffe hissen," I cried, with the ring of triumph in my voice, "an' he towd me, too, if ever I fun out who'd peached, aw'd his permission to break every bone in his body, an', by God, if yo'r not off this hillside before aw count twenty, aw'll take him at his word," and I strode with uplifted arm towards the craven that shrank away. He needed no second telling, and his mother followed him crest–fallen: and never but once again did Ben Walker, to my knowledge, set foot on the threshold he had trod so often as a tolerated if not a welcome guest.

"Whatever did ta mean, Ben?" said my mother to me, when she had watched the pair part way down the hill, to make sure, she said, they pocketed nought: "Whatever did ta mean?"

"Never yo' mind, mother," I replied. "There's no good i' talking overmuch about such things. Anyway, it's been enough for yon' lot an' that should be good enough for you."

"Aw do believe he made it," said my mother to Mary, in a tone of admiration. And from that day she conceived a higher respect for my intellect than years of honest truth had been able to inspire.

Only once again, I say, did Ben Walker, to my knowledge, sot foot on our doorstep. He tarried in Huddersfield for some months and his money flowed like water. Then he disappeared, and it was said he had gone to America with a woman who was no better than she should be. Truth was, the Brigg was getting too hot to hold him. The men who had been in the Luddite business began to pluck up heart as the time went on and no more arrests were made. And one fine night the man who kept the toll–gate at the Brigg heard loud cries for mercy, and rushing out was just in time to see the heels of a dozen men and to drag a drowning wretch out of the cut. It was Ben Walker, and he was all but done for. Then, I say, he vanished, and for years I heard no word of him. Then one wintry night—November I think it was—Mary and I were sat in the house by the fireside, she in the rocking chair my mother had loved of old and knitting as I had seen her that was gone knitting so often that the thread seemed a very part of my own life's warp; and I was sat smoking my evening pipe in the chair he that was gone had made to us more sacred than any monument in church or chapel, and the old clock was ticking steadily on to the bed–hour as sturdily as it had ticked for more years than I can tell. Only there was not to be heard through the rafters the heavy snoring of 'Siah as it had been heard in my father's days. 'Siah was snoring, I doubt not, but in a bed and a house of his own, and the not too gentle breathing of Martha swelled the harmony of his own.

There came a knock at the door that gave us both a start. We had heard no footstep, and Vixen, a waspish daughter of the Vixen of other days, had not given tongue.

Who could it be?

"Does Mister Bamforth live here?" queried a voice that stirred a memory of I knew not what, but something painful, and my mind, without my willing it, was off on the scent.

"He does. Dos't want him?" I said, barring the entrance but holding the door half open, whilst Mary had risen to her feet and held the light above her head, to see the better.

"Aw've tramped fra Manchester, an' awn had newt to eit sin break o' day, an' aw beg yo' for the love of God to gi' me a crust an' th' price o' a bed or let me lie me dahn i' th' mistal."

And as he spoke and his face struck stronger at me, it all came back.

"It's Ben o' Buck's," I cried.

"It's Ben o' Buck's," he said in a low voice, and hung down his head and said no more. I was for banging the door in his face, the hot blood surging to my face and anger and scorn in my heart.

But Mary took the loaf and a slice of cheese from the table where our supper lay, and a coin from the window sill where the milk money was, and gave it to him, but turned her eyes from him as she gave it. And I knew that Mary had taken the better part, and there was no longer anger in my heart and I closed the door upon the figure that slouched away into the cold dark night.

Yes: Mary and I were wed, and for the life of me I cannot remember that I ever asked Mary to be my wife. I always tell her she did all the love–making. Did she not put her arms about my neck, and did she not tell Long Tom she meant to wed me. To be sure it was a Leap Year, and that accounts for it.

I overheard Mary telling Martha that our wedding day was fixed. It was to be in October—on the sixteenth—to be exact.

"Then that settles it," said Martha.

"Settles what?" asked Mary.

"Th' day for t' spurrins," replied our maid; "'Siah's been puttin' it off, an' puttin' it off, tho' awn egged him on never so; but nah, aw'll ha' no more dallyin'. Aw'd fixed i' mi mind to be wed on th' same day as yo' and Ben, if aw couldn't afore, an' not another day longer will aw wait. If 'Siah winnot put 'em up aw'll do it misen, an' that aw'll let him know."

"But perhaps 'Siah doesn't want to get wed," suggested Mary.

"What's that to say to it?" asked Martha. "If he doesn't know who'll mak' a good wife, aw know who'll mak' a good husband. An' 'Siah's just that soft, aw sud be feart o' any other 'ooman puttin' on 'im, an' that 'ud just fret me to skin an' bone, to see onybody else puttin' on 'im an' me no right to stan' up for him."

"But a woman cannot put th' spurrins up," objected Mary.

"Then aw'st ma' 'Si."

"But how if he's loath?"

"Aw'st bray him."

"What! 'Siah?"

"Aye, Mary, an' if yo'll tak' my advice, an' yo' may need it now yo're goin' to be wed yersen, never let on to be fleyed o' yo'r man. First time aw gay' 'Si' a bat, mi heart come into mi mouth an' mi knees knocked one agen t'other, yo'd a thowt aw wer' playin' a tune on th' bones under mi petticoat; but, Lor' bless yo', he just oppened his mouth an' gaped at me an' scratted his yed—'Well awm dalled,' says he, 'if this doesn't beat th' longest day!'—an' so aw fot 'im another clout wi' mi neive, an' bar tellin' me to be careful aw didn't hurt misen, an' to hit wheer it wer' soft, if a soft place aw could find, 'Siah said nowt; but it's done him gooid. He's more fleyed o' me nor ony two i' th' Colne Valley," concluded Martha with legitimate pride.

And Soldier Jack and Faith made a match of it. We were all married on the same day, in the same church, by the same parson. It was Mr. Coates, the vicar at the Parish Church at Huddersfield, tied us, for neither at the Slaithwaite Church nor at the Powle could that then be done. And a gradely wedding we had, as is only right when three couples, all friends, and all of a family after a fashion o' speaking, get wed on the same day.

Faith and Mary were just enough to send a man off his head, as they stood in their veils, and even Martha looked comely, for love put its halo about her head. Mr. Coates couldn't keep his eyes off Mary and Faith, for I reckon he didn't see two such pictures every day, and when we went into the vestry to sign th' register:

"The Rose," says he, handing the quill pen for Mary to sign her name. "And the lily," he added, with a smile and a courtly bow, like the gentleman he was, to Faith.

"Nay, sir," said Mary, with a happy laugh, "Nay, sir, the lilies come fra Golcar."

And now, my children, my story is told. You know more about the Luddites, perhaps, than when you began to read it. You know how vain was their attempt to stop the introduction of machinery. And no doubt machinery has been a great boon. Why, I myself, as you know, run my own mill by it.

But don't tell me the Luds were a bad lot—misguided, short–sighted, igno-rant, if you like, but rogues, and idle, dissolute n'er–do–weels——No! and still no!

THE END.

Lector House believes that a society develops through a two-fold approach of continuous learning and adaptation, which is derived from the study of classic literary works spread across the historic timeline of literature records. Therefore, we aim at reviving, repairing and redeveloping all those inaccessible or damaged but historically as well as culturally important literature across subjects so that the future generations may have an opportunity to study and learn from past works to embark upon a journey of creating a better future.

This book is a result of an effort made by Lector House towards making a contribution to the preservation and repair of original ancient works which might hold historical significance to the approach of continuous learning across subjects.

HAPPY READING & LEARNING!

LECTOR HOUSE LLP
E-MAIL: lectorpublishing@gmail.com